A SOLDIER'S RETURN

Taller, even, than she remembered, he was dressed in ragged jeans and a denim jacket over a black T-shirt. His features were gaunt; his dark hair was in need of cutting; his body was all bones and sinew. But there could be no mistaking the defiant attitude he'd never lost. She was looking at Jake O'Reilly.

"Hello, Kira." He'd paused a few steps away, one hand balancing the backpack that was slung over his broad shoulder. A haunted look flickered in his eyes. If she'd passed him on some city street, she might have assumed him to be homeless.

"Hello, Jake."

SUNRISE CANYON

JANET DAILEY

ZEBRA BOOKS
KENSINGTON PUBLISHING CORP.
http://www.kensingtonbooks.com

ZEBRA BOOKS are published by

Kensington Publishing Corp.
119 West 40th Street
New York, NY 10018

All Kensington titles, imprints and distributed lines are available at special quantity discounts for bulk purchases for sales promotion, premiums, fund-raising, educational or institutional use.

Special book excerpts or customized printings can also be created to fit specific needs. For details, write or phone the office of the Kensington Sales Manager. Attn.: Sales Department. Kensington Publishing Corp., 119 West 40th Street, New York, NY 10018. Phone: 1-800-221-2647.

Zebra and the Z logo Reg. U.S. Pat. & TM Off.

First Kensington Books Hardcover Printing: November 2016
First Zebra Books Mass-Market Paperback Printing: March 2017
ISBN-13: 978-1-4201-4010-1
ISBN-10: 1-4201-4010-8

eISBN-13: 978-1-4201-4011-8
eISBN-10: 1-4201-4011-6

10 9 8 7 6 5 4 3 2 1

Printed in the United States of America

CHAPTER ONE

The sky was still dark above the high gate of the Flying Cloud Ranch. The desert foothills lay pooled in shadow. Stars were fading above the Santa Catalina Mountains, which rose to the east. Beyond their rocky ridges, the coming sunrise burnished the sky with streaks of pewter.

The narrow trail wound downhill among stands of paloverde and towering giant saguaros. Razor-spined chollas glistened like cut crystal in the silvery light. A kangaroo rat darted across the path, the flash of movement causing the mare to flinch and snort.

"Easy, girl," Kira Bolton murmured, soothing the animal with a gentle touch of her hand. "It's all right. You're fine."

Too bad she couldn't calm herself with the same words. These dawn rides usually brought her peace. But Kira felt no peace this morning. She'd been in turmoil since last night, when her grandfather had given her the news she'd hoped never to hear.

"That investigator I hired has found Jake. He's in Flagstaff, working at a garage. I'll be driving up there tomorrow to get him and bring him back."

"What if he doesn't want to come?" Kira had asked, hoping she was right.

"He'll come. I'm not leaving without him. Jake needs this ranch, and Paige needs her father."

Kira had known better than to argue with the determined old cowboy—even though the last person she wanted to see again was Jake O'Reilly. After three years, she was still coming to terms with her cousin Wendy's death. Jake's presence would rip open all the old wounds—wounds that were still raw below the surface.

But this wasn't about her, Kira reminded herself. This was about Jake. More important, it was about the vulnerable five-year-old girl who still kept his and Wendy's wedding photograph on the nightstand next to her bed.

Halting the mare on a level ridge, she watched the morning shadows flow like water across the desert below. Here and there, small ranches and luxury estates dotted the landscape. Farther to the west, in the blue distance, Kira could see the outskirts of Tucson and the network of roads leading into the city.

The day promised to be a showstopper. Spring in Arizona's Sonoran Desert was a time of renewal—a time when the cactuses burst into glorious bloom and the earth teemed with life. Now, as dawn broke, the air rang with birdsong. A family of quail called from the branches of an ironwood tree. A cactus wren piped its song from a clump of blooming golden brittlebush. A tiny elf owl settled into its home—an old woodpecker hole in a giant saguaro—and closed its eyes.

Kira loved this country, and the ten-acre ranch that perched on a plateau at the crest of a small, hilly canyon—a canyon known only by the name she and Wendy, as children, had given it years ago. They had called it Sunrise Canyon, for its magnificent view to the east and for the way the dawn painted the rocky cliffs with rose-gold light.

All too soon, the sunrise faded. It was time to go back, Kira told herself. Anytime now, the ranch would awaken, the horses needing to be fed, her teenage students, as she liked to call them, waking up in the guest cabins and needing attention. On this, their first morning here, the three girls and four boys would be tired, hungry and probably cranky. They would need a lot of guidance and a healthy measure of discipline to get them through the day. It would be Kira's job, as a licensed equine-assisted therapist, to give it to them.

Tucker, the ranch's nine-year-old Australian shepherd mix, came wagging out of the gate as Kira rode in. Dismounting, she reached down and scratched his shaggy head. A friendly, mellow dog, Tucker played his own vital role in the ranch's therapy program. Now he followed Kira as she led her mare toward the stable.

The aromas of coffee, bacon and eggs wafted from the kitchen. Consuelo, the Mexican cook, stepped onto the back porch and struck the metal triangle that hung on a chain. The clanging sound echoed across the yard, a signal that breakfast was ready.

The seven students, most of them barely awake, trudged out of the three guest cabins—three girls in one, two boys in each of the others. None of them looked happy about being rousted out at six a.m. But as her grandfather—Dusty, as he liked to be called—had told them in last night's welcome speech, if they didn't get up, they would miss breakfast. If they didn't work, they wouldn't eat. They were to keep their cabins clean, do their own personal laundry and change their own beds with the sheets provided. If they broke the rules, their parents would be called to come and take them home.

The rules, as Dusty had explained, were simple. Anybody who harmed an animal or another person, left the ranch without permission, took what didn't belong to them, used alcohol or drugs, or fooled around sexually (hanky-panky, he'd called it), would be gone the next day. The youngsters had raised their hands to show they understood and accepted the rules.

They weren't bad kids, but each one, in his or her own way, was in pain. That pain could manifest itself in any number of behaviors—bullying, withdrawal, self-mutilation, night terrors and other problems. Kira had read each of their files and spoken with the parents before admitting them to the program. They would be here for four weeks. All of them had been excused from school on the recommendation of doctors or counselors for the session. Most had brought homework assignments to do on their laptops or tablets.

Kira gave them a smile and a friendly wave as they trooped into the dining room for breakfast. Then she turned her attention to unsaddling Sadie and brushing her down. Dusty's big Jeep Wrangler was gone from its place in the parking shed. Her grandfather would already be headed north to Flagstaff, to pick up Jake—and bring a whole new set of complications to their lives.

She would miss Dusty today, and likely tomorrow as well. Together, the two of them made a perfect team—Kira with her master's degree and experience in counscling, and her grandfather with his imposing presence, his no-nonsense approach to kids and his deep knowledge of ranching and horses. She could—and would—make it through the day without him. But things wouldn't be as easy, for her or for her students.

"Hi, Aunt Kira." The little girl had climbed the paddock fence and was perched on the top rail, next to the gatepost.

"Hi, yourself." Kira led the mare into the grassy paddock and closed the gate. "Have you had breakfast?"

"Not yet. I was waiting for you. Where did you go?"

At five, with her mother's fiery curls and her father's intense dark eyes, Paige was a small bundle of stubborn independence. Only in quiet moments did her sadness flicker through—for Wendy, the mother she barely remembered, and for Jake, the father who'd gone to fight for his country and had never come back for her. After three years, she still mentioned her parents in her bedtime prayers.

How would it affect her if Jake returned—especially if the war had changed him from the gentle, fun-loving father her imagination had built around his picture?

"Where did you go, Aunt Kira?" she asked again.

"Just for a ride, to see the sun come up."

"Why didn't you take me with you?"

"You were asleep. I checked." Kira boosted Paige off the fence and lowered her to the ground. "Come on, let's go chow down."

By the time they arrived in the dining room, the teens were refilling their plates. Good food, and plenty of it, was part of the ranch experience. Kira gave them a smile as she took her place, with Paige next to her, and filled their plates. "Eat up," she said. "You're going to need your energy today."

"What are we going to do?" a husky boy named Mack asked her. "My folks told me we'd get to ride horses!"

"So you will," Kira said. "But not right away. First you'll be learning how to take care of a horse—feed it, groom it and keep its quarters clean. Then you'll learn how to work with it on the ground. Next will come things like putting on the saddle and bridle. After that, if you've learned your lessons and your horse trusts you, you get to ride. But keep one thing in mind. Nobody rides until the whole group is ready. That means if one person is slow catching on, the rest will help them. We go forward together or not at all. Got it? Raise your hand if you understand."

Seven hands went up.

"How long does that part usually take?" Lanie

was petite and dark-eyed, her sleeves buttoned at the wrists to hide the razor cuts on her arms.

"A couple weeks, at least," Kira said. A mutter went around the table. She smiled and shook her head. "Riding your horse is a privilege—one you'll be expected to earn. At the end of every day, we'll sit down in a group and talk about our experiences and what we've learned from them. You'll also have weekly one-on-one sessions with me to talk privately about anything that concerns you. Any questions?"

Heather, a plump, freckle-faced girl, raised her hand. "When do we start?"

Kira glanced at the clock on the wall. "You've got twenty minutes to finish eating, bus your dishes and go back to your cabins to brush your teeth, use the bathroom and whatever else you need to do. Then meet me out front at seven fifteen sharp."

Kira waited until everyone had scraped their plates and carried their dishes to the plastic tub on the side counter. Then, as her charges scattered to their cabins, she went outside. With Paige and the dog tagging along, she filled the feeders in the paddock with hay, and turned the stabled horses out with Sadie. All the horses were older animals, patient and wise. In the weeks ahead, they would have much to teach the troubled youngsters who'd come here to heal.

Today the students would get a chance to observe the horses from outside the fence—their body language, how they interacted, supported each other and resolved differences. If this group of teens was typical, they would already be picking out their favorites.

But their first lesson would be the one waiting when they came outside this morning—a reality that anyone working with animals had to deal with. Forcing her worries to the back of her mind, Kira set out two wheelbarrows, seven sets of gloves and seven shovels. It was time to muck out the stable.

"This must be your lucky day, O'Reilly! Some old geezer just paid your fine!"

Startled out of a doze, Jake sat up on his bunk and swung his feet to the concrete floor. "Are you messing with my head? I don't know any old geezer."

"Well, he must know you. He just showed up with a receipt from the court clerk for a thousand dollars cash. Here." The deputy tossed Jake a plastic trash bag containing his clothes and boots. "Get dressed. You can pick up the rest of your stuff up front."

Knowing better than to ask questions, Jake stripped off the hated orange jumpsuit and scrambled into his clothes. He could barely remember the bar brawl that had landed him here—a blur of angry words and fists crunching into flesh and bone. But the memory of his hearing before the judge was crystal clear, including the pro bono lawyer who'd asked for leniency on the grounds that Jake was a war hero.

He'd been allowed to plead the assault-and-battery charge down to disorderly conduct, but the sentence was still a stiff one. A thousand-dollar fine or thirty days in the Coconino County Jail. Not having the money, Jake had been forced to do time—which meant losing his construction job and missing his rent payment. By now, the damned landlord had probably sold everything he owned—not that it would be much of a loss. His small monthly veterans' benefit would be direct-deposited to his bank account, which he could access with a debit card. But he'd used the last payment for his rent, and the next one wouldn't be there for a week. Except for the few bills in his wallet, he was dead broke.

But today, out of nowhere, somebody had paid his fine and set him free. *"Some old geezer,"* the deputy had said. That couldn't be right. There had to be a catch—there always was. Maybe it was a case of mistaken identity. If so, when the truth came out, he could expect to be thrown right back into that cell.

Whatever was going on, Jake told himself, he mustn't get his hopes up.

After hooking his belt and shrugging into his denim jacket, he opened the cell door, which was unlocked, and stepped out into the hall. The deputy was waiting to escort him down the corridor, past the security desk, to the reception area.

As he stepped into the open space, a tall figure rose to greet him—whip-lean, with stooping shoulders, a hawkish nose, silver hair and a neatly trimmed mustache. "Hello, Jake," he said.

"Dusty?" Jake froze, struck by the shock of recognition. He hadn't seen Wendy's grandfather since her funeral, three years ago, and they'd barely spo-

ken that day. "I don't understand," he said. "What are you doing here? What do you want from me?"

"Get your things, boy," the old man said. "We can talk later, while I treat you to a good steak dinner."

"Thanks, but I can buy my own food—and I'll find a way to pay you back for bailing me out." Jake collected his bagged personal effects from the checkout counter—his wallet with forty-eight dollars in it, his cheap Timex watch, and his keys— one to his apartment and the other to the '95 Ford pickup that had thrown a rod, trashing the engine, two days before the fight that had led to his arrest.

The old man headed for the parking lot. Striding after him, Jake inhaled the crisp mountain air as he tried to recall what Wendy had told him about her grandfather. Dusty Wingate had been a national bronc riding champion back before Jake was even born. After too many injuries on the rodeo circuit, he'd retired to manage the family dude ranch near Tucson. Now in his seventies, he still made an impressive figure—like a modern-day Buffalo Bill in jeans and boots, a fringed leather jacket and a bolo tie strung through a hunk of silver-mounted old-pawn Navajo turquoise.

His wife, who'd died of cancer in her fifties, had given him two daughters. The firstborn, Wendy's mother, Barbara, was running a charity mission with her second husband—a preacher she'd met at her first husband's funeral—in Uganda or some other godforsaken place. When Wendy got pregnant and married Jake, the woman had pretty much disowned her. She hadn't been there for the wedding. Hell, she hadn't even bothered to come home for her daughter's funeral.

Dusty's other daughter had perished in a small plane crash with her doctor husband, leaving Wendy's cousin Kira an orphan at seventeen. Funny he should remember even that about Kira. Something in him didn't want to remember her at all. Something else couldn't let go of her.

He knew, of course, that Kira had taken in his daughter to raise. But he'd long since made up his mind not to contact her. As long as Paige was safe and well cared for, she was better off not knowing the haunted, sometimes violent man her father had become.

Dusty led the way to a late-model white Jeep Wrangler and clicked the remote to unlock the door. "Climb in," he said. "There's a good steak house ten minutes from here. I know they don't starve you in jail, but you look like you could use a decent meal."

"Thanks . . . I guess." Jake climbed into the passenger seat, closed the door and fastened his seat belt. "I've got some questions for you. For starters, how did you know where to find me?"

Dusty started the engine and pulled out of the parking lot. "A few months ago, I hired a private investigator to track you down. He didn't have an easy time of it. You don't seem to settle anyplace for long, do you?"

"I guess not." That mind-set had evolved after Jake checked himself out of the VA hospital. *Don't stay around long enough to get attached to people, to places or even to animals. No love, no loss, no grief.* So far, it seemed to be working for him. In his good moments, he'd managed to feel almost numb.

They drove in silence for a few minutes before Jake spoke again. "So my next question is, what made you think a bum like me was worth finding?"

Dusty braked the Jeep at a red light. "That answer's going to take some time. What d'you say we leave it till our supper's on its way?"

Jake settled back into the cushy leather seat, his eyes tracing the silhouette of tall ponderosa pines against a blazing Arizona sunset. He'd been in jail two weeks, barely half his sentence. It felt damned good to be out. But he sensed that the old man was reeling him in like a hooked fish. Not knowing why made him edgy.

He would listen, Jake decided. But he'd be damned if he was going to talk. There were no words for the hellish things he'd seen and even done in Afghanistan. If Dusty tried to pump him, he would get up from the table and walk away.

Dusty pulled up to a restaurant with a log exterior and a name Jake recognized as a high-end steak-and-ribs chain. Inside, the aromas coming from the kitchen made him weak in the knees. After two weeks of jail fare and, before that, eating from fast-food dollar menus, this was like stepping into a forbidden paradise. But he'd insisted on paying his own way, and he could only imagine what a really good meal would cost here.

The hostess showed them to a booth. Dusty ordered two Coronas while Jake perused the menu. The cheapest item, a burger with fries and coleslaw, was fifteen dollars. That would have to do him.

"My offer to buy you dinner still stands," the old man said. "They've got great prime rib here."

"Thanks, but I've got it. And I'll buy yours, too." Jake gave his order to the waitress—a burger.

Dusty shrugged. "I'll have the same." As the waitress hurried off with their order, he turned back to Jake and thrust one of the chilled Coronas across the table. "You're a stubborn man, Jake O'Reilly. At least I'm buying the beer."

"Thanks." Jake took a swig, savoring the coldness and the taste. "What I really need is to know what your game is. I never expected to see you again, and now you show up and spend a thousand bucks bailing me out. What's in this for you? What do you want?"

The old man's eyes, a deep, startling shade of blue, gazed into Jake's. "It's simple enough. I want to take you back to Tucson and give you a job on my ranch."

"What the hell?" Jake stared at him. "I don't know anything about ranch work. I've never even been on a damned horse."

"Maybe not. But there's plenty you could do. I know about your engineering degree, so you should be handy with tools. And some of the kids we work with could use another man around the place."

"The kids?"

"Teenagers with troubles—at risk, that's what Kira calls them. She runs a horse therapy program to help them."

Kira.

Why was this all beginning to make some kind of crazy sense?

"What about Paige?" he asked.

"Your little girl needs to see her father, Jake. She's getting old enough to wonder why you never came back for her."

Jake's fingers tightened around his glass, hard enough to whiten his knuckles. "I never came back for her because I'm not fit to be a father. The nightmares in my head, the memories of what happened over there—I could scare her, even hurt her without meaning to. I shouldn't be with kids. I shouldn't really be with anybody."

"So you just plan to keep running. Is that it?" The wise blue eyes seemed to skewer him to the back of the booth.

"I spent five weeks in the VA hospital before I got tired of talking to their shrinks. 'Give it time,' they said. 'Maybe it'll go away.' That was almost two years ago. It hasn't."

Dusty set down his beer and leaned across the table. "Come home with me, Jake. Come and do some good where you're needed."

"Nobody needs me," Jake said.

"That's where you're wrong. I need you because I'm getting old. Paige needs you because you're her father. And Kira—she needs you, too."

"Why would Kira need me?" He pictured Wendy's cousin, so smart, so driven. How could a woman like Kira need anybody?

"Kira needs you to forgive her for what happened. Maybe if you can do that, she'll finally be able to forgive herself."

Jake stared down into his glass. He'd seen the police report. Kira's Toyota Corolla, with Wendy in the passenger seat and two-year-old Paige strapped into her car seat in the back, had been hit by a drunk driver, late at night. The big SUV had T-boned the small sedan, killing Wendy outright. Kira had walked away with cuts and bruises. Paige, thank God, had been untouched.

"You know Kira didn't cause the accident," Dusty said.

"I know." *But if Kira hadn't been out at that hour, on that street, with his wife and daughter in her car, Wendy—his one hope of becoming a whole man again— would still be alive.*

The waitress, arriving with their meals, broke the tense silence. The burger was first-rate—as it should have been for the price. Jake could've wolfed his down, but he forced himself to eat slowly, matching the old man bite for bite. They were almost finished when Dusty spoke.

"Let me make you a practical offer. You owe me a thousand dollars, money you promised to pay back. I'll hire you on as a maintenance man at twenty dollars an hour, half of that to go toward repayment, the other half to you. Once the loan's paid, you're off the hook. You can stay or go. I've got an empty guest cabin where you can live rent free, meals included. That's the best deal you're going to get anywhere."

Jake scowled down at his empty plate. It was a generous offer, more than generous. And if he said no, he'd be welching on a loan he'd be hard-put to repay, sacrificing the one thing he had left—his honor.

The old man was no fool. He had sprung a clever trap, and Jake was caught in it.

"So what do you say?" Dusty asked.

Jake exhaled slowly. "I'll need to go by my place and pick up a few things."

"Fine. I'm pretty beat after driving up here. We can get a motel for the night, or if you're up to driving, I can sleep on the way home."

Jake rose, leaving his last two twenties on the table with the check. "I've had nothing to do but sleep for the past two weeks. Let's go."

CHAPTER TWO

Kira gathered her students in the living room after dinner for their nightly lecture and discussion. She'd found that the cozy setting—the timbered ceiling, the overstuffed leather furniture, the shelves stocked with books, along with the crackling blaze in the tall sandstone fireplace—helped the teens relax and feel more like talking, which was essential to their therapy.

Tonight most of them looked ready to fall asleep. They'd had a strenuous day, cleaning the stable and hauling fresh bedding for the stalls, observing and taking notes on the horses and taking a midday hike to a spring above the ranch for a picnic. She would cut tonight's session short, Kira decided.

"Before we start our discussion, I want to tell you a little about the ranch," she began. "Take a look at the painting above the fireplace. That beautiful white horse is Flying Cloud. He belonged to my great-great-grandfather. It was the money that Flying Cloud won racing, back in the 1920s, that bought the land for this ranch. Some of the horses you'll be working with are his descendants."

Kira glanced around the circle of young faces. Two of her students were yawning. Dusty usually handled this part of the lecture, and he did it like the showman he was. Without him, she would just have to make do.

"The ranch started as a cattle operation, but after the Great Depression, much of the land had to be sold off. That was when my great-grandfather turned it into a guest ranch—or a dude ranch, you might call it. During its heyday, in the 1950s, we had some famous people staying here, including movie stars and politicians. Their autographed photos are hanging out in the hall. You can see them as you walk between here and the dining room."

"I looked." Heather spoke up without raising her hand. "I didn't know any of those old creeps."

"It was a long time ago," Kira said. "But they were famous in their day. If you google them, you might learn a thing or two."

There was no response, only a circle of blank faces. Kira continued.

"A few years ago, my grandfather was going to close the ranch and retire. That was when I talked him into opening a horse therapy program. And now, here we are." Kira took a breath. "So let's talk. What did you think of your first job this morning?"

Mack raised his hand. "It sucked! I came here to ride horses, not to shovel shit!"

"Thank you for raising your hand, Mack," Kira said. "So you didn't like it much. Anybody else?"

Brandon, the slender, soft-spoken boy who was Mack's cabin mate, raised his hand. "I didn't like it, either. But animals poop and they can't clean it up by themselves. Somebody has to do it for them. I learned that when I had a dog."

Kira made a mental note to ask Brandon about his dog in one of their private sessions. "So you didn't mind it too much, Brandon?"

"I guess not. Just the smell, maybe."

"I couldn't stand the smell," Lanie said. "It almost made me throw up. Do I have to do it again?"

"Only if you want to work with the horses," Kira said. "Nobody's going to force you, Lanie, but if you don't want to help, you might as well not be here."

"Sheesh!" Lanie picked at one bitten thumbnail. "This is as bad as being home!"

"Thank you for telling us how you feel, Lanie," Kira said. "Now let me tell you all something. We'll be starting every day by feeding and watering the horses and cleaning their stalls. Today it took a long time. When you learn to work together, and work faster, you'll have more time to spend with the horses. Now, to move on, what did you learn from observing the horses together? What did you write down in your notebooks?"

The discussion that followed brought out some good observations, with all the students taking part except one. Faith, a fifteen-year-old Taylor Swift look-alike, had done her share of the work, but had barely spoken all day. She sat a little apart from the others, her manicured hands folded in her lap. Kira had learned that the quiet teens were often the most deeply troubled. But the horses could work wonders—Kira had seen it happen. She could only hope it would happen again.

When the youngsters showed signs of nodding off, Kira dismissed them with a reminder that they'd be getting up early the next morning. She was tired, too. Getting through a long opening day without Dusty's help had been exhausting. And unless he'd turned right around and driven back from Flagstaff, she'd be on her own tomorrow as well.

What had possessed her grandfather to hunt down Jake and try to bring him home? The last time she'd seen Jake, on leave for Wendy's funeral, he'd been cold and distant, as if his emotions were encased in granite. Even when she'd told him she'd be taking care of Paige until his current deployment as an Army Ranger was over, he'd barely found the words to say a thank-you before he turned and walked away.

How could she not believe he'd blamed her for his wife's death—or that he blamed her still?

The most disturbing thing was, he'd never come back for Paige. When he'd failed to show up after the end date of his deployment, Dusty had contacted the VA. According to their records, he'd checked into a veterans' hospital in Virginia, suffering from post-traumatic stress disorder. Weeks later, Jake had checked himself out and disappeared without a trace.

And now, if Dusty succeeded in his quest, Jake would be living here, on this ranch. And every day of dealing with the man would be a new challenge.

Emotions churning, she wandered from room to room, putting things in order for tomorrow and turning off the lights. Consuelo, who lived with her retired husband on the outskirts of Tucson, had her own room and bath off the kitchen. When the students were here, she usually stayed, but tonight she'd gone home. Except for Paige, asleep in her room, Kira was alone in the house.

As part of the nighttime routine, she took a flashlight, stepped outside and made a circuit of the guest cabins and grounds to make sure her students were settled in. Everything was quiet—no surprise, since they'd all looked exhausted tonight. But something told Kira she wouldn't fall asleep so easily. There was too much weighing on her mind.

The desert night was cool, with a light breeze blowing off the mountains. Out here, away from the lights of Tucson, the stars spilled glory across the deep dark of the sky. Kira remembered nights as a child, when she and Wendy would come to visit their grandfather here on the ranch. They would spread a blanket on the ground and lie on their backs, gazing up at the sky, picking out the constellations and talking about the things they wanted to do when they grew old enough to make their own decisions about life.

It was a mercy, she supposed, that neither of them could've known how their lives would turn out.

With a final glance around the yard, she went back into the house and locked the doors behind her. She would look in on Paige, then get ready for bed and try to get some rest.

Tiptoeing down the hall, she eased open the door to the little girl's room. Paige slept with a night-light, a little angel figure that plugged into the outlet next to her bed. Lit by its soft glow, she was curled on her side, her profile sweet in sleep, her curls tangled on the pink Disney Princess pillowcase.

A framed photograph of her parents on their wedding day sat on the nightstand, where Paige could see it when she lay down to sleep and when she first woke in the morning. She had no memory of the fatal car crash. She accepted what she'd been told—that her mother was an angel, watching over her from heaven. Her father's absence was harder to explain. She'd been told early on that he meant to come back for her. But as months turned into years, that chance had faded. Paige was mostly a happy child, secure in the love of everyone around her. But now and then, she still asked where her father was and when he was coming back.

Kira hadn't told her that Dusty had gone to get him. How would it affect her now, having Jake show up—a very different Jake from the smiling man in the wedding photo?

Standing next to the bed, Kira studied the picture in the glow of the angel light. She'd been Wendy's maid of honor that day, awkward in an unflattering pink ruffled dress, which she'd never worn again. But Wendy, in a strapless mermaid-style gown that fit every curve of her stunning figure, had taken breaths away when she walked down the aisle on Dusty's arm.

Growing up, the two of them had been almost as close as sisters—Wendy, the beautiful one with her emerald eyes and Titian hair, and Kira, known as the plain one, the smart, ambitious one. For as long as she could remember, Kira's decisions had been guided by reason and common sense. But impulsive, passionate Wendy had always led with her heart. She had followed her heart to the very end of her life.

As for Jake . . . Kira's gaze lingered on the handsome, smiling face. He'd looked so dashing that day, in the dress uniform of an Army Ranger, and he'd seemed so much in love with his beautiful bride.

That was the last she'd seen of him until Wendy's funeral, three years later. At the time, she'd assumed his haunted look was nothing more than grief. Even then, she should have known it was more.

Turning away, she slipped back into the hall and closed the door, leaving it ajar. Maybe Jake would be gone when her grandfather got to Flagstaff. Or maybe Jake would refuse to come home with him. Surely, that would be for the best.

Wouldn't it?

It was after midnight when Jake drove into Phoenix and negotiated the freeway connections that would get him off I-17 and onto I-10. From there, the drive to Tucson shouldn't take more than a couple of hours.

Simple enough. But as he made his way through the interchange and onto the route that would take him due south, it was as if a gate was closing behind him. Phoenix was where he'd spent his years as a foster kid. It was where, after turning eighteen and being booted out of the system, he'd signed up for ROTC and managed to get into college. It was where he'd met Wendy, at a big rock concert, when she'd climbed onto some boy's shoulders and fallen into his arms. These days, he couldn't even remember the name of the band. But at least the big, sprawling desert city was familiar; and not all his memories of the place were bad.

Leaving Phoenix felt like leaving a fortified base on a combat mission into hostile territory. The thought of the unknown, and all the things that could go wrong, was a fear he'd battled and conquered hundreds of times. But it never went away—not even here, in the good old USA.

Beside him, on the reclining passenger seat, Dusty was snoring like a bassoon. Jake wouldn't have minded turning on the radio and getting some late-night music, but he didn't want to wake the old man, who probably needed his rest. As it was, there was nothing to take his mind off what lay ahead.

Had he made the right decision, letting Dusty talk him into coming to the ranch? The longer he drove, the more doubts crept into his mind. If he'd stayed in jail and done his time, at least he could've walked away a free man—his *own* man. He could've left Flagstaff, found another job somewhere else, with nothing to tie him down. Now, it was as if he felt invisible walls closing around him.

It wasn't too late, he reminded himself. He could pull off the freeway, park the Jeep in a safe place, like a busy service station, lock the keys inside and walk away. When Dusty woke up, he'd be gone. He'd pay back the money, of course—just drop the payments in the mail from different places. He was good at disappearing. By the time the old man tracked him down again, he'd be someplace else.

Someplace where nobody cared that he woke up from nightmares in a cold, shaking sweat, that he started at any sound that resembled a gunshot or explosion, or felt a welling panic every time he walked past a shadowed alley; someplace where nobody cared enough to be hurt by his outbursts of rage and terror. His demons were his own. He would deal with them in his own way. They were nobody else's damn business.

The next off-ramp was coming up. There'd be a gas station or fast-food joint at the bottom. Could he do it? Jake's pulse quickened as he steered into the exit lane.

He was heading down the ramp when Dusty woke with a snort, opened his eyes and sat up. "Are we there?" he asked, blinking in the glare of neon lights.

"We're in Phoenix," Jake said, knowing his chance for a quiet getaway was gone. "I was thinking I could use some coffee and a restroom. How about you?"

"Sounds good if you'll let me buy this time."

Jake thought of his almost-empty wallet. "Sure," he said.

They pulled into a convenience store, used the

men's room and took their coffee back to the big SUV. "Want me to drive?" Dusty asked. "I've had a good rest."

"I'm fine." The last thing Jake wanted was to fall asleep and have one of his bad spells. "Tucson's a straight shot from here, but you'll have to give me directions to the ranch."

"No problem. It's easy enough. You've never been to the ranch, have you?"

"Nope." Jake swung into the driver's seat. "Wendy told me it was quite the hangout in its day. Movie stars and all."

"It's still pretty nice. I bulldozed the swimming pool when I retired from dude ranching. Too much upkeep. Now that Kira's bringing those kids in, she's wishing I'd kept the blasted thing."

"How's Kira doing, anyway?" Jake forced himself to ask. "Did she ever get married?"

"Nope. According to her, she's too involved in her work to look for a man, or need one—not that I really believe her. Anyway, she's got Paige for family. She's done a fine job, raising that little girl of yours."

Something clenched inside Jake at the thought of being around his daughter. And what about Kira? By now, Paige would be like her own child. She couldn't be too happy about having the little girl's father in the picture.

Hell, this was a bad idea. When Dusty showed up at the jail, he should've told the old man to mind his own business and walked right back into that cell.

"Does Kira know I was in jail?"

Dusty chuckled. "Nope. I told her you were

working in a garage. Far as I'm concerned, that'll be our secret."

"And Paige? Does she know I'm coming?"

"Kira didn't plan to tell her. She didn't want Paige to be disappointed if you didn't show up."

"Then do this for me—and for her." As soon as he spoke, Jake knew his idea was the only way. "Don't tell her I'm her father. As far as Paige is concerned, I'm just a man you met who needed work."

"You don't think she'll recognize you?"

Jake recalled the image he'd glimpsed in the mirror of the convenience store restroom—the bloodshot eyes and gaunt cheeks, the shaggy hair streaked with premature gray, the scruffy growth of beard on the lower part of his face. "She won't recognize me," he said.

"All right." Dusty nodded. "For now, that's not such a bad idea."

"What about Kira? Will you make sure she knows about it?"

"I'll tell her right off," Dusty said.

"I have a feeling Kira won't be overjoyed to see me."

Dusty didn't answer. He was looking out the side window, already watching the freeway signs for the exit to the ranch.

Kira untangled the covers from her legs, punched her pillow and, lying back, willed herself to drift into slumber. It was no use. She'd been awake most of the night, too agitated to sleep and too tired to get up. She wanted to be in top form for her students tomorrow. But if she didn't get some decent rest, she'd be a stumbling, coffee-swilling wreck.

She'd closed her eyes and was doing her best to relax when she heard the familiar rumble of Dusty's Jeep coming up the drive. She sat bolt upright. A glance at the bedside clock told her it was barely two in the morning. Her grandfather was back sooner than expected. Maybe he hadn't found Jake after all.

Spurred by hope, she sprang out of bed, flung on her flannel bathrobe and shoved her feet into her leather-soled slippers. Headlights cast moving shadows through the window blinds as the Jeep pulled into the yard.

Kira rushed down the hall, through the living room and out onto the front porch. By then, the big vehicle had come to a stop, its engine and lights switched off. Lit by the risen moon, the doors on both sides were opening. Two people. Her heart plummeted.

The lanky figure climbing out of the near side was her grandfather. He moved wearily, his back and limbs stiffened from the long ride. Kira hurried down the steps to lend a supporting arm. She had just reached him when the driver came around the front of the Jeep.

Taller, even, than she remembered, he was dressed in ragged jeans and a denim jacket over a black T-shirt. His features were gaunt; his dark hair was in need of cutting; his body was all bones and sinew. But there could be no mistaking the defiant attitude he'd never lost. She was looking at Jake O'Reilly.

"Hello, Kira." He'd paused a few steps away, one hand balancing the backpack that was slung over his broad shoulder. A haunted look flickered in his eyes. If she'd passed him on some city street, she might have assumed him to be homeless.

"Hello, Jake." Her voice betrayed her unease. "I suppose you'll want to see Paige, but she's asleep right now. Tomorrow I'll need time to prepare her. She wasn't told you were coming. It might be a shock, especially . . ." She looked him up and down, leaving no doubt what she meant.

"Your grandfather has something to tell you, Kira," Jake said. "Hear him out before you say any more."

Dusty cleared his throat. "On the way here, we decided it would be best not to tell Paige that Jake's her father. That'll give her some time to get used to him, maybe even figure things out for herself. For now, he'll just be a man we hired to do some maintenance around the place. Does that set all right with you?"

"It's fine. Good idea." Kira turned back to Jake. "Your cabin is the one on the far end. It's unlocked and ready. The key's on the dresser. If you're hungry, you can help yourself to any leftovers in the fridge. Breakfast, if you want it, is at seven, or you can fix your own in the kitchen. I'll let the cook know you're here tomorrow, so she won't be startled when you walk in."

"I'm not hungry now. Anything else?" His gaze

narrowed. Kira realized she'd been talking in a nervous stream of words, none of them welcoming. But why should she be anything but honest? She wasn't happy to have him here—this stranger who had the power to shake her world.

"I said, anything else?" He shifted on his feet, his voice edgy.

Kira shook her head.

"Then I guess I'll turn in." He shouldered his pack, walked away a few steps, then paused to look back at her grandfather. "Thanks, Dusty. I'll do my best not to make you sorry."

"I know you will, Jake. Now get some rest." Dusty let Kira support his arm as they mounted the porch. A glance across the yard told her that Jake was already striding toward the cabin.

"I don't have a good feeling about this," she said. "I wish you'd left well enough alone."

The old man crossed the threshold and waited for Kira to close the door behind them. "I know you do. But Jake gave up a happy life with his wife and child to fight for his country. Now he's not only broken, he's fallen through the cracks. A hero deserves better than what he's gone through."

"And Paige?"

"I know you want to protect her. So do I. But she doesn't deserve to grow up wondering why her father didn't care enough to be there for her. Bringing Jake here might turn out to be a mistake. But leaving well enough alone, as you say, could be an even bigger mistake." He gave Kira's shoulder an affectionate squeeze. "Give it a chance. That's all

I'm asking. Now go back to sleep. Things won't look so bad in the morning, you'll see."

Kira returned her grandfather's hug, trudged back to her room and crawled into bed. The old man believed he was doing the right thing, she told herself. But it was as if he'd brought home a wounded wolf he'd rescued from a trap and asked her to take it in.

She wasn't entirely heartless. She would do her best to help Jake feel at ease here. But she wouldn't lower her guard with him—especially where Paige was concerned. And she would keep her students at a distance from him. She'd seen her share of PTSD in her training. She knew the symptoms—depression, sleeplessness, bursts of anger, sudden flashbacks—and she knew they didn't just go away. Until he proved otherwise, she'd have to assume that, whatever his intentions, Jake O'Reilly was a troubled man. She couldn't afford to trust him.

The cabin was more luxurious than Jake had expected, with floors of red Mexican tile, arched doorways and a bathroom with a shower spacious enough for a Hollywood-style orgy. The massive bed, with its cushiony mattress and hand-carved headboard, beckoned to his weary bones. But he wanted to get clean before he slid between those pricey-looking sheets.

The walls were decorated with signed photos of the old-time movie stars who'd stayed there—John Wayne, Audie Murphy, Ann Sheridan, Maureen

O'Hara—probably filming their Western movies in Old Tucson and the surrounding desert.

One thing for sure—this place was a far cry from the jail where he'd spent the past two weeks, and he wasn't about to complain. Stripping off his clothes, he stepped into the shower and lathered up with the scented soap he found. Rinsed, toweled and smelling like a damned Victorian flower garden, he turned down the covers and rolled into bed.

Bone-weary after the long drive, he'd expected to fall asleep as soon as his head settled onto the downy pillow. Instead he lay there with his eyes open, staring up at the shadowed beams that crossed the ceiling.

Kira.

Some people didn't change. She was much as he remembered her—tall and boyishly slim, light brown hair raked carelessly back from her face, and those cool, penetrating gray eyes that seemed to see right through him.

Tonight the look she gave him had felt like being stabbed with an icicle. And the way she'd machine-gunned those words at him, as if already laying down the law. . . . The woman wasn't thrilled to have him here, and she'd made no effort to hide it.

"Kira needs you to forgive her for what happened. Maybe if you can do that, she'll finally be able to forgive herself."

The old man's words came back to him, raising painful questions. Did he really blame Kira for the accident that had killed Wendy? A deeper question—did she have reason to blame herself?

True, it was a drunk driver who'd plowed into Kira's car that night—a bastard who'd backed away and driven off with nothing more than a dented grill on the front of his big SUV. But what had Kira been doing out at one in the morning, in an unsavory part of town, with his wife and daughter in her car?

Maybe it was time he asked her.

But no, he hadn't come here to confront anybody or open up old wounds. All he wanted was to keep his head down, earn enough to pay back what he owed Dusty and leave. The last thing he wanted was to get in Kira's face.

Or in his daughter's. Paige would be better off with a memory than with the reality of what her father had become.

His eyelids were growing heavy. He was drifting now. His awareness was clouding over, as if blurred by windswept sand. . . .

The young girl was standing in the middle of the rutted road, right in the path of the armored Humvee. She appeared to be about fifteen, wearing a dark jacket, a long, loose cotton dress and a tangerine-colored scarf that wrapped her head, hiding her face except for her dark, expressive eyes.

The driver blasted his horn. The girl didn't move.

"Should I stop, sir?" the driver asked.

"No, it could be a trap," Jake heard himself answer. "Go slow. Honk again. Maybe she'll move."

Horn blasting, the massive vehicle lumbered closer.

The girl stood fast, as if bolted to the spot. Ten feet. Five feet. There was a blur of movement, then a hellish burst of flame and sound. The driver slumped over the wheel. Blood splattered the broken windshield, inside and out. In the dead hush that followed, a tangerine scarf fluttered upward, riding a dust devil into the sky.

Jake woke, his jerking body drenched in sweat, his throat constricting in silent screams.

CHAPTER THREE

Raw-eyed and edgy after a sleepless night, Kira was up before dawn. On most mornings, she looked forward to a day with her students and the horses. But right now, she wasn't ready to deal with seven impulsive teens, let alone Jake's presence on the ranch. She needed to get outside, to move, to stretch her cramped muscles and calm her frayed nerves before facing the day.

Deciding on a walk instead of a ride, she pulled on a clean shirt, jeans and tennis shoes, splashed her face and brushed her teeth. After checking on Paige and her grandfather, and finding them both asleep, she stole out of the house.

The cabins were dark, the ranch yard quiet. The call of a passing crow and the subtle stirring of horses in the barn deepened the morning peace as she crossed the yard and passed under the high arch of the gate.

The moon was a fading crescent in the western

sky, the sun barely streaking the east with the colors of dawn. The air was cool on Kira's damp face. She closed her eyes a moment, filling her lungs with its freshness.

Cactus blossoms, still in bud yesterday morning, had unfolded into full bloom. The saguaros were crowned in white. Crimson clusters fluttered from the tips of ocotillo spears. A low hedgehog cactus bore flowers of blazing pink.

As she strode down the trail, Kira could feel her mind and body coming awake. She could always count on these desert mornings to freshen her spirit and prepare her for the day—and today, of all days, she would need to stay calm and positive. Whatever happened, she mustn't let Jake's presence distract her from her work.

Her path wound among stands of mesquite and paloverde and outcroppings of chunky rust-hued rock. Just ahead lay an open spot with a view. Kira was nearly there when she came around a bend in the trail and discovered she had company.

Seated on a flat boulder, gazing out over the valley, was the last man she wanted to be alone with today.

Tension shot through her body. She wheeled in her tracks, hoping to slip back the way she'd come. But she was too late. Jake had already turned to look at her.

His startled expression froze, then hardened into something unreadable. "Good morning, Kira," he said.

"Goodness, you're up early!" she said, feeling

awkward. "I was thinking you might want to sleep in, this morning."

"I wasn't that tired." His gaze scanned the cactus-studded foothills as if searching for some hidden enemy before he glanced back at her. He looked as if he'd been awake all night, just as she had. "Feel free to sit if you want," he said. "There's room."

"Thanks." She lowered herself to the space on the boulder beside him. Maybe a little polite conversation would help to ease the tension. Her mind raced through a list of off-limits topics—Wendy, the accident, his war experiences, his PTSD, maybe even Paige. She would have to weigh every word.

"You're up pretty early yourself." He was wearing a faded brown tee, with what appeared to be a traditional Army Ranger tattoo just visible below the short sleeve.

"I like to start my morning with a little quiet time. It helps get me centered for the rest of the day, which can become pretty hectic."

"Dusty told me you were working with kids."

"We've got seven of them here, getting four weeks of therapy with the horses. Three girls and four boys. They're not bad kids, or violent, just troubled."

"Troubled?"

"Self-destructive behaviors, mostly. Or problems getting along with others. A lot of the kids who come here are depressed, some of them traumatized."

"And I'm guessing they're rich and spoiled."

He seemed to be prodding her, looking for a sore spot. Refusing to give him the satisfaction, Kira answered calmly.

"Unfortunately, the program's expensive. Right now, while it's new, we can only afford to take students whose families can pay. Later on, if we can expand our services or get some government funding, we're hoping to include some low-income kids. I've stayed up nights writing grant applications. So far, nothing's come through."

"I see." He fell silent, his hands resting on his knees. In the stillness, the rise and fall of his breathing mingled with the cry of a circling hawk.

Kira shifted on the rock. She was about to get up, make some excuse and leave, when he spoke again.

"So what is it with the horses?"

Kira settled back into place. At least it was easy to talk about her work. "There's a lot to it. The students choose a horse and work with it every day, taking care of it and earning its trust. If they can do that, they eventually get to ride it."

"And that's therapy?" He picked up a pebble and tossed it down the slope, startling a flock of mourning doves into flight. "Sounds like more bother than it's worth. Why not just get the kid a damned dog?"

"Dogs are too easy. What you get from a horse, you have to earn. The horse doesn't care who you are, only how you behave with it. That's the therapy—creating trust, creating cooperation, learning to get along, to be relaxed and peaceful and follow the rules. I've seen it work with these kids, time and time again."

She met his skeptical gaze. His eyes were the color of black coffee, brimming with hidden secrets. "Do you ride?" she asked.

"Hell, no. I've never been on a horse. I don't even like them."

"Why not? There has to be a story behind that."

"Maybe." He tossed a pebble down the canyon, watching as it bounced out of sight. "If there's any kind of story, it goes way back. My father was a rodeo cowboy, and not a very good one. I couldn't have been more than three or four years old when I saw him get bucked off an outlaw bronc that damn near trampled him to death before they pulled it away. He was in a lot of pain after that. Couldn't work. Got into heavy drinking, beat on my mother and on me—she let him. The state finally took me away and put me in the foster system."

Kira knew he'd had a rough childhood. Wendy had told her that much. But she'd never heard the details. "What happened to them—your parents?"

He shrugged. "My mother's long gone. My father was in prison, last I heard. It's not like we're close."

"I'm sorry." Kira might have said more, but she sensed that this proud, wounded man wouldn't welcome her sympathy. She rose, glancing at her watch. "Time for my students to start the day. I need to be getting back."

"So do I. Dusty promised to put me to work. I just hope it doesn't involve the horses."

He stayed a few steps behind her as she wound her way along the narrow trail. At least they'd gotten off to a decent start this morning. But she doubted it would last. There were too many memories between them, too many painful truths left unspoken.

"I have one question," she said. "If you'd wanted to be here, you would have shown up a long time ago. How did my grandfather get you to come with him? I can't believe it was easy."

His chuckle sounded more cynical than amused. "Easier than you think. He paid the fine to bail me out of the Coconino County Jail. I owe him a thousand dollars."

Kira stifled a gasp, then shook her head. Why should anything about this man surprise her? "He told me you were working in a garage," she said.

"I know. But why lie about it? It is what it is."

"What did you do?" She paused, turning back to face him.

"Punched a smart-ass college kid in a bar. Cracked his jaw and knocked out one of his front teeth."

"Why? What did he do?"

"Made a comment about our troops. When I told him to shut up, he took a swing at me. I swung back. Direct hit. If I had it to do over, I wouldn't change a thing."

"Even if it meant going to jail?"

"Believe me, there are worse places to be than jail."

They were walking again, moving steadily up the trail, toward the ranch. The rising sun flashed above the crest of the mountains, flooding the land with light. In the valley below, a road construction crew, widening a narrow highway, had already started their workday. Muted by distance, the drills chewed into the rock, boring holes for the dynamite that would be rammed deep and detonated.

"How's your cabin? Is it all right?" Kira asked, making small talk.

"It's amazing. When I think of the old-time stars that have stood in that shower—"

He broke off as the booming roar of a dynamite blast echoed up from the valley. "Incoming!" he shouted. "Get down!" Diving for Kira, he shoved her to the rocky ground and flung himself, spread-eagled, on top of her. Facedown, she spat dirt as she thrashed and struggled, pinned under his solid weight. As she fought to get free, she could feel his heart pounding against her back, racing as if in terror.

Suddenly the truth hit her. Having dealt with veterans suffering from PTSD, it was something she should have already known.

Jake was trying to shield her with his body. He was trying to protect her.

At once, she stopped fighting him and willed her muscles to relax. "It's all right, Jake," she said in a calm voice. "There's no danger. It's just the men working on the road. They're blasting the rock with dynamite."

He was still for a moment, as if weighing what she'd said. As the crisis passed, she became aware of his warm, masculine weight pressing down on her, the hardness of his body, its pressure against her hips. Then the breath eased out of him. He rolled off her and, with a muttered curse, sat up.

"Did I hurt you?" he asked.

"No." Kira scrambled to her knees. She had a skinned elbow and a cactus thorn pricking her leg, but she couldn't let that matter. "You scared me at first, but then I realized you were trying to protect me."

"Protect you from a damned silly noise. *Booyah!*" He pushed to his feet, his expression dark. "I shouldn't even be out here with you."

"It's all right." Standing, Kira brushed herself off and plucked the cactus thorn out of her jeans. "The cook should be here by now. Let's go back and get some breakfast."

"You go back. I need a minute." He motioned her away. "Go!" he growled when she hesitated. "Damn it, don't mother me! I just need to be alone."

Kira left then, striding up the trail, her mouth fixed in a taut line. It didn't matter, she told herself. Jake wasn't her patient. He wasn't even her friend. The last thing he wanted was her sympathy, let alone her help. *Well, fine.* If he wanted to be ignored, she'd be happy to accommodate him.

The ranch was stirring to life. Consuelo's car was parked outside the kitchen. Paige was in the yard, tossing a stick for the dog. As Kira came through the gate, she saw Dusty on the porch, a worried look on his face.

"Is everything all right?" Kira asked.

"I was just wondering if you've seen Jake? He's not in his cabin."

"I met him on the trail. He'll be showing up soon." Kira mounted the steps. "I still don't think it's a good idea having him here. You know he's got issues. And he doesn't seem to want any help."

"Did you ask him?"

"I didn't have to."

Thrusting his hands into his pockets, the old cowboy gazed toward the gate. "Well, now that he's here, I can't just throw him off the place for no reason, can I? Jake must've had some god-awful experiences fighting for his country. He deserves a chance—or at least some patience and understanding."

"Fine. But he's your rehabilitation project, not mine. I've got my students to worry about—and Paige." Kira strode off toward the cabins to make sure her charges were getting ready for breakfast. Her grandfather was a wise old man, but he was wrong about Jake. All her instincts told her, war hero or not, the man was trouble.

Jake had walked back down the trail to where he could look out over the valley. From here he could see the construction crew working on the road, their massive earthmoving machines made as small as toys by distance.

The dynamite blast had flung him back to Afghanistan and the roar of exploding mortar shells that the Taliban had fired onto their patrols. In the moment, the memory—the fear, the need to protect—had been absolutely real. And in that moment, when he'd flung Kira to the ground and held her down, he'd made a fool of himself. But it wasn't going to happen again. He wouldn't let it.

For a few minutes, he watched the men work, listening to the whine of their pneumatic drills as they bored into the rock. Knowing they were there, and that they'd be blasting, would help him control his reaction when it happened again.

Even so, there were no guarantees. Any sound that might be mistaken for bombs or gunfire could be enough to throw him into panic.

It was a hellish way to live. At least his body had survived in one piece. In that way, he'd been luckier than some of his buddies. But holding down the most menial job was always a problem; and the idea of an intimate, lasting relationship was a joke. What woman would stay with a man who had a way of jumping at shadows or waking up from dreams in a murderous rage?

Or trying to kill himself?

Jake had walked that dark line more than once. So far, he'd managed to stop himself before stepping over the edge. But the notion of ending the pain was still there, whispering like a seductress.

Would things be different now if his wife hadn't died?

Remembering, he turned and moved back along the trail.

The few months he'd spent with Wendy before

his first deployment had been the happiest time of his life. During his first yearlong tour of duty, she'd been his rock. They'd kept in frequent touch by Skype, her face and her voice pulling him back from the nightmare of the war and reminding him of what he had waiting on the home front.

When she'd greeted him at the airport, with their baby girl in her arms, and he'd held his family close, the horror had receded like the memory of a bad dream. Their time together had been bittersweet—fiercely tender, desperately loving, but marked by strain. The war had changed him in a way she couldn't understand. But still, Wendy had stood by him, true blue. And when the second deployment had shaken him even more deeply than before, she'd been a call away, to anchor him to the things that were important—home, family, trust and love.

He'd been nearing the end of that second deployment, ready to come home and heal in her arms, when he'd gotten word of the accident.

Wendy's death had shattered him. Granted leave to attend the funeral and make needed arrangements, he'd felt no attachment to any part of his home life. Even his daughter, a toddler who barely remembered him, was like a stranger. When Kira had offered to take the child, it had been all he could do to mutter a word of thanks and walk away. He'd returned to Afghanistan, finished his tour and signed up for another one. The war had become his world, and now there was nothing in this world to quiet the monsters he still carried in his head.

The ranch gate was in sight now. He could hear the sounds of morning—voices, horses and the clang of the steel triangle that signaled breakfast was ready. Jake knew he should eat, but the thought of sharing a table with Kira, Paige and seven curious teens had killed his appetite. He'd just grab coffee in the kitchen and hope Dusty could find a way to keep him busy. If he got hungry later, he could go inside and make himself a sandwich.

Coming here had been a mistake. There were too many shared memories, too many people who knew his past. And there was one little girl who'd be better off not knowing him at all.

He would stick to his work, Jake resolved, avoiding Kira and her students, avoiding Paige. As soon as he worked off his debt to the old man, he'd be out of here. And he wouldn't waste time looking back.

Kira forked hay into the outdoor feeders and filled the big steel trough with fresh water from the hose. Then she opened the stalls and turned the horses out of the barn, into the paddock. Soon the students would be coming outside to clean the stable. After that, Dusty would be introducing them to the horses.

Dusty knew more about horses than anyone Kira had ever met. It would be his vital job to teach the students about horse handling, just as it was hers to deal with their personal issues and the therapy sessions. As a team, they worked well together. Neither of them could imagine doing the program alone.

As the students headed to their cabins for a quick after-breakfast break, Dusty came out onto the front porch. Brushing the hay dust off her jeans, Kira joined him.

"Did you ever find Jake?" she asked. "I didn't see him come back."

"I caught him in the kitchen while you were at breakfast. He'll be cleaning out that old shed behind the cabins, sorting things and separating out the junk. Somewhere in there, I remember a big batch of cedar shingles. After he digs them out, I'll put him to patching the barn roof and maybe oiling it, too. That should keep him busy for a while."

"You may want to keep an eye on him." Kira told Dusty what had happened on the trail when Jake had been startled by the blasting. "He practically tackled me. And he didn't let me up until I explained what was going on. Oh, and he's not much for horses, either. He says he doesn't even like them."

"That's what he told me. I'll keep it in mind. Did you talk about Wendy, or about Paige?"

"No, I thought it best to steer clear of emotional subjects. I suppose that'll come in time, but I don't think he's ready. Frankly, neither am I."

"That's fine. It'll happen when it happens." He glanced toward the guest cabins. "Right now, here come your students. Time to get to work."

Kira's charges finished cleaning the stable, shortening yesterday's time by almost a third. There was some complaining, but it was mostly hushed by other students who just wanted to get the job done. All to the good. They were already learning to work together, but they had a long way to go.

Once Kira had collected the gloves and shovels, Dusty took over. After lining the students up along the paddock fence and inviting them to sit or stand, he began his basic horse lecture.

"Today you'll get to walk into the paddock, choose any horse and make contact with it. But before you walk up to a horse, there are a few things you need to understand.

"First of all, horses can be dangerous. You approach an animal that weighs ten times as much as you do, an animal with hooves that can kick and teeth that can bite, you'd better know what you're doing. And that's why you'll be given helmets to wear whenever you work with them, even when you're not riding. Understand?"

The students nodded in wide-eyed silence.

"Second, when you're around a horse, there's one thing to remember. What that big animal wants most is to be safe. For the few million years horses have been around, they've been food for predators. That fear of being killed and eaten is hardwired into every last one of them, from a Derby winner to a Shetland pony. If anything scares them— a noise, a moving shadow, a person making the wrong move—the horse won't take time to figure it out. He'll take off running, or if he can't run, he'll fight. Keep that in mind. Your number one concern will be to make sure your horse feels safe."

A faint smile tugged at Kira's lips as she observed her students. Dusty was a master showman. He had those kids in the palm of his hand.

"There's one other thing a horse wants. He wants to get along. He wants to know who's in charge and to do what it takes to fit in and be comfortable. In that way, he's not so different from you. Once he knows you're his boss and understands what you want him to do, the natural thing will be for him just to do it. But we'll talk more about that later."

As Kira stood by, watching and listening, she could hear the faint thumping and rustling of things being moved in the storage shed behind the cabins. Jake was hard at work and staying out of the way, which was fine. She knew he wanted to work off his debt to Dusty and leave. But what if it was Dusty's plan to keep him on as part of the ranch family?

And what about Paige? As her father, Jake would have custody of the little girl. If he wanted to take her, Kira would have no legal recourse except to let him—unless she could prove he was an unfit parent.

If it came to a battle, things could get ugly. But whatever happened, Kira vowed, she wouldn't stand for Paige being torn from her loving, secure home to share her father's rootless lifestyle and endure his bouts of PTSD. She would fight Jake with everything she had.

"Kira?" Her grandfather's voice pulled her back to the present. This, she realized, was the point in his lecture where she would walk into the paddock and demonstrate how to approach a horse safely.

"Yes . . . ready." She walked to the paddock gate, opened it carefully and, after stepping through, closed it behind her.

"That's the first thing to remember," Dusty said. "You close the gate. You don't want to let the horses out. The second thing is to be aware of *all* the horses, not just the one you're after. You don't want to startle them. Make sure they all know you're there."

Kira demonstrated by whistling, then speaking softly. The seven horses raised their heads and pricked their ears. "Read their body language," Dusty said. "Look at the ears. They're friendly and curious. If a horse has its ears laid back, that means it's upset, and you should keep your distance. But these animals are all fine."

Kira chose a buckskin gelding named Buddy, who was standing a little apart from the others. Speaking softly, she walked toward it. "Remember what I told you," Dusty said. "Always approach a horse from the left side, never from straight on in front, and never, ever from the back unless you want to get kicked. Horses have good eyesight, but they can't see straight in front of their noses or behind their rear ends. You'll always want your horse to know where you are."

"Why not the right side?" one of the boys asked.

"They're not used to that. Horses are trained to be handled and mounted from the left."

"Unless they're Indian horses." The speaker was

a small, bespectacled boy named Calvin. "Indians mounted their horses from the right."

"That's true," Dusty said. "But it was a long time ago. These days, I'm betting even Native Americans mount from the left."

"Smart-ass!" Mack poked Calvin in the ribs.

"None of that." Dusty gave him a scowl. "Now, watch Kira's hand, how she holds it flat for the horse to smell—palm down so he'll know she's not offering any treats. When he's had a good sniff, she'll pet him—not on the nose or the face, but back by his shoulder, on his withers. Now watch how she walks away, easy, looking out for the other horses. That's what each of you will be doing today, just to get acquainted. Your helmets are right here, by the fence." He glanced around the group. "So who wants to go first?"

The metal storage shed was about ten feet by twenty and crammed shoulder high with what looked like sixty years' worth of junk. Standing in front of the open double doors, Jake shook his head. He was no longer concerned about Dusty having enough work for him. Sorting out this mess would keep him busy for at least a solid week. Maybe he could put his entire wage toward paying the old man back—twenty dollars an hour instead of ten. He could manage it, as long as he had food and lodging. And that would get him out of here in half the time.

He took a few moments to analyze the task. A

triage approach might work—one pile for worth-less trash to be hauled off, one pile for things that were clearly worth keeping and a third pile for items that Dusty would need to look at before de-ciding what to do with them. With no rain in the forecast, it wouldn't hurt to leave things outside for a few days.

Taking a deep breath, he set to work. A crushed wicker basket? Trash. A worn-out saddle? Almost trash, unless it had sentimental value. Ask Dusty. A box of what looked like old family photographs? Keep. A set of half-worn truck tires? Ask.

A shaggy brown dog came trotting around the cabins and lay down in a shady spot next to the shed. Jake liked dogs. He'd made friends with one or two that hung around the camps in Afghanistan. Unlike people, they didn't get on his nerves or try to sneak up on him. This one seemed more inter-ested in having something to watch and a comfort-able place to nap than in making friends. Jake spoke a word to the animal, then went on working.

He was making slow progress, but the task was like shoveling away at a mountain. The desert sun beat down on him, hot in spite of the mild spring day. As he paused to lift the brim of his baseball cap and wipe the sweat off his forehead, he sensed a movement behind him—and it wasn't the dog.

Danger instincts on hair-trigger alert, he dropped to a half crouch and spun around, prepared to fight for his life.

Standing a few feet away was a small person in shorts and a pink tee with a kitten on the front.

Russet curls framed a heart-shaped face. Dark eyes, fringed by long lashes, widened as Jake straightened and exhaled. The little girl looked startled, but she stood her ground, one hand holding out a peace offering—a can of root beer. The can was so cold that moisture trickled down the outside.

"Hi, mister," she said. "I'm Paige."

CHAPTER FOUR

Jake's mouth went dry. His daughter was a younger image of Wendy, except for her eyes. Those eyes were his.

"You looked thirsty." She held out the root beer can. Jake took it and popped the tab.

"Thanks," he said, finding his voice. "Does anybody know you're out here?"

She shook her head. "Everybody's busy. What's your name, mister?"

"My name is Jake. I guess you can call me Mister Jake."

She studied him with a thoughtful frown. "My daddy's name is Jake," she said. "But he doesn't look like you. He doesn't have whiskers."

"There are a lot of Jakes around." He turned his back on her and began rummaging in the shed, holding the can in one hand. The ice-cold root beer tasted good, but his throat was so tight he could barely swallow it. Maybe if he ignored her, she'd go away. He needed her gone. Having her here, so close, was tearing into his heart.

"What are you doing, Mister Jake?" she asked.

"I'm working for Dusty. He's paying me to clean out this shed." He hoisted part of a rusty bedframe and dumped it on the designated trash pile.

"Can I help?"

"You're too little. This stuff is pretty heavy. And some things have sharp edges. You could get hurt."

"Okay. I'll just watch." She plopped down onto a tire that had rolled off the pile.

Jake glanced at her from beneath the rim of his baseball cap. She had fair skin, like Wendy's, and she was sitting in the hot sun. "You'd better go someplace shady," he said. "You'll get sunburned out here."

"No, I won't. Aunt Kira makes me wear sunscreen every day. She likes me to wear a hat, too, but sometimes I forget."

Jake lifted a heavy cardboard box off the stack in the shed and lowered it to the ground. "It sounds like your aunt Kira takes pretty good care of you."

"Uh-huh," Paige said. "Aunt Kira's like my mom. But she isn't my real mom. My real mom died when I was little. She was in a car crash."

Jake felt the familiar sensation, like a steel auger boring between his ribs. He knew he should stop right there, but he felt compelled to go on, to drive the pain a little deeper. "Do you remember your mother?" he asked.

"Not much. But I've got her picture. She was really

pretty. She's up in heaven now. But I still talk to her. Sometimes it's like I can feel her listening."

Do you really believe she listens to you?

Jake didn't voice the thought. Early on, after the accident, he'd tried talking to Wendy. But he'd given up on that. It was like leaving voice mail for somebody who would never return your call. Kind of like prayer, which he'd also given up.

"What about your father?" he asked, knowing the question was a bad idea.

"He's in the army. He was supposed to come back, but he didn't. I think maybe the army won't let him. They need him to stay and fight the bad people."

The auger twisted, driving deeper, all the way to his heart. "I guess you don't talk to him, do you?"

She shook her head. "He isn't in heaven. He can't hear me."

"Paige!" A motherly-looking Mexican woman in her fifties came bustling around the row of cabins. "*Ay de mi!* I've been looking all over for you. What are you doing out here, bothering this poor man?"

Jake and Consuelo had met briefly in the kitchen that morning when he'd stopped by for coffee, so no introduction was needed. "She isn't bothering me," he said. "But this might not be the safest place for her. She's probably better off going with you."

"Come on, *chiquita*." Consuelo took Paige's hand. "I'm making cookies in the kitchen. You can help me."

As she was being led off, Paige glanced back at

Jake. "I'll bring you some cookies when they get done. Chocolate chip. They're really good," she said, giving him her mother's smile.

The dog roused himself, got up and followed them back around the cabins. Watching his daughter go, Jake quivered from the strain of controlling his emotions. That little girl's smile held the power to destroy him. Lord, he should never have agreed to come here. He should have stayed in jail, where he, at least, felt safe.

"He isn't in heaven," she'd answered when he'd asked her about talking to her father.

She was right about that. It was more like he was in hell.

"This horse hates me! I want a different one!" Mack, the big boy with anger issues, was red-faced with frustration. He'd chosen a docile bay mare named Bella. She'd let him come close enough to offer his hand for a sniff, but every time he tried to stroke her, she edged away.

"That's not how it works, Mack." Kira stood a few steps away, coaching. "If you give up, she'll know she got the best of you, and she'll do it again. Step back now and try to relax. She can tell you're upset. It's making her nervous."

"I can't do this! She hates me!" Mack yanked off his helmet and flung it on the ground.

"Nobody hates you, Mack. Not me, and certainly not the horse. She only wants to feel safe. Now put on your helmet, take a few breaths and think about how easy this will be—or if that doesn't work, close your eyes and think about your favorite song."

Mack put on his helmet and closed his eyes. The students who'd gone before him had done all right, including Lanie, who'd been terrified at first. Being the first one to fail would embarrass him and worsen his anger issues.

"Got the song?" Kira asked, and saw him nod slightly. "Good. Now open your eyes, and as you go to the horse again, sing it very softly, just for her. Try it. That's it. Now let her smell your hand. Keep singing."

Kira couldn't hear the song, but she could see Mack's lips moving. The mare might not be a music lover, but if singing helped relax the boy, that could make the difference. She held her breath as Mack stood to the left of Bella's head and put out his hand, palm down.

Bella was curious. Her ears pricked forward, a small sign of acceptance. This time she allowed Mack to touch her and stroke her withers. A tiny shudder of pleasure passed through her body. Mack glanced back at Kira, his eyes wide, his mouth grinning. "Hey, she likes it!"

"And I think she likes *you*," Kira said. "Good job."

The last two students had watched the others and had no trouble with their horses. Feeling good about the session, Kira seated the group by the fence. "Tell me some of the things you learned today," she said.

Calvin raised his hand. "I tried to go on the right side of my horse, like an Indian. The horse didn't like it."

"So what did you learn from that?"

Calvin grinned. "I learned to listen to Dusty."

"Good thinking," Kira said. Calvin, small, solitary and extremely bright, had been bullied at school and online. His parents had signed him up for horse therapy after he attempted suicide; they hoped it would give him confidence and make him feel less like a victim.

Lanie raised her hand, her sleeve sliding back to show a glimpse of ugly, healing cuts. "If you're scared or mad, the horses can tell. It's like they can read you."

"That's right," Kira said. "You might be able to fool people, but you can't fool a horse. And the horse will never try to fool you. Horses are honest to the bone, and they expect the same from you."

After a few more comments, Kira dismissed her students to wash up and get ready for lunch. The morning had gone well. They were off to a good start, but there were bound to be some bumps down the road. These kids weren't here because they were happy and well-adjusted. They were here because they needed help. It would be her job as a therapist to see that each of them received that help.

In the afternoon, they'd be taking a field trip to the Arizona-Sonora Desert Museum—a twenty-one–acre educational showplace for the desert's plants and animals. By the time they returned to the ranch, the teens would be worn-out and ready for dinner. After that, Kira would have her first one-on-one session, starting with Heather.

Dusty's SUV, with an extra bench seat installed in the back, was the go-to vehicle for hauling students around. Kira had been planning to have Dusty drive, as usual. But while the teens were at lunch, he'd taken her aside. "It'll be a long afternoon, and I don't know if I'm up for it," he said. "I've asked Jake to drive you."

Kira gazed at him in sudden concern. Her grandfather had been strong and active for as long as she could remember. But he was in his midseventies now. Maybe it was time she faced the fact that he needed to slow down.

"Are you all right?" she asked.

"Fine." He patted her shoulder. "Just not as young and spry as I used to be. Jake drove that Jeep all the way back from Flagstaff. He'll do fine."

A moment flickered in Kira's memory: Jake's reaction to the dynamite blast that morning—the warm, manly weight of his body as he'd held her down, and her unexpected response. She swiftly dismissed it. That had nothing to do with now. Her concern was for her students. How would it affect them if he had another such episode? Would they be safe with him?

Even without that concern, she didn't feel ready to spend the afternoon with the man. Being with Jake stirred memories of the past, with secrets that were best forgotten.

"It's all right," she said. "I can drive the Jeep myself."

"Now, Kira, I know you like to focus on the kids, not on the road. And it never hurts to have another grown-up along. Anyway, I already asked Jake. He said he'd do it."

Kira sighed, giving in. "Fine. Will Paige be all right staying here? I was going to take her along, but with Jake there—"

"She's already met him," Dusty said. "Consuelo found her out by the shed with Jake this morning."

Kira's pulse skipped. "Does Paige know—"

"No. And neither does Consuelo. As far as they're concerned, he's just a stranger I hired to do some work. Stop fussing about it, Kira. Sometimes things need a little shaking up."

"But not where Paige is concerned. Jake isn't stable. I don't want him upsetting her, or maybe even scaring her."

"He's her father."

"And right now, that can't be allowed to matter. I'm leaving her here. She won't be happy about it, but she'll be fine with you and Consuelo. Meanwhile, I'm going to have my hands full—not just babysitting my students, but worrying about Jake. Ask me next time, before you get him involved."

Washed, combed and wearing a clean T-shirt, Jake wandered into the kitchen. From the dining room, he could hear Kira's teenage gang laughing and talking over lunch. He'd been invited to join them, but he didn't want to be stared at or questioned. Even agreeing to drive them this afternoon was probably a mistake.

Consuelo was at the sink, loading the dishwasher. "Hi," he greeted her. "I was hoping I could make myself a quick sandwich."

"There's some already made." Consuelo pointed to a stacked plate on the counter. "Have all you want. And there's Diet Coke in the fridge."

"Thanks." Still standing, Jake picked up a sandwich and took a bite. Turkey, bacon and tomato on whole wheat. It was first-rate. "And thanks for the cookies," he said. "Paige brought me two of them before she had to run back to the house."

Consuelo laughed. "That little sneak. I thought there were a couple of cookies missing from the pan. She seems to have taken a fancy to you."

Something tightened around Jake's heart. "Don't ask me why," he said. "I haven't been all that friendly to her."

Consuelo's dark eyes took his measure. For a moment, Jake feared she might have figured out who he was. But her gaze lingered on the Army Ranger tattoo—a traditional winged skull with a flag—that decorated his upper arm. "You were in the army?" she asked.

"Yeah, for a few years." He popped the tab on a can of Diet Coke.

"My son was in the army," she said. "They sent him to Iraq. He'd been there a month when he was killed by a roadside bomb."

And a bastard like me is still alive. Where's the justice in this world?

"I'm sorry," Jake said, thinking about the buddies he'd lost and the times he'd yearned to trade places with any one of them. It was the thought of those men that had kept him from putting a bullet through his own head in the dark times. They had died for a cause. How could he throw away his own life—the life that fate and luck had spared—for nothing?

"We're all sorry," Consuelo said. "We've got two girls, but he was our only boy. Losing him almost killed my husband, and me too. But what do you do? You accept it and move on." She gave him a brave smile. "It's nice to meet somebody who came back from that awful war in one piece."

"A lot of good men didn't." Jake crumpled the empty soda can and tossed it in the recycle bin. "Thanks for the sandwich. If there's anything you need while I'm here . . ."

"Thanks. I'll remember that." She gave him a smile as he left the kitchen. *A good woman. A wise woman. "You accept it and move on."* It sounded so easy, the way she'd said it. But Jake had tried. The horrors that he'd not only witnessed, but had taken part in, were burned into every nerve cell in his body, and were woven into the fabric of his soul. They had become the man he was—the man he would be for the rest of his life.

The Arizona-Sonora Desert Museum was on the west side of Tucson, a drive that took about an hour. Before their departure, Jake had stood by listening while Kira went over the rules with her students. They'd be set free to explore the two miles of trails and animal exhibits, but they were to practice the buddy system. No going off alone or going off the trails. And they were to check in at least every hour with their cell phones. If she didn't hear, Kira would call them and, if need be, track them down. By four o'clock, everyone was to be back at the visitor center for refreshments and the ride home.

That was the Kira he remembered, perfectly organized and in charge. Did she ever loosen the tight grip she kept on herself and those around her?

Silly question, Jake thought. He wouldn't call her a control freak, but Kira was one of the most focused people he'd ever known.

He'd assumed his duties would be limited to driving, but he was wrong. With the kids scattering like sailors on shore leave, he'd been about to find a seat in the shade of the visitor center when Kira gave him his orders.

"Come on, we need to keep an eye on them."

"I thought you were turning them loose on their own," he said.

She gave him a rare grin. "That's what they think, too. But this is one more way to observe them from a distance—who's getting along, who's breaking rules, who's not fitting in. It all goes into their therapy. It's also a way to make sure they're safe."

"Fine. But why do you need me to spy on them? That's your job. I'm just the chauffeur."

Her eyes narrowed. "These kids all have problems, and four of them are boys. It never hurts to have a man along in case things get out of hand— bullying, teasing the animals, sneaking a joint in the restroom, you name it. That's one reason why I like bringing Dusty on these outings. All it takes is a word from him to keep the kids in line."

Jake hung back, still reluctant to get involved. "Sorry, I don't have much experience at babysitting. Besides, I don't know if an ex-jailbird is the best role model for your kids."

"Forget that. You're US Army. Just tug up your sleeve and flash that tattoo. They'll be shaking in their boots. Come on." She seized his hand to pull him along with her. The contact tingled against his palm, sending a heat flash up his arm. As if she'd felt it, too, she pulled away. "Please," she said. "I need your help this afternoon."

Relenting, he moved with her down the path, matching her long, purposeful strides. She was tall, but Jake towered over her by half a head. Now he looked down at her, his gaze tracing her stubborn profile. "Don't you ever back off, Kira?" he asked her.

"I don't know what you mean."

"I think you do. Don't you ever stop charging ahead like a one-woman army? Wendy always said you were the most motivated person she knew. But where does it stop?"

The mention of Wendy's name passed like a brief shadow between them before she spoke. "Everything I've done—my degree, my practice—has been due to hard work and discipline. I can't afford to back off, as you say. I owe myself, and my students, too much for that."

"Do you?" He studied her upturned face, the fine-drawn features, the thoughtful gray eyes, the ripe, sensual mouth, which seemed to contradict everything else he knew about her. How many times had that mouth been kissed? Jake found himself wondering. Had she ever been in love, or had her all-consuming discipline left no time for such trivial things?

"Do I what?" she asked.

"Do you owe your whole life to your work? What about fun? What about having a family?"

"You're a fine one to talk." She looked away, as if wishing she'd bitten back that last remark. "Anyway, I have a family of sorts. I have my grandfather and Paige. . . ." She glanced up at him in sudden alarm. "Oh, but Paige is yours. I mustn't let myself forget that."

"I didn't come to take Paige away from you, Kira. She seems happy where she is. And I'm no fit father for a little girl."

He sensed her relief. "Dusty told me you met her."

"She came out to the shed and introduced herself. She was . . . Oh, Lord, she took my breath away."

"Paige is a joy. I think she got the very best of both you and Wendy."

"You could say that." He didn't want to talk about Wendy, how she'd died or how much he still missed her. Wendy had been his lifeline; and now that she was gone, there was no road back to where they'd been and what they'd had. He was lost, with no hope of ever being found.

Ending the conversation, he opened his copy of the visitor map, which Kira had handed out to each of the students and to him. The twenty-one–acre complex, which integrated cactus gardens, natural desert and animal exhibits, was a maze of trails, paved and unpaved. Their path had taken them past the hummingbird aviary and outdoor pollination garden, a mass of blooming scarlet, pink and gold flowers. So far, they hadn't seen any of the students.

"Where now?" Jake asked.

Looking past his shoulder, she pointed to the map. "Most kids like to head up here, to Cat Canyon and the desert loop trail. Let's go that way."

Jake shook his head, surprised that he was almost enjoying this. "It feels like you're plotting a spy mission. What do we do when we find them? Hide behind the rocks?"

"If we see them, and they're okay, we keep our distance. If they see us, we wave and keep walking." She strode out, Jake keeping pace with her. Other visitors strolled the paths, but on a weekday, with most children in school, the park wasn't crowded.

A few minutes later, they spotted the three girls, who'd stopped to watch the otters in the stream-life exhibit.

"Well, they look okay," Jake said.

"Yes. But take a closer look. Heather's the dominant one. She's got Lanie in hand, and they're both ignoring Faith. See how she's standing apart, not even involved with them and acting like she doesn't care? That's an issue right there."

"I see what you mean." The tall girl, pretty enough to be a model, was being shunned by the other two. Growing up, Jake had seen girls behave that way.

Could be some jealousy involved, but that was Kira's business, not his.

Kira moved on up the trail, Jake keeping pace with her. He'd grown up in Phoenix, but never spent much time in the higher desert country around Tucson. He'd forgotten how beautiful it could be in the spring, with cactuses and wild-flowers bursting into bloom on the hillsides, drawing swarms of birds and nectar-seeking insects.

They'd reached the beginning of the loop trail when Kira's cell phone rang. Jake couldn't make out words, but the boyish voice on the other end of the call sounded frantic.

"Slow down, Calvin," Kira said. "Tell me what happened." She listened a moment. "We'll be right there!" she said.

Jake caught her as she raced up the trail. "What is it?"

"It's Patrick. He went off the trail, climbed up some rocks and took a fall. He's conscious, but he's got a bleeding cut on his head and who knows what else. Poor Calvin sounded frantic."

She surged ahead, with Jake plunging after her. A memory flashed in his head: charging up a hill under AK-47 fire from the Taliban dug in on the ridge; seeing the young corporal on his right go down, seeing his face. . . .

Jake wrenched himself free of the memory. This was no time to go off the deep end, when a child was injured and Kira needed his help. *Pull yourself together, damn it!*

Now, rounding a bend in the trail, they could

see the two boys. One was sprawled faceup on the gravel. The other, a small boy with glasses, had stripped off his T-shirt and wadded it against his companion's head.

"Good work, Calvin." Kira dropped to her knees beside the injured boy, a skinny redhead. "How are you doing, Patrick?"

His face was pale, his freckles standing out as if they'd been painted on his skin. His eyes gazed up at her. "I'll be okay," he said. "Please don't call my mom and dad."

"I'll need to call them," Kira said. "That's a rule I have to obey. But if you'd obeyed *your* rules, this wouldn't have happened. Why did you go off the trail?"

"There was a lizard on the rocks. I wanted to catch it."

"Well, there you go. I hope you've learned your lesson. Now let's have a look."

Kneeling next to Calvin, Jake watched Kira ease the wadded, blood-soaked shirt away. The gash at the boy's hairline, most likely caused by a sharp rock, didn't look too bad, but it was bleeding like a fountain. Jake knew that scalp wounds, even the nonserious kind, tended to bleed a lot. Once the flow was stanched and the boy was checked out by a doctor, he'd probably be fine. But the blood reminded Jake of the men he'd seen who'd never go home whole, and the innocent women and children who should never have been in the way. So much blood . . .

Remembered horror clenched his gut. He battled the urge to clamber to his feet and get away from here. Kira needed him. He had to get himself under control.

"There's a first-aid station in the visitor center," she said. "I don't think it would be wise for Patrick to walk that far. If you'll carry him, Jake, I'll stay next to you and keep the pressure on his wound. There's an emergency clinic not far from here. Once he's bandaged and cleaned up, you can drive him to get checked out. I'll stay and keep an eye on the other students till you're back." She gave Calvin a smile. "You come with us, too, Calvin. Once we've taken care of Patrick, I'll owe you a new shirt. You can choose any shirt you want from the gift shop."

Patrick's arms and legs dangled as Jake carried him the half mile over winding trails to the visitor center—just as he'd carried wounded men and maimed children, bleeding, dying in his arms as bullets and mortars rained around him. This wasn't the same—a warm, safe spring day and a foolhardy boy who would soon recover. But as he walked the trail, with Kira beside him, he could almost smell the burning fuel and feel the grit of exploding earth blasting his face. Remembered cries and groans echoed in his head, drowning out even the recollected roar of gunfire.

Panic was setting in, squeezing him like a vise. If he could hold on till they got some help and he could put the boy down, maybe he'd be all right. Ahead, he could see the modern lines of the adobe-colored visitor complex. To his mind's eye, it was like the high double wall of sand-filled HESCO bags that had given the outpost camps a measure of protection. If he could make it to that wall with his precious burden . . .

"My goodness, somebody's had an accident." The voice of a park docent broke into his thoughts. "Here, let's get him where we can have a look."

Barely holding himself together, Jake lowered the injured boy's feet to the pavement and allowed Kira and the docent to help him inside the building, with the shirtless Calvin trailing behind.

Jake spotted a restroom sign and headed for it. Inside, the place was empty. For now, at least, he was alone. Apart from the faint trickle of water, the only sound he could hear was his heart pounding against his ribs.

Shaking, he made it into a stall and managed to bolt the door before the dam broke inside him. Choking on sobs, he slammed his fist against the metal wall, again and again, until his bruised knuckles numbed to the pain.

CHAPTER FIVE

By the time Patrick was cleaned up, bandaged and ready to be driven to the emergency clinic, Jake had regained his self-control. A cold numbness had set in, a welcome condition in which he could think clearly but felt very little. It was this state of mind that enabled him to work and function in everyday life. It made that life bearable—most of the time.

The directions to the clinic were easy to follow. It was only a few miles from the museum. But Patrick's constant barrage of questions made the distance seem endless.

"That's a cool tattoo, Jake. Did you get it in the army?"

"Uh-huh." Not really *in* the army, but Jake didn't care enough to explain that.

"I want to get a tat when I turn eighteen. Did it hurt to get it?"

"Some."

"Wow! That would be cool, being in the army. What rank were you?"

"Lieutenant. I went through a program called ROTC, where the army trained me in college and then I had to serve."

"Did you fight?"

"Uh-huh."

"Where? Iraq?"

"Afghanistan."

"Wow. Did you kill anybody?"

"Uh-huh." Jake held on to the numbness, willing it to deepen, to freeze him to the core.

"Cool. What did it feel like?"

"You don't want to know."

"Did you win any medals?"

"Uh-huh." Jake recalled the day he'd taken the two Bronze Stars, the Purple Heart and the rest, and then tossed them off a bridge into some nameless river.

"Did you—"

"Patrick."

"Huh?"

"Enough questions. Just be quiet." Mercifully, by then, they were turning in to the clinic parking lot.

Kira had used her personal credit card to pay for Calvin's new shirt—navy blue with a roadrunner emblazoned across the front. She'd given Jake the business credit card, along with the keys to Dusty's Jeep, when he left to take Patrick to the emergency clinic.

It had occurred to her that if he got it into his head, he could leave the boy at the clinic and take the Jeep and the credit card, hitting the open road. But she'd had little choice except to trust him. Patrick needed to be checked by a doctor, and her other students couldn't be left here unsupervised. Still, Jake's appearance had worried her—his expression unreadable behind the dark sunglasses he wore, his knuckles freshly bruised as if he'd been fighting.

By any measure, Jake was a volatile man. But Dusty trusted him, she reminded herself. And her grandfather's instincts about people were almost as good as his instincts about horses. All the same, she felt a wave of relief when, more than an hour later, the Jeep pulled into the parking lot. Patrick climbed out of the passenger side, wearing a shaky grin and a fresh gauze dressing taped to his head.

Jake got out and came around the vehicle. "Three stitches, but no concussion. The doctor says he'll be as good as new."

Walking up to where Kira stood, he handed her the credit card and the receipt. "The doctor also said Patrick should take it easy for the rest of the day. No running around in the hot sun."

"Fine. Calvin's in the gift shop, looking at books. I'll send Patrick in to join him." She took a moment to inspect Patrick's new bandage, then directed the boy inside.

Jake gazed out across the parking lot at the color-burnished hills. "Calvin was pretty cool this morning, using his shirt to stop the bleeding while he called you on his phone."

"He's a great kid," Kira said. "It breaks my heart that he was almost cyberbullied to death before he came here."

"You're kidding!"

"I'm sorry," she said, catching herself. "Please forget what you just heard. It's unethical for me to share information about my students."

"Kind of like doctor-patient privilege?"

"Exactly. All I can say is that every one of these kids is hurting. In that way, they're not so different from you."

He flinched. "That's a low blow."

"Is it? What happened to your hand?"

"That's none of your damned business." His voice was flat, emotionless. "I'm not one of your sick, rich teenagers, Kira."

His words stung. "Are you saying you don't have a problem?" she demanded.

"All I'm saying is that I don't need any help from do-gooders like you and your grandfather. And I'll be damned to hell if I'm going to let you poke and prod me like a bug under a microscope. As soon as I've paid Dusty back for bailing me out, I'll be gone like a shot. You'll never hear from me again!"

"And what about Paige?"

A groan rumbled in his throat, like the sound of a lion in pain. "What about her?" he asked.

"Does she deserve to grow up without knowing her father—or knowing that he cared enough to be there for her?"

"Does she deserve to know that her father was a burned-out train wreck who won a bunch of medals for blowing up men, women and children—even little girls like her?"

Shocked into silence, Kira stared at him. She was saved from having to respond by the sound of her cell phone.

"That'll be the girls checking in." She turned away from him to take the call. "Yes, come on back here," she said. "If you see Mack and Brandon, tell them to come back, too. It's time to get some ice cream and head home."

She made a quick call to Brandon's cell phone, then turned back to see Jake walking away from her, toward the parking lot. "Where are you going?" she called, half-afraid she'd made him angry enough to drive off and leave them stranded.

He turned and gave her a withering look. "Calm down. I'm going to wait in the vehicle, maybe take a nap if I can manage it. Come on out when you're ready to go."

With that, he wheeled and strode away.

Half an hour later, they were on the road again. They'd left earlier than planned, but the students were all tired. When they got home, there'd be the horses to feed, then dinner, and then her first private interview with Heather, while the others did their schoolwork or watched a video in the den. And she'd need to phone Patrick's parents as well. It would be best to have the boy there when she made the call. That way he could reassure them he was all right and make sure they knew the accident had been his own fault.

Buckled into the passenger seat, Kira glanced at Jake. He'd barely spoken to her since their heated exchange in front of the visitor center. But if he was still upset, he showed no sign of it. He drove calmly and carefully, his hands relaxed on the wheel, and the radio tuned to a mellow country station.

Behind them, the sun was low over the western hills, casting the saguaros into long shadow. By the time they'd passed through Tucson and taken the road into the Santa Catalina foothills, some of the students had fallen asleep.

Kira's gaze traced the line of Jake's profile against the fading sky. She'd always told Wendy he was too handsome for his own good. Even after some very rough years, he was still a striking man. Not that she should care. The last person she wanted to be involved with was her cousin's widower, who'd loved his beautiful wife so blindly that he could never have seen what was coming.

But why was she even thinking along those lines—especially knowing that Jake had every reason to resent her?

Only as they were driving through the side gate to the house and Kira saw the lights of the house—the living room strangely dark—did the premonition strike her that something was wrong. When she saw Consuelo waiting on the porch with Paige, she knew she'd been right. Reaching over the console, she touched Jake's arm.

"Let me out here," she said, unclipping her seat belt. "Then park by the cabins. Tell the students to go get ready for dinner."

"Is everything all right?" he asked.

"I don't know." Kira opened the door and sprang to the ground. As Jake pulled away, Consuelo hurried down the porch steps. She clasped Kira's hands, her face ghostly pale in the porch light.

"It's your grandfather, *querida*," she said. "He had a heart attack this afternoon. They Life-Flighted him to that heart care center on St. Mary's Road."

For the first instant, Kira went numb. No, she hadn't heard right. There had to be some mistake. Her grandfather was strong. She'd never even known him to be sick. How could this have happened?

Then, as reality sank in, she realized she had to be the one in charge. There was no one else.

Questions—what to ask first? Kira struggled to stay composed. "How is he? Will he be all right?"

"I don't know. Paige heard the dog barking and found Dusty lying in the barn. I called nine-one-one and tried to do CPR, but I only knew what I'd seen on TV. Then the helicopter came and took him."

"Oh, Paige!" Turning, Kira gathered the little girl into her arms. The small body shook with sobs. "What a brave girl you are," she murmured. "Can you be brave a little longer?"

Paige gave her a tearful nod.

"Why didn't you call me, Consuelo?" Kira asked, looking up at the distraught woman.

"I wanted to. But didn't have your number. I knew it was on Dusty's phone, but I couldn't find that phone anywhere. He must've had it on him when they took him away."

Jake came around the side of the house. "What is it?" he asked.

Kira told him. "I've got to go to the hospital," she said. "Consuelo, can you stay here tonight?"

"Of course. I was already planning to be here."

"I can drive you, Kira," Jake said.

"No," she told him. "I need somebody to be in charge of the students and the horses. That'll have to be you."

Jake's expression said, *I didn't sign on for this.* But he didn't argue.

"If I'm not back in the morning, get the students to help with the horses," Kira said. "Paige can tell you a lot—she's been watching the rest of us for years. Consuelo, the kids will be hungry. They'll need their supper. After that, you can put in a movie for them to watch."

"Don't worry, there's lasagna in the oven. I'll take care of them," Consuelo said. "You need to go."

"Yes. I'll call you as soon as I know something." Kira found her keys and raced for her own eight-year-old Subaru Outback, which she'd bought used and kept in the vehicle shed. Minutes later, as the sun sank over the distant hills, she was speeding down the road toward the highway and Tucson.

Dread was a cold weight in her chest. For the past ten years, since her parents' deaths, her beloved grandfather had been the one constant in her life. Strong and wise, he had always been there to support her. His willingness to be her partner in the horse therapy program was what made it work, for her and for the troubled young people they helped.

He had to be all right. He just had to be.

Jake stood at the foot of the steps, watching Kira's taillights vanish around the first bend in the road. He forced himself to take deep breaths as reality sank in. Dusty was in the hospital fighting for his life—a battle he might have already lost. And Kira had rushed off to be with her grandfather, leaving him in charge of the ranch—a place where he'd never wanted to be in the first place.

Consuelo touched his shoulder. "You must be hungry. Dinner will be ready soon."

"Thanks. Don't wait for me." He gave her time to go inside before he mouthed a few choice curses. Kids? Lord, he'd never been a fan of teenagers, and the time he'd spent with this bunch hadn't changed his mind. Horses? They were nothing but big, spooky brutes that would just as soon kick you as look at you. And now he was supposed to deal with them. Just for good measure, he uttered more curses he'd picked up in the military, where profanity was natural speech.

Something soft brushed his hand. "Mister Jake, my grandpa says you're not supposed to use those words."

Paige stood looking up at him. Dusty would be her *great*-grandfather, but since she'd never known her grandparents, the technicality wasn't worth explaining.

"Sorry," he said. "I'll have to watch my mouth around here, won't I?" He waited for her to go inside. When she didn't budge, he said, "Shouldn't you go in and get ready for dinner?"

She took his hand, pulling him toward the barn. "Grandpa always says you mustn't fill your own belly while you've got hungry horses. We've got to feed them before we eat."

"How the h—" Jake swallowed the forbidden word. "How do we do that? I've never fed a horse in my life!"

"That's okay. I can show you what to do." She tugged him across the yard, the dog tagging along behind them. It was getting darker, and Jake didn't have a flashlight. But his daughter seemed to know where she was going.

The horses were still loose in the paddock. "How do we get them in the barn?" he asked.

"Sometimes we leave them outside. They'll be okay tonight," Paige said. "But they need to eat. Wild horses eat all day. These horses aren't wild, but their digestion works the same. They mustn't go too long without food, and there's not enough grass for them in the paddock."

"Digestion?" "You know some pretty fancy words for a little girl," Jake said. "And you seem to know a lot about horses, too."

"I just listen to my grandpa," Paige said. "You can learn a lot if you listen." She was still for a moment as if fighting tears. Jake could imagine what a shock it must have been, finding Dusty unconscious in the barn and having to run for help. His daughter was one brave little girl.

"Grandpa would want us to take care of his horses," she said.

As Jake gazed at the light and dark shapes moving in the paddock, something tightened in his gut. He still had occasional nightmares about the bronco that had turned his father into a broken, alcoholic ruin. "Do I have to go in there with them?" he asked.

"No. See those bins by the fence? Those are the feeders. You fill them up with hay. It's easy. You just throw it over the fence. There's a wheelbarrow and a pitchfork in the hay shed. Come on."

The rising moon lent enough light to see the way. Jake followed the small, darting figure through the shadows. The hay shed, open in front, was behind the stable. An empty wheelbarrow, with a pitchfork leaning against it, stood next to what was left of a large, cylindrical hay bale.

"So I just fork the hay into the wheelbarrow and take it out. Is that the idea?" he asked.

"Uh-huh. Once we found a rattlesnake in the hay." She paused. "But don't worry. It was dead."

"Thanks." Jake shuddered as he plunged the pitchfork into the hay bale. He hated snakes.

It took him a couple tries to get it right, but he soon had the wheelbarrow heaped with fragrant hay. With Paige giving directions, he wheeled it to the paddock and refilled the feeders. One horse wandered over and began to munch, followed by another, then more, chomping the hay with their big, flat teeth. Jake could smell their earthy scent.

He could hear them breathing, nickering and passing gas. Why did some folks make such a fuss over horses? They were dangerous, messy, expensive and a hell of a lot of work.

"Now they need water." Paige handed Jake the hose and pointed to the trough. "You can fill it through the fence. I'll turn on the tap. Tell me when it's full."

They finished the task and walked back to the house together, the dog trailing behind. After sending Paige inside to get ready for dinner, Jake sank onto the top step. The dog settled beside him. He scratched the shaggy ears. It was too soon for any word from Kira. All he could do was hope her grandfather would pull through. Dusty was a good man. He'd gone to a lot of trouble and expense to get a burned-out human wreck out of jail and bring him here. Jake still didn't understand why he'd done it. If the worst had happened and Dusty didn't make it, maybe he never would.

As she swung into the hospital parking lot, Kira reminded herself that the Carondelet Heart and Vascular Institute had a reputation for excellent care and the latest technology. But none of that would matter if Dusty had arrived too late to be saved.

Sick with worry, she screeched into the first parking place she found, bolted out of the car and rushed to the hospital entrance. By the time she reached the front desk, she was out of breath.

"Mr. Wingate?" The receptionist checked her

computer screen. "Yes. He's stabilized and in the ICU. They can tell you more at the nurses' station. I'll give you directions."

Stabilized! The word sang in Kira's head as she raced down the hall to the elevator. Her grandfather was alive. She even dared hope that he might recover and be all right.

"He's resting," the ICU nurse told her. "The doctors did an angioplasty and put a stent in the blocked artery that caused the heart attack. He's not out of the woods yet, but if everything looks good, he should be able to go home in a few days. After that, he'll need to take it easy for about three weeks while the stent heals."

"Can I see him?"

"For a few minutes. But don't expect much. He's an old man and he's been through a lot. The best thing for him right now is rest."

"I won't be long." Kira hurried down the hall and tiptoed into her grandfather's room. He lay with his eyes closed, his spare old body hooked up to a maze of tubes and gauges. The monitor above the bed beeped softly, tracking his pulse, blood pressure and oxygen level—all stable, thank heaven.

Dusty had always been a tower of strength. Now the sight of him almost broke her heart. He looked so small and fragile in that bed, his face pale, his cheekbones jutting like ledges above the oxygen tube that was clipped to his nose.

Leaning over the bed, Kira slipped her hand into his and gave it a gentle squeeze. Her heart skipped as he squeezed back and opened his deep blue eyes. "Hello, honey." His voice was weak and hoarse.

"Hello, you old rascal." Kira smiled at him through welling tears. "How are you feeling?"

"Like shit. How do you think?"

"I'm just glad you're still here," Kira said. "You gave us all quite a scare."

"The ranch—the kids—" He was straining to sit up. Kira laid a hand on his shoulder, holding him back.

"Don't worry, everything's fine. Jake's there to help. We can muddle along fine until you're completely well. Right now what we all need most is for you to rest."

The nurse had come into the room; her look sent a clear message that it was time for Kira to leave.

"I've got to go now." She brushed a kiss on his forehead. "I'll be back tomorrow. Rest and do as you're told, all right?"

"You know me better than that, girl," he joked feebly as Kira exited the room. The tears she'd been fighting spilled over as she found her way to the main entrance and hurried outside to her car. Dusty was the linchpin that anchored her world. How could she have survived if she'd lost him?

She was climbing into her Subaru when she remembered the call she'd promised to make. People at the ranch would be worried about Dusty, too. She found her phone in her purse and scrolled down to the number of the landline phone.

Consuelo answered the call. "How is he?" she asked. "*Ay diós,* we've been worried sick."

Kira passed on the good news. Consuelo put the phone aside to tell Paige and perhaps Jake, if he was close by.

"Is everything all right there?" she asked when Consuelo was back on the line. "How are my students?"

"Fine. They're still eating dinner. Will you be back tonight?"

"Yes. There's not much I can do here. Dusty just needs to rest."

"*Bueno.* I'll tell Jake to expect you."

"What about the horses? Is somebody taking care of them?"

Consuelo chuckled. "The horses are in the paddock. Paige showed Jake how to feed them."

Kira had to smile. "I knew I could count on her, and on you. Do you need anything from town while I'm here?"

"Eggs. Juice. Maybe some chocolate milk and donuts for snacks tomorrow. All right?"

"Sure. I'll pick some up. See you in an hour or so."

Kira ended the call and slipped her phone back in her purse. She sank back into the seat to collect her thoughts before starting home.

At least, tonight, there was hope that her grandfather would recover. Meanwhile, she mustn't allow herself to be crushed by the load of extra duties—the students, the care of the horses, the lectures she'd usually left to Dusty, to say nothing of the counseling sessions she handled herself. As always, she would have to be there for Paige, who would be worried and would miss her beloved great-grandfather. And she'd also need to check on Dusty at the hospital. Right now, it all seemed overwhelming.

"Jake's there to help." Those words—her own—had been part of her reassurances to Dusty. But could she really count on Jake—a footloose man with a wounded soul, a man who avoided kids and disliked horses, a man who suffered from unpredictable spells of PTSD?

For all she knew, Jake could turn out to be more of a burden than a help. And with Dusty gone, he could easily take it into his head to disappear.

She'd be a fool to count on Jake, Kira concluded. Until Dusty was well again, the whole burden of the ranch and the program would be on her shoulders. She was on her own.

The teenagers had acted like tired, cranky three-year-olds at dinner. The quiet ones had withdrawn into sullen silence. The others had bitched and complained through the whole meal.

Jake had joined them for the first time. For most of the meal, he'd managed to ignore them. But when four of them had walked away from the table without bussing their dishes, leaving Consuelo to clean up, he'd had enough. The army would never have put up with such slipshod behavior, and neither would he.

"You—all of you—stop right there!" he'd barked in his sharpest command voice. The students turned in the doorway to stare at him. "You four." He

pointed out Heather, Mack, Brandon and Patrick.
"You know the rules. Get back here and bus your
dishes. And while you're at it, each of you apologize to Consuelo. She's not your personal maid."

Consuelo had come to the kitchen doorway.
Jake saw her smile as the offenders trooped forward with their dishes and a muttered apology.

"The rest of you, watch and learn," Jake snapped.
"You do your share around here, or you don't eat.
And you don't leave until you're excused. Do you
copy?"

"Y-yes, sir." The shaky voice was Calvin's.

"And another thing. While you're here, you're
to be respectful—to each other and to the adults
here. I want to hear 'please' and 'thank you.' I want
to hear 'yes, sir' and 'no, sir.' And, you gentlemen,
you're to treat Kira and Consuelo as the ladies they
are. Do you understand?"

The students nodded.

"I want to hear it loud and clear. Do you understand?"

"Yes, sir!" the students chorused.

"Fine." He gave them his sternest glare. "Dismissed."

After the students had gone to their cabins, Jake
wandered outside and sat down on the front steps
to clear his head. The dog came up behind him
and thrust its nose under his arm. He made room
for the shaggy creature beside him, one hand
scratching its lopsided ears.

Consuelo had passed on the good news about Dusty a big relief. But even if the old man made a full recovery, he was going to be out of action for weeks, leaving Kira with the full burden of the ranch, the students and the horses. Whether he liked it or not, she was going to need his help.

Need.

Jake had never liked the word. It implied guilt on one side, dependency and weakness on the other. The only person he'd ever truly needed was Wendy. When she died, it was as if something vital had been torn by the roots out of his soul. He'd made a vow never to need anyone—or to be needed—again. Until today he'd managed that. Now here he was, trapped, indebted and *needed*.

He had stopped petting the dog. It whined and nudged his hand, wanting more. Jake obliged, using his fingers to untangle a bur lodged under its collar.

It was dark now, the house quiet. Overhead, the night sky blossomed with stars. Bats swooped low, catching insects in midair. In the paddock, the horses were stirring, their low snorts and nickers sounding like murmured conversation.

He remembered how Paige had shown him the way to feed the big animals. Such a smart, confident little girl, like a miniature of her mother, but with gifts of her own. She'd be in bed by now, lost in childish dreams.

The thought of her triggered an ache in his chest. Even if he were free to love his daughter, there was no way he could claim her or think of staying. The time would come—and soon—when he'd have to walk away. He would do it, knowing it was best for her, even though it would be like ripping out a piece of his heart.

Lord, why had he let the old man bring him here?

Why hadn't he realized it would be the biggest mistake of his life?

CHAPTER SIX

Jake was still on the porch when Kira's Outback drove in the side gate and pulled up to the house. The dog rose to greet her, tail wagging, as she climbed out of the driver's seat and walked around to open the back. Inside were several tall paper bags filled with groceries.

"Let me give you a hand with those." Jake hurried down the steps and scooped up two of the heaviest-looking bags.

"Thanks." Kira grabbed a third bag. "Consuelo only asked me to pick up a few things, but I got carried away."

Jake started up the steps again. "How's Dusty?"

"Holding his own. It was hard seeing him so helpless. But he's a tough old man. He's got to pull through. I can't imagine this place without him."

"You want these bags in the kitchen?"

"Right. The eggs, milk and juice go in the fridge. The rest can be left out till morning. In case you're hungry, I bought extra chocolate milk and donuts."

Was that an invitation to stay? Jake put the groceries on the kitchen counter, leaving the question open. Kira came in with a single bag and set it on the kitchen table. She looked burned-out after the long, rough day. Shadows rimmed her storm-gray eyes. "There are two more bags in the car," she said. "Do you mind?"

"No problem." Jake went out and retrieved the rest of the bags. When he came back into the kitchen, Kira had just finished stowing milk jugs in the refrigerator.

"I have to put the car in the shed," she said. "Stick around. I need to talk to you about tomorrow." Without waiting for a reply, she hurried outside again. That was Kira. Always focused and charging ahead, even when she was exhausted. Her constant drive tended to set his teeth on edge. But he was here to help, Jake reminded himself. He would do his best to give her what she needed.

Jake heard her vehicle start up and pull away. Having nothing left to put in the fridge, he wandered into the living room to wait. When she didn't return after a few minutes, his restlessness drove him to explore.

A floor lamp, behind the sofa, cast a low light over the room with its well-worn leather furniture, sandstone fireplace and timbered ceiling. Leading off to Jake's right was a shadowed hallway, lined with several doors. At the far end, a sliver of light and the muted theme of a popular telenovela flowed from the crack under a closed door. That, Jake guessed, would be the room where Consuelo was enjoying a well-earned rest.

The other doors were closed, except for one that stood a few inches ajar. Against his better judgment, he found himself walking toward it, moving lightly down the hall, until he could look into the dimly lit room.

Something tightened around his heart. Paige lay sleeping in the glow of her night-light, her eyes closed, her hair tousled on the pillow.

She was so beautiful, she almost took his breath away. But he knew he shouldn't be here looking at her. If Paige woke up and saw him, she might be startled. And if Kira found him in the hallway, she was liable to be upset, or even angry. Nobody needed that kind of confrontation tonight.

He was turning to go when he noticed something on the nightstand. He recognized it at once. It was the framed portrait that he and Wendy had posed for on their wedding day.

Paige had been little more than a toddler when her mother died; and as her father, he'd scarcely been there at all. Any real memories of her parents would be very dim at best. But Jake could imagine how the smiling pair in the picture could become an idealized version of her father and mother. Their happy faces would greet her every morning when she woke. They would watch over her at night while she slept. They would never hurt her, never scold her, never grow old or go away.

But people in a photograph were a sad substitute for the real thing. They could never laugh with her, play with her or teach her. They could never love her.

Driven by impulse, Jake slipped through the door, took the picture and carried it back to the light in the living room. Looking at those faces was like twisting a knife in his gut, but right now, feeling the pain was better than feeling nothing at all.

The young man in the portrait looked like a stranger—the trusting eyes, the boyish grin. He was marrying the woman of his dreams, and he would do everything in his power to make their lives perfect. Even the thought of his upcoming deployment couldn't dim that confident look. There'd been no doubt that he would serve his country with honor and come home whole, finding his wife waiting with their child in her arms.

The poor, stupid bastard.

And Wendy—Lord, but she'd looked so beautiful in her ivory gown and veil. They'd been so happy then, and so much in love. If only he could have chosen to die in her place. She could have been there for their daughter. She could've followed her own dreams and made a fulfilling life for herself without him.

Instead he'd survived—a useless wreck of a man who could barely make it from one day to the next; a man whose real life had ended on a dark city street, in a crumpled mass of metal.

"Give me that picture, Jake." Kira's soft voice startled him. He hadn't heard her come back into the house. Gently but firmly, she took the photograph from his hand.

He'd expected her to be angry, but all she said was "Let me put this back. Paige will be upset if she wakes up and finds it gone."

Jake watched her walk into the shadows, slim,

erect and utterly self-possessed. Nothing seemed to touch her—at least not from the outside.

"Kira needs you to forgive her for what happened. Maybe if you can do that, she'll finally be able to forgive herself."

Dusty's words came back to him as Kira vanished into Paige's room and came out a moment later without the photograph. She didn't act like a woman who needed forgiveness. For that matter, Jake wasn't sure he was ready to forgive her. But after three years, maybe it was time he stopped walking around the tragedy and tried to learn the whole story.

As she stepped into the light again, Jake forced himself to speak. "We've never talked about that night, Kira—the night of the accident. If I understood what happened, maybe it would help me move past it."

Kira glanced away, her hands arranging an afghan on the back of the couch. "There's not much to understand," she said. "Wendy had gone to a bachelorette party with a couple of her girlfriends. They'd picked her up at her place. Since I'd agreed to babysit, they dropped Paige off at my apartment on the way.

"Toward midnight, when she wasn't back, I started to worry. I was just about to phone her, when she called me. She said she wanted to go home, but her friends were drunk and didn't want to leave the party. I offered to come and get her."

"Wendy wasn't drunk?" Jake remembered how his wife had enjoyed getting tipsy. It had never been a problem between them. But he sensed—or perhaps only imagined—a slight hesitation before Kira shook her head.

"I didn't ask, but she sounded sober," Kira said. "Paige fussed when I woke her up and buckled her into her car seat, but she was fast asleep by the time I picked up her mother half an hour later."

"How did Wendy seem? Was she all right?"

"She was fine, just tired and glad to be away from there. But . . ." Kira's voice trailed off. She crossed the room and stood gazing out the front window.

"But?" Jake demanded, his impatience getting the better of him.

She stood silent a moment more. "It was late, and I was dead tired," she said at last. "I wanted some coffee to perk me up for the drive home. I spotted an all-night drive-through and stopped long enough to buy a cup." Her throat moved as she swallowed. *"Just long enough."*

There was no need for Kira to finish the story. Jake could guess the rest. The brief time it had taken to pull up to the drive-through window, buy the coffee and leave had put them directly in the path of the drunk driver, who'd run the red light, slammed into Kira's small car and killed Wendy.

A few seconds more, or a few seconds less, and nothing would have happened.

"My God," he said, staring at her.

"Yes, now you know." She turned away from the window. "For what it's worth, the driver of the SUV wasn't hurt. And because his family had political connections, he got off with a slap on the wrist. He was killed, driving drunk again, six months later. I guess you could call it karma."

She made a shrugging motion, like someone shedding an uncomfortable coat. "But this isn't why I asked you to stay. Since my grandfather's in the hospital, I'm going to need your help with the students and the horses. I know you don't owe me a thing, but I hope you'll lend a hand, out of respect for Dusty."

Jake was still reeling from the story she'd told him, but he feigned indifference. "As long as I'm getting paid, I'll do whatever. But I don't know a damn thing about horses."

"Well, you can learn. All you need to do is stay one step ahead of the students. Let me get a few things and meet you in the kitchen for chocolate milk and donuts. We can take some notes and go over the plans for tomorrow."

As Jake watched her stride back down the hall, he couldn't help wondering what lay beneath that coldly efficient manner of hers. She had just told him a gut-wrenching story, one that had left him shaken to the core. Then, as if nothing had happened, she'd simply shifted gears and moved on to the next order of business.

If he could see into the depths of her soul, would he find a hidden cache of warmth and vulnerability? Or would he only see more of the same, all the way to her frozen, protected heart?

Dawn's first light crept over the Santa Catalinas, brushing the desert foothills with shades of mauve, violet and gold. Mourning doves, nesting in a mesquite thicket, woke to fill the air with their gentle calls. A jackrabbit, its huge ears as long as its body, scampered down to a streambed for a morning drink. A Gila woodpecker drummed on the ribs of a giant saguaro.

Dressed for the day, Kira walked out to the paddock. For a few moments, she stood by the fence, sipping her coffee and watching the horses. She'd told Jake to meet her out here at first light, but there was no sign of him. If he didn't show up in the next five minutes, she would have to go and roust him out of bed. That would be awkward, to say the least.

From the moment Jake had shown up here, she'd known that the details of Wendy's death would come to light. Over and over, she'd rehearsed the story in her mind—every word true, or at least as true as it needed to be. As for the rest, what Jake didn't know was best left unsaid.

She'd been brutally honest about the coffee stop that had put her car in the wrong place at the wrong time. For that, if Jake needed somebody to blame, she would accept the burden. It was the least she could do.

Last night, after the painful revelation, she and Jake had spent an hour in the kitchen, going over the plans for today and what he needed to know. The subject of the accident hadn't come up again. It was as if a door had been closed. She could only hope it would never be opened again.

Except maybe by Paige, when she was old enough to ask questions.

Paige was another worry. Kira could sense that Jake and his daughter were already bonding. With Jake filling in for Dusty, the two of them would be spending more time together. Kira felt powerless to stop what was happening, but one thing was certain: if Jake broke his little girl's heart, she would never forgive him.

She glanced at her watch. Jake's time was up. If she had to march into his cabin and drag him out of bed by one leg, so be it.

She was turning to go, when she heard his voice.

"There you are! I was wondering when you were going to show up!" He was coming around the barn, fully dressed, pushing a wheelbarrow loaded with hay. "I was just about to give these babies their breakfast," he said, glancing at the horses. "As long as you're here, you can lend me a hand."

Kira's gaze took him in. He was wearing worn jeans, a khaki-colored tee, which outlined his muscular arms and chest, and a battered straw hat somebody had left behind in the tack room. He looked fit and relaxed—except for his eyes. They were rimmed in red and framed in shadow, a sign that he'd spent a sleepless night.

"Are you just going to stand there, or are you going to pitch in and help?" He spoke in a teasing tone.

Kira pulled on her work gloves. "Tell you what. Let's put the hay in their stalls. Then we can bring the horses inside."

"Have you checked on Dusty this morning?" Jake asked her as she walked beside the wheelbarrow.

"I called first thing. He had a calm night, and

he's resting. All good, I suppose. I'll be taking a break to visit him later. For now, let's get to work."

Since the horses had spent yesterday and last night in the paddock, the stable was already clean. The students could shovel out the paddock, then go into the stalls to practice brushing and grooming their horses.

It was a well-designed and well-equipped stable. The open-topped box stalls were roomy enough for a horse to move around or even lie down in the straw. Each stall had a feeder, a place for a water bucket and a post on either side with a metal ring for cross-tying. In addition to the stalls, there was a tack room, a room for veterinary care and an area with a hose and a drain, where a horse could be bathed.

This morning the stable was clean and quiet. Kira found an extra pitchfork and helped Jake pile the sweet-smelling hay into the feeders. When he went back to the hay shed for more, she used the time to fill the water buckets and get eight soft nylon halters and leads out of the tack room. She tossed these over the gate of an unused stall.

Jake was back a few minutes later, wiping hay dust off his face. "Paige said that somebody found a dead rattlesnake in the hay. Is that true?"

"We've found more than one." Kira forked hay into a stall and moved on. "The snakes like the hay fields because there are plenty of mice there. A few unlucky ones get picked up by the baler. But in case you're wondering, no, we've never found a live one."

Jake shuddered. "Sorry, I can't stand snakes."

She gave him a smile. He was standing close, reaching past her to fill a feeder with hay. His body smelled of clean sweat and the lavender soap stocked in the guest cabins. Kira had never thought of lavender as a masculine scent, but on Jake, it was. The thought flitted through her head that he could wear Chanel No. 5 and still smell like a man.

Not that she was attracted to him. He was too raw, too edgy and dangerous to be her type. The few men she'd been involved with had been cultured and highly educated. Still, she found herself inhaling Jake's nearness, her senses swimming in his male aura.

Heavens, what was going on with her?

Kira was about to draw back when the highway crew in the valley below set off the first dynamite blast of the day. The explosion boomed, echoing like thunder off the canyon walls.

Jake's body went rigid, his eyes narrowed to slits. Kira laid a hand on his arm. She could feel his straining muscles as he fought an inner battle against the rising shock waves. This time he would know what he was hearing, and that it wasn't a danger. But long exposure to war had programmed his nervous system to react.

Her fingers tightened on his arm. "It's all right, Jake," she said. "It's only the highway crew."

"I . . . know." With a long exhalation, he brought himself under control again. His body was shaking. Kira checked the impulse to wrap him in her arms and hold him like a frightened child.

"It's bound to happen again," she said. "They could be blasting all day. Will you be all right?"

"I'll be fine. I'm fine now. Don't fuss over me," he growled. "So what do we do next, just open the gates and let the horses run in?"

"Not quite." Kira gathered the halters and ropes. Walking outside, she selected one set and laid the rest over the paddock fence. "We'll have to lead them in. Come on. It's lesson time."

Jake followed Kira into the paddock, where ten horses waited. All of them were calm. They'd probably done this drill hundreds of times. But he didn't like horses, and he didn't like being here, especially with a bossy female who thought she knew it all. No doubt, Kira had a good heart. But her take-charge ways were getting to him like a bur under his jeans.

"Come over here," she said. "We'll start with Sadie. She's my own mare." After separating one rope and halter, she thrust the rest of the tangled gear into Jake's hands and strode toward a fine-boned animal that raised its head at her approach. Stepping around a pile of steaming manure, Jake followed her.

"Always the left side. Remember that, and make sure the students remember it."

Jake watched as she slipped the nylon halter over the mare's head, as easily as one might slip a harness onto a dog. When the halter was fastened in place, she clipped the end of the rope to a ring under the chinstrap. "See, it's easy," she said, handing the rope to Jake. "The important thing is to stay calm and let her know you're in charge. Now walk close to her, on the left. Lead her out of the paddock and into the first stall—the one on the right. She'll know where to go."

Jake took Kira's place to the left of the mare's shoulder. She swung her massive head around to look at him. Her big, soft eyes held a glint of suspicion. For a nickel, he would have walked away right then, but he had to man up and show Kira he could handle this job. Maybe then, she'd stop treating him like one of her troubled kids.

The mare snorted and shook her head. "She can tell you're nervous," Kira said. "Calm her down. Talk to her and stroke her above the shoulder. She likes that."

Jake laid a cautious hand on the mare. Beneath his palm, her coat was like warm satin. He could feel the taut, quivering muscle underneath. Could she be as uncomfortable with him as he was with her?

"Easy, girl," he murmured, running a hand along her withers. "You're all right. Nobody's going to hurt you."

He could feel the mare relaxing. The strange thing was, he could feel himself relaxing as well. "Easy, now." He ran his hand down her shoulder, letting the sleek warmth and earthy, animal aroma creep into his senses. "That's it. Good girl." Keeping a grip on the rope below the halter, he moved forward a couple of steps. The well-trained mare stayed even with him. "Come on, Sadie, let's go get breakfast."

Kira opened the paddock gate and closed it behind them. They moved at a brisk pace, crossing the short distance to the open door of the stable. "Don't let her bolt for the hay," she coached. "Take her in easy. Then unclip the lead and let her eat. Careful now. That's it. Stay clear of her hindquarters as you leave."

Kira was grinning as she closed the gate of the box stall. "See? Nothing to it. Come on, let's get the others inside."

They finished stabling the horses in time to join the students for breakfast. Kira couldn't help but notice the change in their behavior. Yesterday they'd been boisterous and pushy, whining and teasing each other like siblings on a long car trip. Today they were meek little lambs. Calvin even got up to pull out her chair before she sat down.

The looks they gave Jake combined fear and hero worship. Consuelo had mentioned his reading them the riot act last night. Whatever he'd said to them, it must've sunk in. They all seemed to be on their best behavior.

Kira was happily surprised with the way Jake was handling his new duties. But she could sense the rebellion seething beneath his compliant surface. This ranch was not where he wanted to be; and she was not the person he wanted to be with—especially after what she'd told him about her role in Wendy's death. He had to be counting the hours and adding up the wages, just waiting for the time when he could write off his debt to Dusty and hit the road.

But why should it matter? Kira asked herself. She hadn't wanted him here in the first place. And with so many painful memories between them, she certainly didn't want him to stay.

Did she?

After breakfast Jake dismissed the students with instructions to meet outside the stable in fifteen minutes with their work gloves and helmets. Jake was about to go back to the stable, but Kira stopped him on the porch. "What did you say to them last night?" she asked.

"'Say to them'?" Jake raised an eyebrow, feigning innocence.

"You know what I'm talking about. Yesterday they were acting like spoiled pests. This morning they were saying 'please' and 'thank you.' They bussed their dishes and actually thanked Consuelo for breakfast, and they didn't leave until you dismissed them. You must've really put the fear into them."

Jake gave her a mysterious glance. He was enjoying this. And he was enjoying the way Kira looked when her guard was down and she wasn't giving orders. There was a softness to the angular planes of her face and a tempting fullness to her glossed lips.

"What did you do?" she asked again.

"Nothing much. I just pretended I was back in the army and the kids were a bunch of recruits. You told me to flash my tattoo. That's pretty much what I did."

Her mouth curved in a smile. "Well, whatever

you did, it worked. Thanks." She paused, and Jake could sense a mental shift. By now, he knew what to expect. "I still need to call Patrick's parents," she said. "While I'm doing that, you can get the students started on cleaning the paddock."

"Roger. I take it you'll still want Patrick there when you make the call. I'll send him in."

"Thanks. It shouldn't take more than a few minutes. I doubt Patrick's parents will be surprised. The boy has issues with rules and with impulse control. What he did yesterday, climbing on those rocks, was typical behavior—the sort that equine therapy has a good chance of helping."

Jake turned to go, then paused. "Didn't you say it was unethical to talk about your students?"

"I did. But that was before you were working with them. Now that you're part of the team, you'll need to understand a little about each one. The counseling sessions will still be confidential, but I can, at least, fill you in on their backgrounds."

"Part of the team." It shouldn't matter, Jake thought. But for some reason, it felt good.

He was about to leave again when Paige came out onto the porch. Since he hadn't seen her at breakfast, Jake guessed that she must've eaten in the kitchen. She was dressed for the day, except for her sneakers, which trailed their laces as she walked.

"Hi, Mister Jake." She gave him a heart-melting smile. "Would you help me tie my shoes?"

Kira stepped forward. "Mister Jake has to go, honey. Come here, I'll help you."

"No." Paige's face assumed an adorable pout. "I want Mister Jake to help me."

Jake glanced at Kira. She shrugged and rolled her eyes. Was she put-out, maybe even hurt? Feeling awkward, Jake bent and tied the pink laces into bows. "How's that?" he asked Paige.

Paige looked down at her shoes. "It's fine. Can I help you feed the horses, Mister Jake?"

His discomfort growing, Jake shook his head. "Sorry, Paige, the horses have already been fed. I was able to do it because you showed me how last night. You were a good teacher. Maybe another time, okay?"

"Okay." Paige sighed.

Kira straightened the straw hat on Paige's head. "The students will be grooming and leading the horses. You can watch if you'll stay out of the way. But you'll have to wait here while I make a phone call."

"Can't I just go now with Mister Jake?"

Kira's eyes met Jake's above the little girl's head. He'd half-expected to see jealousy in her gaze. Instead what he saw was concern—a concern he shared. This headstrong child, for whatever reason, had attached herself to him and would not be turned away. How would she take it when he walked out of her life a second time?

"Please, Aunt Kira," Paige's look would have melted stone. "I won't be any trouble."

Kira sighed. "All right. I'll be along in a few minutes. You stay with Mister Jake and do what he says. Promise?"

"Promise." The little girl skipped after Jake, who'd already headed for the stable. Halfway there she caught his hand. Jake felt his heart fracture as the small fingers slipped into his palm. He'd done his best to ignore the blood bond with his daughter. But it was as if Paige, in her innocence, had sensed it at once. Whatever lay ahead for them was bound to be painful—even frightening.

As they crossed the yard, another dynamite blast shook the air, echoing up the canyon to ring in Jake's ears. Taking deep breaths, he let the sound wash over him as he walked, holding tight to his little girl's hand.

CHAPTER SEVEN

Kira sat on the living-room couch, sipping an iced tea and waiting for Heather to come in. Her first one-on-one counseling session had been set for yesterday, but Dusty's emergency had preempted everything. This afternoon she was playing catch-up with the program schedule.

When she'd phoned the hospital after lunch, the nurse had said her grandfather was asleep. Later, Kira would drive into Tucson to visit him again. Right now, she would give her full attention to the troubled girl who needed her help.

While she waited, she reviewed the notes she'd taken when she'd talked with Heather's parents. Fifteen-year-old Heather was bright, but she was a few pounds overweight and felt less attractive than her pretty, popular older sister, Megan. She hid her lack of confidence by being pushy and sarcastic. Her issues with her sister had come to a head when Megan had been elected homecoming queen. The afternoon before the dance, Heather had stolen into Megan's room and used a pair of scissors to slash her sister's gown. Her parents, good people, desperate for help, were hoping that the horse therapy program would ease Heather's hostility and raise her self-esteem.

At the sound of the front door opening, Kira slid the folder under the couch and rose to greet her student. Heather came in dragging her feet, a scowl on her face. "Do I really have to do this crap?" she asked.

"You do. But only once a week. And you get to choose what you tell me—or don't tell me. I'm here to listen, not to judge. Have a seat."

"Fine, but I'm not here to talk." Heather sank onto the far end of the couch, grabbed a Diet Coke from the cooler on the floor and popped the tab.

"That's up to you," Kira said. "But the time will go faster if we chat. How are things working out for you here? Are you enjoying the horses?"

"They're okay. But I don't like shoveling their poop."

"Nobody does. But it's part of having horses. They don't clean up after themselves. Hey, you did great with the leading today. That mare went right along with you."

Heather shrugged and took a swig from the red-and-white can. Her nails, Kira noticed, were bitten to the quick.

"Is your cabin okay? How are you getting along with your roommates?"

Heather shrugged again. "Lanie's okay. But Faith is a bitch. Always in the bathroom primping. We can't even go in and pee without asking Her Royal Highness's permission. She reminds me of my sister."

"Reminds you how?"

"Oh, you know, it's all about her and how she has to look perfect all the time, so everybody will see her and think how beautiful she is. It sucks, having a sister like that." Her hands tightened around the can, making it buckle. "But I got back at Megan. I got her good."

Kira saw an opening. "I know what you did to your sister's dress. Your mother told me."

"The dress?" Heather's fist crushed the can. A spurt of Coke spattered the tile as she dropped it on the floor. "That stupid dress was nothing compared to what I did before that."

"What did you do?" Kira felt a tingling premonition.

"You really want to know?"

"Only if you want to tell me. I meant it when I said I wasn't here to judge."

"And you won't tell my parents?"

"I'm your therapist. What you tell me is private."

"Okay." Heather's hands were clasped on her knees, the fingers interlaced. "Megan's boyfriend, Kevin, came by the house when nobody was home but me. I told him that if he wanted it, I could give him something better than kissing bitchy Megan. So . . . I did."

"You had sex with him?" Kira willed herself not to appear shocked.

"Yup. But that isn't all. It gets even better. A lot better." Her tone was sarcastic.

"Better how?" Kira asked.

Heather gazed down at her clasped hands, then back at Kira. A tear glimmered in her eye. "I'm pregnant."

Kira didn't get away to visit Dusty until dinner-time. Another session with the horses—approaching them in the paddock, putting on their halters and returning them to their stalls, along with the follow-up discussion—had taken much of the afternoon. That activity had gone well, as had the phone call to Patrick's parents and the one-on-one with Calvin, a sweet, gifted boy who just wanted acceptance.

Jake had been quietly supportive, stepping in where he was needed to adjust a halter strap or encourage a hesitant youngster. At the same time, he'd kept his distance from Kira, leaving her to do her job.

She was grateful for his help, even though his presence brought to mind a gentle wind that could blow in a thunderstorm. Jake O'Reilly was a mass of contradictions—a strong and decent man plagued by inner demons. Kira's instincts told her that his coming here would end badly. But right now, she needed him—and she had little choice except to trust him.

Sunset streaked the sky as she drove through the desert foothills. Kira switched on the headlights, knowing it would be dusk by the time she reached the hospital. Dusty had been on her mind all day. Last night the old man had looked like a frail stranger. Tonight she could only hope he'd be well enough to enjoy her visit.

Kira had long since learned that for her, the only way to function was to divide her concerns into mental boxes. There was a box for the horses, a box for the program, a box for Paige and now a box for Dusty. Close one; open another. That was how she made it through each day.

Some boxes she opened every day. Others, like her parents' deaths, were sealed shut. Wendy's box had been sealed shut, too, until Jake had forced her to open it, look inside and see things she only wanted to forget.

Now she'd added a new box—Heather, and what to do about her pregnancy. Since the secret had been privileged communication, she couldn't discuss it with anyone—not Jake, not Dusty, not even Heather's parents. But the girl needed support. She needed a doctor. She needed to make decisions and plans for the baby.

Then there was the liability issue—cold but a real concern. Should anything go wrong, having allowed Heather to work with the horses while pregnant could leave the program open to a lawsuit.

All things considered, Heather would have to leave. And the girl would have to tell her parents why. Tomorrow, after breakfast, Kira would call her into the office, lay out the realities and hand her the phone.

As Kira drove into the hospital parking lot, she closed Heather's box and opened Dusty's. Worries weighed on her as she hurried into the building and took the elevator to the third floor. What if the stent wasn't working? What if the old cowboy had suffered another heart attack?

Outside the door of his room, she paused to take a deep breath. Then she gave a light rap on the door, opened it and stepped into the room. Her grandfather was sitting up in bed, finishing a dinner of roast chicken and looking almost his usual self.

Giddy with relief, she strode to his bedside and planted a kiss on his cheek. "You're looking so much better," she said. "How are you feeling?"

"Rarin' to get up and get the hell out of here." His hoarse voice betrayed his weakened condition. "Fool doctor says I have to stay another couple of days. But I've had it with getting poked and prodded and eating this damned hospital food. Maybe the next time you come, you could smuggle me in some of Consuelo's tamales."

"I'll see what I can do." Kira pulled a chair close to the bed and sat down. "Meanwhile, don't tax yourself worrying or trying to get up. The nurse says the best thing for your heart is rest."

"Rest! Hell, I'm going stir-crazy!" He reached out and pressed her hand. "How are things at the ranch? Is Jake working out all right?"

"Jake's been a lot of help. He can't lecture like you do, and he still doesn't like horses much, but he runs those students like they're new recruits at boot camp—and they eat it up. It's like they think he's Superman."

Dusty grinned. "I knew that bringing Jake to the

ranch would turn out to be a good thing. How's Paige doing?"

"She tags around after him like a little puppy." Should she tell Dusty about her concern that Paige was headed for a broken heart? But why worry the old man now, when the last thing he needed was stress?

"Paige still doesn't know he's her father?"

"I don't think Jake wants her to know—ever. He's still not planning to stay."

"He told you that?"

"Yes, the day after he arrived." She remembered their early-morning clash on the canyon trail. "But he does mean to repay you before he leaves. So he should be around for a while—at least until you're back on your feet."

"I see." Dusty looked disappointed. "How's he dealing with the PTSD?"

"It's there. But he does a good job of masking it around Paige and the students."

"I was hoping that being on the ranch, with the horses, might help him."

"It might. But that remains to be seen." Kira rose. "I'm wearing you out. It's time I drove home and let you get some rest. I'll be back to see you tomorrow."

"Bring Jake next time," Dusty said. "Or send him in your place if you can't leave the kids. I could use a word with him."

"Of course. Rest easy." Kira brushed a kiss across his forehead and left. On the way to the car, she found herself wondering about her grandfather's intent. Had Dusty known all along that he had a bad heart? Was that why he'd gone to so much trouble to find Jake and bring him to the ranch, so someone would be there to help her? Had he done it for her, for Paige or for Jake himself?

She took her time driving back to the ranch, stopping for more donuts, playing the radio and doing her best to clear her head. Tonight, in her absence, the students were being treated to an outdoor cookout, with a blaze in the big fire pit east of the house. They'd be roasting hot dogs and toasting marshmallows to make s'mores for dessert. If Dusty had been there, he would have regaled them with stories of his rodeo days. Jake didn't have that background, and Kira knew he wouldn't want to talk about the war. But she had little doubt that her charges were in capable hands.

It was ten fifteen when she pulled through the side gate and parked her car in the vehicle shed. From there she could see the glow of the burning fire, but no one was moving in the yard. Except for the front-porch light and the dimmed lamp in the living room, the house windows were dark.

As she walked closer, a lone figure rose from one of the stone benches that rimmed the fire pit. Silhouetted against the flames, Jake stood waiting.

By the time Kira finally showed up, Jake had begun to worry about her. A lone woman on the road after dark—anything could go wrong. An accident, a blown tire or car trouble could leave her vulnerable to any human predator who happened along.

He'd tried to tell himself he was being ridiculous, that Kira was a strong, capable woman who could take care of herself. But overprotectiveness was one aspect of his PTSD. And it wasn't something he could turn off like a switch. He'd lost too many good men on his watch—men he cared about as friends and brothers. Now, whether he liked it or not, he was beginning to care about Kira.

About her, not *for* her.

It wasn't the same thing, he reminded himself as she walked into sight. He wasn't fit for a romantic relationship with any woman. But the relief he'd felt at the sound of her car was strong enough to make his pulse leap.

The firelight sharpened the planes of her face and veiled her eyes in shadow. She was a protector, too, watching over everyone and everything on this small ranch. Tonight she looked as if she needed a break, Jake thought. When was the last time anyone had protected *her*, or cradled her in his arms and made her feel that it was all right to let go?

Not that it should be any of his business.

"Where is everybody?" she asked.

"Asleep, I hope. Paige and the students are tucked in their beds, and you gave Consuelo the night off." He wouldn't tell her about tucking Paige in and hearing her bedtime prayer, or how deeply he'd ached when she'd asked God to bless her daddy and bring him home.

"How's Dusty?" he asked.

Her smile showed some strain. "Better. Strong enough to complain. All he wants to do is come home. But the doctors are keeping him a couple more days. That's probably a good idea. Oh—he wants you to come visit him tomorrow. He said he could use a word with you, whatever he meant by that."

"He didn't say what he wanted?"

"Not a hint." Kira shrugged her slim shoulders. "Since one of us needs to be here with the students, I'll probably let you go alone."

"You don't mind my taking the Jeep?"

"Take my Outback. It gets better gas mileage. Just don't let Dusty talk you into smuggling him out of the hospital. I wouldn't put it past him to try it." She turned back toward the house.

"Don't go yet." The words escaped Jake's mouth before he had a chance to consider them. "Sit down. If you're hungry, we've got a few hot dogs left. I can cook you one. Or if you'd rather have a s'more, I know how to toast a perfect marshmallow. One of my many hidden talents."

She made an effort, at least, to laugh. "How can I turn down an offer like that? I don't care for hot dogs, thanks, but since you offered, I'll take a s'more. Maybe I can learn something from your technique."

"Coming up." Jake chose a sharpened willow stick from the bundle the students had used and eased a fresh marshmallow onto the point. "It's important not to squeeze it," he said with mock seriousness. "You'll want a nice, round shape that will toast evenly."

Kira giggled—a sound like a little girl's laugh. She needed to giggle more often, Jake thought.

"Now you hold it over the coals, not the flame," he said, demonstrating. "Close, but not too close.

And you turn it, very slowly. See that little curl of smoke? That means it's browned enough on one side and needs to be turned. There . . . see? Perfect."

He'd no sooner spoken than the marshmallow burst into a miniature flaming torch. By the time Jake snatched up the stick and blew out the fire, there was nothing left of it but crisp black carbon.

Kira was laughing—really laughing. Seeing her in the firelight, Jake noticed how her eyes crinkled at the corners, and how her generous smile made tiny dimples in her cheeks. He'd never thought of Kira as pretty—especially compared with Wendy. But tonight she possessed a different sort of beauty—strong, vulnerable and as elusive as a moonbeam.

"I'll tell you what," she said, taking another sharpened willow from the bundle. "Let's have a contest. You can toast another marshmallow for me, and I'll toast one for you."

"Okay." He passed her the bag of marshmallows. "But what's to stop you from burning mine on purpose?"

She grinned. "If I do that, I'll lose. And I don't like to lose."

"You're on." He speared a marshmallow. When they were ready, they held their sticks above the coals, turning them carefully as the white surfaces darkened to golden brown.

"Done!" he said, raising his stick. "I'd say we've got a tie."

Kira studied the marshmallows with a playful frown. "I could argue that mine is brown on top, and the one you toasted is only brown on the sides.

But all right. Let's call it a tie. Here's your masterpiece. Let's make our s'mores."

A tray on a folding camp table held leftovers from the cookout. Layering graham crackers and squares of chocolate with the hot, melted marshmallows, they carried the messy treats back to the fire, sat down and took the first dripping bites.

"Good?" he asked, licking marshmallow off his lip.

"Mmmf!" She swallowed the mouthful she'd taken. "We do this cookout every session, but I never eat these. I've forgotten how decadent they are. Right now, I feel like a ten-year-old kid."

"Enjoy." He liked watching her, with a chocolate smear on the end of her nose and a rare, delicious look of pleasure on her face. It was a look he wouldn't mind seeing more of—maybe from above, with her soft brown hair spread on his pillow. . . .

But what was he thinking? An affair with Kira would be a disaster—there was too much shared baggage between them, too much guilt and pain. He imagined tears, accusations, slamming doors and the open road. No, it was best to keep things as they were now, in a state of guarded truce.

"I'm guessing Paige got her share before bedtime," Kira said. "She loves s'mores."

"I think she ate three of them. I hope they won't make her sick."

"Three's about usual for her. She should be fine." Kira finished eating and licked her lips, stirring the fantasies Jake thought he'd just put to bed. Maybe . . . but no, she was giving him her serious look now.

"When do you plan to tell Paige you're her father?" she asked.

The question, coming out of nowhere, caught him off guard. He exhaled slowly as the answer came together. "As things stand now, I think she's better off not knowing. She lost her father once. For her to lose him again when I leave here—that would be cruel."

"She's a bright little girl. What will you do if she guesses the truth?"

What *would* he do? Stay? But he didn't belong here. Since leaving the VA hospital, his survival had depended on change—new places, new work, new people, as often as it took. When the monsters in his mind threatened to surface, it was time to move on.

With strangers, it had been easier to walk away. But here, with people who had a connection to him, the pitfalls were everywhere, waiting to trap him. So far, he'd managed to keep the depression and anxiety under control—or at least hidden from sight. But he couldn't do it forever. Sooner or later, his dark side would come out—a side of her father that no child should have to see.

"What are you thinking?" she asked.

"I'm thinking it might be best just to leave now. I could find a job somewhere and send Dusty payments in the mail. Believe me, I'd do it. I don't like owing anybody favors or money."

Kira gazed into the coals of the dying fire. After

what seemed like a long time, she spoke. "I know you don't want complications. And the last thing either of us wants is for Paige to be hurt. But the truth is, until Dusty's on his feet again, I'm going to need your help. Besides, you've only been here a couple of days. I can't imagine you'd have enough money to get very far. You don't even have a vehicle to drive."

"I've gotten by with less," Jake said, thinking of the early days out of the hospital when he'd hitched rides, gone without meals and slept in shelters until he could find work. He could do it again if he had to. But Kira was right. She'd be hard-pressed to manage her therapy program alone. And when Dusty came home, the old man would be more likely to get needed rest if someone was here to help with the work.

"I'll stay," he said. "For now, at least. But there's still Paige."

"Yes. There's Paige." Her tone was laced with caution. Jake thought of the little girl, trailing him around the yard, often slipping her hand into his. He remembered the bittersweetness of tucking her into bed and hearing her prayers. For the good of all concerned, those tender moments would have to end.

And he knew why. Even now, he could feel the stirrings that signaled a bad spell coming on.

"I'll do my best to keep Paige at a distance," he said. "But I'm going to need your help."

"You'll have it." She laid a light hand on his arm. Her fingers were cool. Her touch penetrated his skin like a gentle electric current. The need for intimate contact—a need he'd too long denied himself—pulsed through his body, awakening hidden hungers. Maybe if he seized her in his arms and kissed her, it would be enough of a distraction to halt the black tide that was creeping over and around him, threatening to pull him under.

But that would only be using her. And if he couldn't control his demons . . . he shuddered inwardly, fearing he might not be able to stop himself from going too far. He'd committed some hellish acts in Afghanistan, but rape wasn't one of them.

He stepped back, away from her. "Go get some rest," he said. "I'll clean up here."

"No, that's fine. I can at least take these when I go inside." She began to gather utensils and leftover food from the camp table, putting everything on the tray.

"Go now, Kira," he said. "I need to be alone."

She turned toward him, the tray in her hands. "I'll just—"

"Go, damn it! Just go!" His voice had dropped to a tightly reined snarl.

Kira gave him a concerned look. "Are you all right?"

"I will be if you leave me alone. Now go!"

Tight-mouthed, she wheeled and strode toward the house. A moment later, Jake saw the kitchen light come on. She'd be all right, he told himself. It would take a lot to rattle Kira. But he wouldn't stand for her treating him like one of her patients. If the shrinks in the VA hospital couldn't help him, neither could she. The monsters in his mind had unpacked their bags and signed a long-term lease. They weren't going anywhere.

Crumbling like a mud wall under heavy fire, Jake sank onto a bench and cradled his head in his hands. He'd sworn off hard liquor after the bar fight that had landed him in jail. Alcohol helped blur his memory, but it also tended to make him violent and get him into trouble. Except for the Corona that Dusty had bought him in Flagstaff, he hadn't had a drop since that night in the bar. But he still craved alcohol. If he had a bottle right now, he'd drink until he passed out. At least it would give him some rest. He'd tried medication, too, in the hospital. It had brought on a merciful numbness, but it made him feel so dull and stupid that in the end he'd refused to take it.

What he needed now was rest. Tomorrow would start early, with Kira and her students needing his help. By then, he would have to be functional and under control. But sleep, if it came at all, could bring the nightmares—so real that they were like living his past hell all over again. He could expect to wake up screaming—or, at least, in a cold, quaking sweat.

Right now he was too restless to sleep. Feeling the urge to move, he stood. The fire had burned down to coals. The house windows were dark, but the motion-sensor light, mounted on the edge of the roof, came on as he moved away from the fire.

Overhead, the Milky Way stretched like a glittering bridge across the heavens. The stars were cold and distant against the dark sky. Jake began to walk, past the stable and out toward the ranch gate. Something cool and damp nudged his hand. He glanced down to see that the dog had joined him. He reached down and scratched the shaggy head. Animals—even horses, he was learning—had a soothing way about them. They didn't judge or lie, offering only the truth of their being. All they asked in return was to be treated decently. Maybe that was the key to Kira's horse therapy. Mastering a horse required patience, respect and consistency—traits that were lacking in the troubled kids who'd come here for help. But Jake could already see the progress they were making.

If only things were that simple for him.

He passed under the gate and took the winding trail down the slope to the flat rock where he and Kira had watched the sunrise. Here and there, ranches and housing developments dotted the land with light. In the distance, Tucson glittered like a jeweled beacon. Construction on the valley road below had stopped for the night.

Today he'd been braced for the dynamite blasting and had been able to keep his reaction in check. In his own way, he was making progress, too. But not enough.

How easy it would be just to keep walking—down the trail to a road, and down the road to a highway, where he could catch a ride to anywhere. He'd done it before—simply walked away, without a word to anyone, or even much of an idea where he was headed. Now, as the blackness inside him deepened, he was tempted to do it again. So easy . . . no entanglements, no complications.

But he had promises to keep and people depending on him. It was time to turn back before the compulsion to escape drove him too far. With the dog at his heels, he climbed the trail and passed under the ranch gate. The motion-sensor light flickered on as he crossed the yard to the guest cabin. Attempting to sleep might be a bad idea, but come morning, if he hadn't rested, he'd be in even worse condition than he was now.

The dog was still with him. When he opened the cabin door, the animal trotted inside and lay down on the cowhide rug next to the bed. Maybe it sensed that this troubled human needed some company. Jake left the door slightly ajar in case the dog changed its mind about staying the night. Then he brushed his teeth, stripped down, crawled between the sheets and closed his eyes.

Watching from the kitchen window, Kira had seen Jake cross the yard and head down the trail. She knew better than to follow him. He wouldn't want that. But she couldn't stop herself from worrying. He'd seemed fine when they were joking and sharing s'mores. Then they'd started talking about Paige, and it was as if a light had gone out behind his eyes. Recognizing the signs, she'd hoped he might open up and talk. But Jake hadn't wanted any part of talking. Nor any part of her.

Seeing him reappear through the gate, she'd felt herself begin to breathe again. At least the dog was with him, and at least he'd had the sense to return. She could only hope he'd get some rest and be all right in the morning.

But "all right" had taken on a whole new meaning. Jake's arrival had brought with it a storm of changes—to the ranch, to Paige and to Kira herself. As a therapist, she'd built a wall around her own needs and emotions. But this pain-stricken man stirred feelings she'd long since put to rest. He'd awakened warm, natural urges—like the ones she'd felt with him tonight.

Not that she planned to act on those urges. Jake was like a half-wild animal, scared, hurt and prone to lash out with no warning. The help he needed was beyond anything she could give him here.

Besides, he was still in love with his stunning, flawless wife—the wife he had never truly known.

It would have been better for everyone involved if Jake had never come to Flying Cloud. But he'd already become part of this place and the people in it. Even if he were to go now, Kira knew that nothing he left behind would ever be the same.

CHAPTER EIGHT

Half-veiled by drifting clouds, the moon's light bathed the desert in silver and shadow. Bats fluttered through the darkness, catching insects in midair. An owl flashed low, snatched a mouse in its talons and vanished into a thicket. From the canyon, the night breeze carried the melancholy sound of coyote calls.

Deep in slumber, Jake was unaware. He had fallen over the edge of memory and into the black pit of a dream.

The night was frigid, the mountain air so thin that every man in his platoon was gasping for breath. Burdened by heavy packs and chest rigs, M240B machine guns, M4 carbines and single-shot grenade launchers, they labored up the rocky slope toward their target—a remote village, situated on a plateau below a mountain ridge. Known to be a Taliban stronghold, the village was little more than a cluster of mud-and-stone huts behind a protecting wall. But the view it commanded made it a constant threat to American troops in the area. Intel had picked up a rumor that a Taliban leader had gone into hiding there. If that was true—or even if it wasn't—it was time to blow the damned place to kingdom come.

Lungs burning, they bellied over the edge of the plateau. They'd expected to meet some resistance, but the village, a scant fifty yards distant, appeared quiet and unprotected. Strange, Jake thought, but he had his orders, and they didn't include asking questions.

Right now the wind was in their favor. But its direction could change, blowing their scent to the village dogs. At a barked alarm, all hell could break loose. There was no time to lose. Jake passed the word down the line and gave the order to fire.

Grenade explosions and gunfire blasted the village, lighting up the night like holiday fireworks. Within minutes the place was nothing but dust, smoke and rubble. All that remained for the platoon was to verify the damage and see if the targeted Taliban leader was among the casualties. Weapons at the ready, Jake's men crept forward, past the crumbled remains of the wall and into what was left of the village. Flashlights came on.

"Oh, my God!" the man behind Jake muttered. Then Jake saw them, too—the burned and blasted bodies of women, children, old people, and babies clutched in their mothers' arms—all of them dead amid the ruins. This might well have been a Taliban village. But the men and boys of fighting age had gone, leaving their helpless families behind.

There was nothing to be done. Sickened, Jake was

about to order his men away when AK-47 fire and rocket-propelled grenades erupted from the ridge above the village. As death rained down on them, the soldiers dived for any shelter they could find. Jake saw three men go down. He and their comrades dragged them along as they retreated down the slope, leaving the horror behind.

Jake's eyes jerked open. The room was dark, with shafts of moonlight piercing the window curtains. Heart pounding, body drenched in nervous sweat, he lay still, struggling to return to the here and now.

The dream had felt so real—he had heard the explosions, smelled the smoke. But he didn't need a dream to remember the rest of what had happened.

He had lost two men that night—men who'd been like brothers to him. Five more had been so badly wounded they had to be medevaced out. One of them had lost a leg. Then there were the others—the women, the children, the elders. "Collateral damage," that was the convenient term for dead civilians. But he knew their innocent blood was on his hands. True, he'd acted under orders, and no one had blamed him for the debacle. But he was the one who'd given the command to fire.

Returning to base, he'd reported in and seen to the comfort of his men. After that, all he could think of was calling his wife. He was desperate to hear her voice, calming him, reminding him that there was a better world beyond this hellish war, with loved ones waiting for him to return. If anyone could pull him out of despair, Wendy could.

Still emerging from shock, he'd been about to reach for the phone when he'd remembered. Wendy was dead.

Something touched Jake's hand. Fully awake now, he turned his head to see the dog standing with its front paws on the bed. Low, whining sounds quivered in its throat. Seeing that Jake was awake, the creature jumped onto the bed and snuggled down beside him. Its fur smelled like hay and stable dust, its breath like the leftover hot dogs it had wolfed down last night. But Jake had to admit that right now having company, even a scruffy dog, wasn't all that bad.

Freeing a hand from the covers, he scratched its ears. The dog's tail wagged ecstatically. "Listen, boy." Jake's morning voice rasped in his throat. "Don't think this is going to be a regular thing. I don't make a practice of sleeping with dogs."

The tail thumped harder. Jake twisted his head to see the bedside clock. It was almost four in the morning—too early to start the day, but not worth trying to go back to sleep and inviting another nightmare.

Sitting up, he nudged the dog off the bed and swung his feet to the floor. In his pack, he found some faded sweatpants, a long-sleeved shirt and a pair of flip-flops. Dressed, he let the dog out ahead of him and stepped into the early dawn.

As he filled his lungs with the cool, fresh air, he

could feel the dream receding. The pain was still there, as always. So was the memory. But he felt strong enough to make it through another day.

He was crossing the yard, toward the fire pit, when the security light came on. Jake mouthed a curse. He could understand the need for lights, with a bunch of mischief-prone adolescents to keep track of. But he'd just begun to feel at peace with the quiet darkness and fading stars.

As if on cue, the back door opened and Kira rushed out. She was wearing an old-style pink flannel bathrobe, with what looked like pajamas underneath. Her hair, usually tied back, floated loose around her face. She looked soft and vulnerable, like somebody's mom, only sexier. *Surprisingly sexier.*

"Is everything all right?" She was slightly out of breath.

"Fine. I was feeling restless, that was all. Sorry I woke you."

She exhaled in relief. "No, that's fine. I just wanted to make sure none of my students were sneaking out."

"Nobody in this bunch seems like the type to do that."

Her mouth curved in a lopsided smile. Jake liked her mouth—always had, he realized. "You'd be surprised," she said. "I hate having to run this place like a prison camp, but I'm responsible for these kids. If they get into trouble, I'm the one who has to answer to their parents. And believe me, if they were little angels, they wouldn't be here."

"You sound like you've seen it all."

"Not quite. Just when I'm thinking there's no way they can shock me, I find out I was wrong."

"I take it you've learned something new—and you can't tell me what it is or even who's involved."

She shook her head. "No, I'm afraid I can't."

They were walking toward the fire pit. She was probably tired and wanting to go back to bed, Jake thought, but he found himself wishing she'd stay.

"You don't have to be out here on my account," he said, giving her an opening to leave. "Go on back to bed. I'm big enough to take care of myself."

"Yes, I know." Her gaze swept up and down, taking in his sleep-rumpled hair, untrimmed beard and the faded, stretched-out sweats he'd pulled onto his naked body. "But I couldn't sleep if I wanted to. And it's nice out here. Early mornings are the only peaceful time I have."

"Too bad we can't turn off that light," he said. "It reminds me of that old fifties movie, *Stalag 17,* the one with William Holden in the German prison camp."

"Dusty loves that movie," she said. "The light's on a timer. If we sit down, it'll go off by itself in a couple of minutes. And the motion sensor shuts off at dawn."

She lowered herself to a bench next to the fire pit. Jake took a seat beside her, close enough for quiet talk. "I had some company last night," he said. "Your dog followed me into the cabin and settled down on the rug. When I had one of my war dreams, he was right there, with his paws on the bed. It was almost like he knew what was happening."

"Tucker's amazing that way," Kira said. "I remember a boy from last year who told me he'd come close to taking his own life one night, but the dog stayed right with him and wouldn't leave until the next morning, when the crisis had passed. Some dogs can sense an epileptic seizure coming on. Some can even detect cancer. Tucker's had no special training, but he seems to have a nose for anxiety. Even Paige—"

"Paige?" Jake's pulse jerked. "Is something wrong with her?"

"She has night terrors. Not often—a few times a year. I'm guessing they're related to the crash. She doesn't seem to have any conscious memory of it, but the shock and the confusion could've stayed with her. Tucker seems to sense when she's stressed. If he follows her into the bedroom at night, that puts us on alert."

"Can't you do something for her?" Jake asked.

"Only at the risk of making things worse. Maybe when she's old enough to deal with what happened . . ." Kira's words trailed off, ending in a sigh. She gazed into the charred ashes of the fire. In the east, the first streaks of dawn grayed the sky.

"Is there any way I can help?"

Kira gave him a sharp look. "Maybe—if you were committed to staying and being a real father. But that would be asking too much. We talked about this. We both know you're not ready."

"What if I were to try it? Just asking."

"Trying wouldn't be an option. Not if there was any chance you'd give up and leave."

"I understand." And he did understand, Jake told himself. Being a father to Paige would involve a lifetime commitment. There could be no trial period, no half measures. His choice would be all or nothing.

Kira was right. He wasn't ready.

Standing, he turned to watch the dawn creep over the mountains. He'd done all right here, helping with the students and the horses. But when it came to what really mattered—his daughter—he was out of his depth. It didn't matter that he'd already begun to love her, or that the feel of her trusting little hand, creeping into his, was the most healing thing he'd ever experienced. This wasn't about him. It was about Paige and her tender young heart. To save her from hurt, he would break his own heart and go. It would be the only right thing to do.

Kira had come up behind him. He felt her touch as she laid a hand on his shoulder.

"You should get married, Kira," he said. "Find a good man who can be a father to my little girl."

"Oh, Jake—"

He turned to look at her. She was gazing up at him, the dawn light pale on her face. Tears glistened in her eyes.

Driven by a hunger too sharp to control, he caught her in his arms and pulled her close. She gasped, then softened against him as his mouth pressed those sweet, sensual lips, nibbling, devouring. Her arms clasped his neck, pulling his head down to deepen the kiss. Her body arched to meet his, slim contours of her breast and hips molding to him through her robe. Jake groaned, half-embarrassed as his male response kicked in. He wanted what any man would want. It wasn't going to happen, of course. In fact, he was crazy to have kissed her in the first place. But with Kira in his arms, so soft, warm and fiercely yielding, he'd be damned if he wanted to stop.

The sound of a car coming up the road broke them apart. That would be Consuelo, arriving early to start preparations for breakfast. Kira spun away from him, stumbling a little. Her hair was wild, her mouth deliciously swollen. Knowing what to expect, Jake watched her pull herself together—spine erect, chin up, expression under control. The Kira he remembered was back.

She turned away, then swung to face him. "This didn't happen!" she said. "Do you understand? It *never* happened!"

With that, she wheeled and fled toward the house.

With the morning under way, Kira forced herself to close one mental box and open another.

With six of her students shoveling out the stable, under Jake's supervision, it was time to deal with Heather. She wasn't looking forward to it.

She led the girl to her small private office, showed her to a chair beside the desk, then closed the door. "This is a first for me, Heather," she said. "I've never had a student show up pregnant before. You've done well here, but I'm afraid we can't keep you in the program. Working with the horses might not be safe for you or your baby."

Heather looked peevish. "So who have you told?"

"Not a soul. That would be unethical. But you can't go through this time alone. I met your parents when they brought you here. They seem like nice people who truly care about you. I'm going to hand you the phone. You're going to call them and ask them to come and get you. You can tell them about the baby now or later. That's up to you."

Heather took the phone, laid it on the desk and pushed it away. Her face broke into an impish grin. "Boy, I really had you going, didn't I?" she said.

"What?" Kira stared at her in utter disbelief. "You mean you were joking? You're not pregnant?"

"No way!" Heather laughed, flashing her braces.

"And you didn't have sex with your sister's boyfriend?"

"That creep? I wouldn't let him touch me for a million dollars! In case you're wondering, I'm still a virgin—for now, at least." She laughed again.

Kira took a moment to breathe and count to

ten. "I don't like being lied to, Heather," she said. "How do I know you're not lying now?"

The girl gave her a smug look. "I can prove it. I'm on the rag. Take me into the bathroom and I'll show you. Or if that's too gross, ask my roommates. They know."

Out of patience, Kira stood. Worry about this girl had kept her awake most of the night. "Let's not make this a bigger deal than it already is," she said. "I'll give you a pass this time. But you've lost my trust. If I catch you lying again, you'll be out of here. Understand?"

Heather gazed up at her like a scolded puppy. "Okay. But don't you think it was funny?"

"No, I don't. Now go outside and get to work."

Kira stood on the porch and watched Heather scamper across the yard to join the others. Had she told the other students about the prank she'd pulled? Probably—or at least her roommates. The girl was hungry for attention. This story would be one way to get it.

This morning, under Jake's supervision, the students had led the horses out of their stalls and loosed them in the paddock while they cleaned the stable. After that, each of them would get to choose the horse he or she wanted to work with for the rest of the session.

Kira didn't anticipate any trouble. Most of the students had already picked their favorites. They would draw numbers to determine the order of choice. But even for late choosers, there wasn't a bad horse in the lot. Like humans, the mares and geldings had their personal quirks, but all of them were docile, sensitive and well-trained. Once the horses were chosen, there would be days of ground-work, followed by saddling and bridling, then, fi-nally, mounting and riding. The last part of the session would be devoted to trail rides in the desert and mountains, ending with an overnight camp-out in a high meadow. Not everyone would finish the rigorous course. But Kira had watched many troubled youngsters build confidence, overcome fear and acquire new self-respect. She would do her best to see it happen for this group.

Kira's pulse skittered as she caught sight of Jake among her charges. He'd been absent at breakfast this morning. Maybe he'd wanted to save himself the embarrassment of facing her. That, or he was avoiding Paige. Maybe both.

She'd tried to lock the memory of that searing kiss into one of her mental boxes. But it kept creeping into her thoughts. The taste of him clung to her lips; and it was as if the feel of his lean, hard body had been branded into her flesh.

"It never *happened."* That was what she'd told him. But it had. He had kissed her. Fool that she was, she'd kissed him back. And for that one fleet-ing moment, she'd felt a heady sense of freedom. Not that it could be allowed to matter. They were broken people, she and Jake. Any relationship be-

tween them would be doomed from the first moment.

Forget it, she told herself. Forget it and move on. But something told her it wasn't going to be that easy.

"Kira?" She felt a tug at her sleeve. Paige stood looking up at her. She was dressed, but her hair was uncombed, her shirt was buttoned wrong and her shoelaces were untied.

"Here, sweetie." Kira dropped to a crouch in front of her. "Let's get you tidied up a little. Have you had breakfast?"

"Uh-huh. I had eggs and toast in the kitchen, in my jammies. Then I got dressed."

"All by yourself, I see." Kira rebuttoned the shirt.

"Uh-huh. Mister Jake said I could help him today."

This would have been before this recent decision, Kira reminded herself. "Mister Jake's busy with the horses," she told the little girl. "You could get in the way and get hurt. We'll find something else for you to do."

Paige's lower lip jutted in a pout. "But I want to help Mister Jake. He said I could."

"And I'm saying no, Paige." Somebody had to be the bad guy. "Let's go inside and braid your hair. Then you can watch *Sesame Street*. After that, you can sit on the fence and watch the students choose their horses. Okay?"

"No!" Paige stomped her small foot. "I don't want to watch stupid *Sesame Street*. I want to go help Mister Jake!" Eyes flooding with tears, she turned and stormed into the house, letting the screen door slam shut behind her.

Kira sighed. Times like this reminded her that Paige was her mother's daughter. Wendy had been an adorable child, loved by everyone. But she could be a little hellion when she didn't get her way. Paige was cast from the same mold. For now, she would give the little girl some time to come around. Maybe they could plan some fun tonight, like a moonlight hike, while Jake was off visiting Dusty.

Paige's wanting to be with Jake was easy enough to explain. When the students were here, they took so much of Kira's time that Paige was often left to entertain herself or hang out in the kitchen with Consuelo. With Dusty gone, she must have been extra lonesome. That was probably why she'd latched onto Jake.

The other possibility—that at some level she'd recognized her father—was too far-fetched to believe. She'd been a baby when he left for that second deployment, and little more than a toddler when he'd come home for Wendy's funeral. All she had to remember him by was the wedding photo. And now, Jake—leaner, scruffier, bearded and graying—looked nothing like the happy young groom shown in the picture. Only his dark eyes were the same.

Give the child some extra TLC, and she'd be fine, Kira told herself. It was just going to take a little time.

* * *

The students had spent most of the day with the horses they'd chosen—leading them around the yard and partway along the canyon trail, brushing them down in their stalls and leaving them for the night with hay and clean water. The pride on those young faces as they paraded "their" horses around the ranch was something Jake wouldn't soon forget. Each of them had worked hard and earned the right to have a special, chosen animal for the rest of the program.

This horse therapy thing of Kira's was beginning to make sense.

His thoughts lingered on Kira as he drove her Outback down the highway. She'd kept her distance most of the day—no need to wonder why. But he'd caught her watching him from the porch. Was she having the same thoughts he'd been having all day? With Kira, you never could tell.

Kissing her had kicked his pulse over the moon. Her response had burned all the way to the soles of his feet. Damn it, beneath that calm, controlled surface, there was a warm, passionate, sexy *woman*! He wouldn't mind seeing more of that woman, maybe getting to know her under cozier conditions. But who was he kidding? Kira's words had made her position clear.

"This didn't happen! It never *happened!"*

And he couldn't expect it to happen again.

Kira had given him directions to the hospital where Dusty was staying. As he drove into Tucson, he watched the street signs and found the place easily. But he couldn't help wondering why the old man had asked for him—unless he just wanted some fresh company.

Dusty, wearing a hospital gown and a tangle of monitor lines, was sitting up in bed, watching a basketball game on TV. As Jake walked into the room, he used the remote to switch it off. "Thanks for showing up," he said. "I'm getting cabin fever in this place."

"Kira already warned me not to try and smuggle you out of here." Jake took a seat next to the bed.

"Damn, I was about to talk you into that." Dusty looked rested, but the old fire was lacking in his voice. "How's Kira doing, anyway?"

"Fine. You know Kira. She's got a handle on everything. The question is, how are you?"

"I'll be fine, once they let me out of this place. The doctor says it'll be day after tomorrow, if I promise to behave myself." Dusty winked. "He doesn't know me very well, does he?"

"You can joke all you want," Jake said. "But you've had a heart attack. You need to rest and get better."

Dusty shifted in the bed. "Kira says you're doing a fine job with her students."

"I'm pitching in where I can. But I'm no substitute for you. I don't have your knowledge, and Kira, good as she is, doesn't have your storytelling gift. We're hoping that once you're up to it, you can handle the lectures and leave the heavy work to me."

"So you've decided to stay on. You know that nothing would make me happier, don't you?"

The words stunned Jake for an instant. Was that what the old man had planned all along, to make him a permanent part of the ranch? He struggled to find his voice. "Sorry, but I never said that. Once you're on your feet, and once I've repaid what I owe you, I'm planning to move on."

Disappointment was written on Dusty's face. "I was hoping, when you saw how much we needed you, you'd change your mind."

"Dusty, any cowboy worth his salt could wrangle those horses and herd those kids around better than I do. You don't need me. Neither does Kira."

"And Paige? I take it she still doesn't know who you are."

"She's the most beautiful thing I've ever seen." Jake shook his head. "But I can't be a father to that little girl. I'm a wreck. I get dark spells that last for days, even weeks. I get nightmares that wake me up screaming. I fly out of control for no sane reason. The longer I stay, the greater the risk that she'll be hurt—if not before I leave, then after."

"Kira's a therapist. She could help you, if you let her. And the horses—"

"I've tried therapy. Nothing works." Jake was feeling the pressure. He needed a break. "Is there a Coke machine on this floor? I'm getting pretty dry."

"I wouldn't know," Dusty said. "But they could tell you at the nurses' station."

"I'll ask. Want anything?"

"I could use a beer. But I know better. So, no, just get your Coke."

Jake walked down the hall to the nurses' station and was directed to the vending machine outside the elevators. The single five-dollar bill left in his wallet bought him a cold Coke and gave him change. He took the long way back to Dusty's room, sipping as he walked.

The old cowboy had been good to him, bailing him out of jail and giving him a job. Jake understood his motives—or at least he could imagine he did. Dusty was getting old, and even before the heart attack, he could've been aware that his health was failing. Aside from Barbara, Wendy's missionary mother in Africa, Kira and Paige were his only heirs. The ranch was Kira's livelihood. He would want her to stay and continue her program there. But she couldn't manage everything on her own. Who better to help her than the man who was closest to being family—Wendy's widowed husband and Paige's father?

For all Jake knew, the old schemer could've even had matchmaking in mind, bringing him back in the hope that he and Kira and Paige would make a family. But that was a joke. Jake was even less fit to be a husband than a father. As for Kira—that kiss had pushed all the right buttons. But marriage involved a lot more than chemistry. And he couldn't imagine prickly, headstrong Kira as anybody's wife.

He returned to Dusty's room. The old man was sitting taller in the bed, looking as if he had more to say. Jake sat down, prepared to listen.

"I never asked how you were getting along with Kira," he said.

Jake flinched, remembering the feel of her in his arms. "Fine. She's pretty much all business, and very protective of Paige."

"That's about what I expected," Dusty said. "But I need you to understand some things about her. Remember when I said she needed you to forgive her for the accident?"

"Yes. She told me about stopping for coffee that night. But the accident wasn't her fault—and that's what I told her. They were in the wrong place at the wrong time. There's nothing to forgive."

"But there's more to Kira than that. Something else you need to know." Dusty cleared his throat. "Wendy may have told you this story. Stop me if you've heard it."

Jake nodded. Wendy hadn't talked much about her cousin in their brief time together. Back then, nothing had mattered except the two of them.

"You may have heard this much," Dusty said. "Growing up, Kira was a gifted pianist. By the time she was in her teens, she was playing as a soloist with community orchestras. She'd even applied to Juilliard and was waiting to hear from them."

"I had no idea," Jake said.

"Kira's father, a doctor, had his own private plane. He and Kira's mother had scheduled a ski trip to Salt Lake City. They'd planned to fly north a day early to take advantage of good weather, but Kira had an important concert that night. She wanted them there, so they put off their flight until the next day."

"Oh, Lord." Jake could guess the rest of the story.

"That's right. They hit a storm and crashed into a mountain."

"And Kira?"

"She sold her piano, gave the money to charity and never played again."

CHAPTER NINE

Two days later, Dusty came home to chocolate cake from Consuelo and cheers from the students. Paige clung to his side as if terrified of losing her beloved grandpa again. Even the dog, usually a calm animal, went wild with joy.

By the following day, the routine was in place. For the next couple of weeks, the old man was under orders not to ride, lift anything heavier than a spoon or exert himself in any way. He could walk around the house and ranch, but his lectures would be given in the living room or from a chair on the front porch.

Having Dusty available to teach freed up both Kira's time and Jake's. With Kira supervising the horse activities, Jake returned part-time to his original task—cleaning out the storage shed. He'd left things in a mess—items piled outside and half the shed's contents left to sort. With a chance of rain in the forecast for next week, he needed to get the good items out of the way of the weather. After a

morning with the horses, he set aside the afternoon to put things in better order. Dusty had told
him where to find a low-sided open trailer behind
the barn. Jake had used the Jeep to haul it to the
spot where he'd piled the trash from the shed.
When it was full, he would empty it at the nearest
landfill and come back for more.

The work was pleasant enough. He liked being
out here alone with nobody to bother him. And
the task gave his thoughts freedom to wander. The
only trouble was, they kept wandering to Kira.

Only now, after hearing the story about the
piano and the plane crash, did he feel that he was
beginning to understand her. In her own way, Kira
was as guilt-driven as he was. The three people
closest to her had died violent deaths because she
had altered their timing. The plane crash hadn't
been her fault. It had been a tragic accident, just
like the wreck that had killed Wendy. But Kira
would go on blaming herself, probably for the rest
of her life.

His own way of coping with pain and guilt was to
run—to keep moving, with no ties to anything or
anyone. Kira's way was to hold everything in, to
guard her emotions, controlling not only herself
but everything around her.

He'd glimpsed a different Kira the night he'd
held her in his arms—soft, vulnerable, even passionate. Part of him wanted to know that side of
her better. But he'd known all along that a relationship between them wouldn't work. Now, at
least, he understood why.

Forcing the thought aside, Jake tried to focus

on his work. Twenty minutes later, he was making good progress when he sensed a presence behind him. Even before he turned to look, he knew it was Paige.

"Hi, Mister Jake." She held out a peanut butter cookie and a cold root beer. Her expression would have melted any frozen heart, but Jake, knowing what had to be done, gave her a scowl.

"What are you doing out here?" he growled. "Don't you have better things to do than bother me?"

Tears glimmered in her big brown eyes. "I was lonesome," she said. "I thought maybe you needed a treat."

"Where's Kira?" he asked.

"She's in her office talking to a boy. Grandpa's taking a nap, and Consuelo's watching her TV show. Nobody's got time for me."

"Looks like you've got Tucker." The dog had come up beside her and was eyeing the cookie in her hand.

"Tucker can't talk. And I want to be with you. Why don't you like me anymore, Mister Jake?"

He had to hand it to the kid. She knew how to stab him right through the heart.

"It's not that I don't like you," he said. "It's just that this isn't a good place for a little girl, out here with all this junk and a scruffy old bum like me."

"'Bum' is a naughty word, Mister Jake. That's what Consuelo says." Her gaze was reproachful.

"Sorry," Jake said. "You can see that I'm not fit company for a proper young lady like you."

The dog chose that unguarded moment to snatch

the cookie out of her hand. With a snap of his jaws, the cookie was gone.

"Bad dog!" Paige scolded the creature with a wagging finger. "Sorry," she said to Jake. "I can get you another one."

"Tell you what," Jake said. "I'll take the root beer, and you go back into the house. Find yourself something to do. You mustn't be out here."

"But why?" She thrust the soda toward him, her eyes brimming once more.

He took the can. "Because I said you mustn't. Now get going."

"That's not fair!" She wheeled and stalked toward the house, the dog at her heels. Jake sighed as he drained the soda can. His daughter was a little spitfire, as adorably strong-willed as Wendy had been. It had damn near killed him to send her away, but it had to be done.

Steeling his resolve, he waded back into the work of clearing the shed, grabbing furniture, boxes, souvenirs and old machine parts that hadn't seen daylight in decades. Next in front of him, standing on end, was an old mattress and box spring set. He could see holes where mice had chewed through the cover. They were probably nesting inside, raising generations of mouse families. Maybe he could drag the pieces out of the shed and onto the trailer without disturbing them too much. Then the little vermin would get a free ride to the happy kingdom of the trash dump.

The mattress was heavy and floppy. Sweating with effort, he dragged it onto the trailer. No mice.

Relieved, Jake wiped his forehead with the back of his glove. At least the box spring, which had a rigid frame, should be easier to move.

Grabbing the heavy box spring, Jake shifted it to one side. He was about to lug it to the trailer, but then he saw what had been hidden behind it. His pulse lurched. Drop-jawed, he stared, feeling like some ancient knight who'd just discovered the Holy Grail.

This afternoon Kira had her one-on-one with Brandon, a slim, polite boy with dark hair and eyes. Even before he began to open up, she suspected his secret. His father, who managed a Phoenix sports team, had sent his fifteen-year-old son to Flying Cloud Ranch in the hope that learning to ride would make him more "masculine." Brandon was doing well with the horses, but Kira knew that the change his father wanted wasn't going to happen.

"How long have you known?" she asked him.

He sipped the bottled water she'd given him. "I've always known I was different. But it's only been in the past couple of years that I've understood how and why."

"And you've never come out to anybody? Not even your friends?"

He managed an awkward smile. "Just you, so far. I figure that when I'm grown up and on my own, it won't be so bad. Gays are pretty much accepted these days. But right now, if I told my dad, he wouldn't be able to handle it. And it would upset my mother, too. For now, it'll have to wait. Meanwhile, I really am enjoying the horses." He stood. "Thanks. It helps to talk about it with somebody."

"Talk to me anytime. And don't worry, nothing we say will leave this room." Kira was impressed with the boy's maturity, but she knew that in the years ahead, he'd have some hard decisions to make. The best she could do was to help prepare him.

After Brandon left, she updated the files, shut down her computer and walked back down the hall to the living room. She found Paige alone on the couch. Her well-worn leather baby book, always kept on a shelf within her reach, lay open on the coffee table. Paige loved looking at the photos of herself as a newborn, seeing her little pink hospital bracelet, a single curl of her baby hair and the tiny ink-prints of her hands and feet. There were pictures of her with her toys and in the bath, pictures of her with her mother and even a few with Kira. But there were no photos of her father. Jake had been overseas during that early part of her life.

"Hi, Aunt Kira," she said. "Are you through working?"

"For now." Kira clicked through her mental list of appointments. Faith would be coming in at two o'clock; and after that, there'd be more work with the horses and a slide lecture about tomorrow's outing to Organ Pipe Cactus National Monument. But right now, she had a little time to relax and be with Paige.

"Goodness, you do love that book, don't you?"

Kira sat down next to her. "Which picture is your very favorite?"

Paige thumbed toward the end of the book. "This one," she said, pointing to an informal color photo with herself as a toddler, on her mother's lap. It was a spectacular shot of Wendy, in an emerald-green blouse with her Titian hair flowing over her shoulders.

"My mom was beautiful, wasn't she, Aunt Kira?" Paige asked.

"She was." Aching a little, Kira gave her a hug. "And she loved you very much."

Hearing a footstep, Kira looked up. Jake had come inside from the kitchen and was standing in the open archway between the dining and living rooms. Dressed in ragged jeans and a damp T-shirt that clung to his body, he looked sweaty and hot. Mostly hot, Kira conceded. Whatever else might be going on with him, Jake was calendar-model material.

He cleared his throat. "Excuse me. I was hoping Dusty would be here. I need to talk to him about something."

Kira stood. "Dusty's been napping, but I hear water running in the bathroom, so he must be up. Hang on, I'll tell him you're here."

As she hurried down the hall, she could hear Paige saying, "Come here, Mister Jake. I want to show you a picture of my mom."

Kira felt something sharp tighten inside her. Whatever was happening behind her in the living room, she feared it would not end well. But right now, there was little she could do.

* * *

Jake moved reluctantly to the end of the couch and stood looking down, past Paige's shoulder.

"See?" Paige pointed to the color photo in the album, one Jake had never seen before. "That's my mom and me."

Jake gazed down at Wendy's vibrant, laughing face. She was gorgeous. In the brief time they'd had together, he'd felt like the luckiest man in the world. Seeing her image, knowing she was gone forever, was like the twist of a cold knife in his gut. Maybe if she'd been waiting when he came home, he could have pulled himself together. But that chance was long gone.

"Isn't she beautiful?" Paige asked.

"She was beautiful—I mean in the picture," Jake corrected himself. "And that little baby is you? Unbelievable!"

"Here's another one." Paige turned to a different photo. "Sit down, I'll show you some more."

"Thanks, but I'd better not—"

Jake broke off at the welcome sound of approaching footsteps. "Maybe another time, Paige," he said. "Right now, I need to talk with your grandpa."

Dusty came into the room, followed by a hovering Kira. He was looking stronger, but the heart attack had taken its toll. He appeared slower and less vigorous than before. "What's this all about, Jake?" he asked. "Sit down. You look fit to bust."

Jake sat, then stood again, too restless to keep still. "What do you know about that motorcycle in the shed?" he asked.

"Oh, that old machine?" Dusty laughed. "It's been there so long, I'd plumb forgot about it. It's a '51 Indian Chief, but you probably know that. Otherwise, you wouldn't be so excited."

"Everything on it looks original," Jake said. "It's got a few dings, but still, it's pure vintage gold. Is it yours?"

"That's a good question. Sometime back in the old days, Steve McQueen brought it here to get around on when he was shooting a movie hereabouts. The picture was about done when the bike broke down and wouldn't start. McQueen left it here—said somebody'd come by and take it when the film crew packed up to leave. Nobody ever came. So there it sits."

"Steve McQueen died more than thirty years ago. After all this time, that bike's got to be worth some serious money."

"Maybe. But I could end up bashing heads with his estate if I put it up for sale. And with these old bones, I sure as hell can't ride it. Tell you what, I've got no use for the thing. Get it running, and it's yours."

"You're kidding!" Jake had to sit down. "What's wrong with it?"

Dusty shrugged. "How should I know? I'm a horseman, not a blasted mechanic. There's no title, but after so many years, it should qualify as abandoned property. I know a fellow at the DMV who can help us with the paperwork. There's just one thing." Dusty's sharp blue eyes narrowed. "If you get that contraption running, there'll be no revving the engine and spooking the horses. Understood?"

"And there'll be no taking the students for rides," Kira added. "The liability insurance would go through the roof."

"Understood," Jake said. "And any time I spend on it will be off the clock. The repair job is liable to take a while—if I can even get parts."

After thanking the old cowboy, Jake left the house and walked back toward the shed. The vintage motorcycle was a thing of pure beauty. But it was much more than that. If he could get it running and licensed, it would be his transportation out of here. It would be his ticket to freedom.

He stood in the yard a moment, gazing around him—at the horses dozing in the sunlit paddock, the weathered outbuildings, the desert hills abloom with glorious color. Two golden eagles, mates most likely, circled overhead. The fresh breeze smelled of hay and horses. Far below, on the road, a dynamite blast echoed up the canyon. The sound no longer shot panic along his nerves. It was almost as if, little by little, he was beginning to heal in this peaceful place. But he knew better than to hope. Sooner or later, some trigger or mood swing would push him over the edge. When it happened, he didn't want to be around people he cared about.

Paige had come out onto the front porch. Glancing to one side, he could see her sitting on the top step with her arm around the dog. As he watched her, she turned and buried her face in the shaggy brown fur. Was she crying? Something in him ached to go to his little girl and cradle her in his arms. But he could only do that as her father—not as Mister Jake, the scruffy stranger who was just passing through.

Was keeping his distance the only way to keep her safe? It would have to be, Jake told himself as he turned away. Kira was right—whatever happened, Paige mustn't be hurt. And right now, he had a job to finish—cleaning out the shed.

Faith walked into Kira's office, her hair French-braided and her makeup flawless. Dressed in skinny jeans and a little black tee with a designer logo on the front, the tall, pretty fifteen-year-old could have stepped straight out of a teen fashion magazine. Even her nails were freshly manicured and painted in a glowing shade of blue.

Kira had reviewed her file before the session. According to her divorced mother, the girl had become withdrawn after some inappropriate texting with her married drama teacher had gotten the man fired. Faith had done well with the horses; but so far, she'd had little interaction with the other students.

"Hello, Faith," Kira said. "Have a seat. Would you like something to drink?"

"No thanks." Faith perched on the edge of the chair. "I know I have to be here. But there's no rule that says I have to talk to you. So don't ask me anything—especially not about my personal life. That's none of your business."

"Fine, if that's your choice." What Kira could see was enough. The girl was making an effort to sound worldly and detached, but her lower lip was quivering. Her fingers twisted the birthstone ring on her middle finger.

"I didn't want to come here," she said. "My mother made me. She thinks I'm depressed. Do I look depressed to you?"

"What does depressed look like?"

"Oh, you know . . . like, you can't get out of bed in the morning, or fix yourself up. I can do all that stuff."

"Well, you seem to be a natural with the horses." That much was true.

"I love the horses. They're a lot nicer than people. They don't lie to you or rip you to pieces behind your back. And they don't turn on you and blame you for stuff that wasn't your fault. I mean— like Mr. Halvorson, he was the one who came on to me. I thought it was cool at first, having an older man pay attention to me. But then it got ugly, and people started talking. When the principal called him in, the jerk claimed it was all *my* fault. He said I'd been stalking him."

She pulled a tissue from the box on Kira's desk and wadded it in her fist. "The kids liked him. A lot of them believed his story. They blamed me for getting him fired." A tear trickled down her cheek, leaving a trail of mascara. "I'm never going back to that school—not ever."

"Where was your father during all this, Faith?" Kira asked.

The girl shrugged. "Somewhere back East, I guess. He left my mom and me when I was six. Since then, he hasn't even sent me a birthday card. Mom sells real estate, but she barely makes ends meet. The money to send me here came from my grandpa. Too bad he didn't just give us tickets to Hawaii. It would've been more fun."

It was time to change the subject. "How are you getting along with your roommates?" Kira asked.

Faith smoothed back a lock of hair. "How do you think? Heather's an obnoxious, lying bully, and Lanie follows her around like a little pup. I can't stand them. Isn't there some way I can have a room to myself?"

"Sorry, there's no space," Kira said. "And even if there were, it's against policy for students to room alone. You might try getting to know those girls better."

"Sure." Faith rose with a sigh. "Well, at least my horse understands me."

After Faith had left, Kira sat and gazed out the window, lost in thought. The girl had some serious trust issues, starting with an absent, uncaring father. It might well have been the hunger for a man's attention that had left her vulnerable to the lure of an older male predator. If the relationship hadn't been discovered, an incident might have become a tragedy.

What if something like that happened to Paige?

When her father had left, Faith hadn't been

much older than Paige was now. So far, Paige seemed satisfied that her father was in the army and couldn't come home. But that illusion wouldn't last much longer. Either way, whether she learned Jake's true identity or not, she would grow up believing her father hadn't cared enough to be around for her. She could become as needy and vulnerable as poor Faith.

Unless Jake manned up and stayed.

Agitated, Kira rose and began a nervous tidying of her office, straightening the items on her desk, dusting her computer, tossing a bouquet of wilted wildflowers into the wastebasket. She'd disagreed with Dusty's decision to bring Jake here. But what if her grandfather had been the wise one? What if he'd been right?

She'd seen how Paige had taken to Jake, even without knowing who he was; and she'd seen how unhappy the little girl was now that her new friend was off-limits. She'd also seen the contentment that had settled over Jake when he'd allowed himself to be with her. Paige needed her father. Jake needed his child.

In her training as an equine therapist, Kira had worked with a number of traumatized combat vets, some of them far worse off than Jake. If PTSD wasn't entirely curable, the symptoms could at least be managed. Kira felt confident that she could help Jake, making it easier for him to stay. But he had to be willing. So far she'd seen no sign of that. For him, the only solution to his pain was to move on, leaving Paige to grow up without him.

If nothing changed, once Jake worked off what he owed Dusty and got the bike licensed and running, he'd be loading his pack and heading for the horizon.

What would it take to keep him here, where he was needed?

Jake forced himself to work on the shed contents for the rest of the afternoon. But he did allow himself a few minutes to dust off the Indian and wheel it out front where he could admire it. It was a beautiful machine, long and powerful like a big cat, with a solid body and curving red fenders. The fact that it had belonged to a legendary Hollywood star only added to its glamour.

As a mechanical engineer, he knew his way around an engine. It shouldn't be too hard to figure what wasn't working. With luck it would be something simple, like the fuel pump or the starter. The next step would be to go online and look for vintage parts.

Once he'd located what he needed, he'd have to find a way to pay for it. But his veterans' benefit payment should be in his bank account before long, and he had a check for a week's wages, minus the first repayment to Dusty. Maybe Consuelo could deposit it on her next trip to town. Then he could use his debit card to order online. If the money wasn't enough, he could always wait another week or two. Once he had the critical part in hand, the repair shouldn't be too hard—unless there was some unforeseen problem. With any luck, his only remaining worry would be testing the engine without scaring Dusty's horses.

"So this is what you were so excited about." Kira had come outside. She stood a few feet away, her cool gray eyes appraising the bike. "It's really something. I can picture Steve McQueen roaring down the roads on it, breaking all the speed limits."

"I still can't believe Dusty let me have it," Jake said. "Did you know it was here?"

"I had no idea. It must've been left here before I was even born." She brushed back a lock of her hair, a graceful gesture. "Consuelo wanted me to tell you that dinner's almost ready."

"Thanks. Tell her I'll grab a sandwich later." Jake lugged a heavy carton of old vinyl record albums to the "ask Dusty" pile. "I'm on a roll here. I'd like to get to a good stopping place before dark."

"I'll let her know." Kira lingered, hesitating. "I have a request of my own. By the end of next week, the students should be riding their horses. After that, we'll be taking some trail rides. I'll need you along to help out."

"Me? On a horse?"

"Yes." She looked vaguely annoyed. "Unless you'd rather bring up the rear on foot, with a shovel."

"I don't know about that." He was needling her, enjoying it. "Leading the critters around is one thing, but I didn't sign up for getting on one."

She made a little huffing sound. "You told me what happened to your father, Jake. But these horses are sweet old darlings. You know that. You've been working with them."

"Sweet old darlings or not, they're still horses. But you're the boss. So tell me what you've got in mind."

"You'll need a head start on learning to ride so you can help the students. It's a nice evening, plenty of moonlight. I was thinking, after dinner, while the group is watching *Seabiscuit* with Dusty, you and I could saddle up for an easy ride down the canyon."

Jake took a moment. He wasn't crazy about climbing onto a contrary half-ton animal, capable of breaking every bone in his body; but a moonlight ride with Kira sounded like the perfect ending to the day. Besides, he reminded himself, he needed a favor in return.

"How about a deal?" he said. "I'll agree to cowboy up and ride, if you'll let me borrow your computer to find parts for the bike."

"Sure. Anytime I'm not using the office. Just let me know ahead." She gave him a roguish look. "And I'll see you after dinner, cowboy."

He watched her walk back to the house, admiring her lithe, confident stride. In the years since she'd been Wendy's maid of honor, he'd never considered Kira his type. She still wasn't a good bet for anything serious. He liked his women soft and yielding, focused on him and on their relationship—women like the one he'd married.

Kira was too driven, too independent. But, damn it, she was growing on him. She challenged him in intriguing ways, and there was something downright sensual in the lean strength of her body and the flickers of emotion that softened her face.

Kira.

Jake was looking forward to the ride.

CHAPTER TEN

Jake had been working steadily for the past hour. Now he paused to stretch, raked back his hair and massaged a twinging muscle in his shoulder. In the sky above Tucson, the sunset had deepened to violet and indigo.

Kira had come outside and was crossing the yard toward him. As she walked closer, Jake saw that she was holding a sandwich on a paper plate and a can of juice.

"Consuelo mentioned you hadn't been inside," she said. "A man's got to eat."

"Thanks." He stripped off his leather gloves, took the plate and sat down on a handy wooden crate. He was hungry, and the sandwich—sliced prosciutto, with carefully layered tomato, romaine, pickles and Swiss cheese on rye—was delicious. "This is decadent," he muttered between bites. "My compliments to Consuelo."

"Consuelo was busy. I'm no domestic goddess, but now and then, I make an effort." She gave him a smile. "Anyway, thanks for the backhanded compliment. Ready to mount up and ride?"

Jake stifled a groan. He was tired, sweaty and sore. The last thing he felt like was getting up on a horse for the first time. But he'd given his word. And he liked the way Kira looked with her shirt collar falling open and the twilight reflecting in her silvery eyes. "Ready as I'll ever be," he said.

He finished the sandwich, emptied the can and crossed the yard with her to the stable. After switching on the overhead light, Kira led Sadie, her blue roan mare, out of her stall. For Jake, she chose one of the extra horses, a drowsy-looking chestnut gelding.

"What's his name?" Jake asked, eyeing the unimpressive animal.

"It's Dynamite. But don't let the name worry you. He was a great cow pony in his day. Now he's the oldest trail horse on the ranch. He's every inch a gentleman."

"You wouldn't be pranking me, would you?"

"Believe me, I need your help too much for that. Let's get started."

They collected their gear from the tack room and she showed him how to place the pad and the saddle on the horse's back, buckle the straps, tighten the cinch and adjust the stirrups to his height. There was a lot to learn and remember. Getting the bridle on, with the bit in place, wasn't easy; but, as Kira had said, the old chestnut gelding was a gentleman, accustomed to fumbling students. He endured Jake's awkward efforts with barely a twitch of his gray-flecked ears.

"Mounting is easy if you do it right," Kira said, demonstrating on her mare. "Left foot in the stirrup, push up and swing your right leg over, just like in the movies. Try it."

Jake battled nerves as he put a boot in the stirrup. The boyhood memory of seeing his father thrown and trampled in the rodeo arena came back to him as if it had happened yesterday. As he swung his weight into the saddle, he half-expected Dynamite to live up to his name and explode into bucking fury. But the placid old gelding merely shifted, exhaled and waited for the command to move.

"Give him a little nudge with your heels, like this." Kira demonstrated. "We'll take it easy, once around the yard, before we head down the trail. That's it . . . soft and light, just so he knows it's time to go. Don't worry about the reins at first. Just hold on. If Sadie and I go ahead, he'll follow us."

Swaying with each step, Dynamite ambled through the barn door and into the yard. By now, it was dark. The rising moon spilled light across the landscape. Kira rode a few yards ahead of him. Jake kept his eyes on her slim, erect back. She sat her horse like a queen, her pale shirt a beacon ahead of him in the darkness.

Jake envied her self-confidence. He hadn't been keen on riding, but he took pride in doing things well. Now that he'd been forced into the challenge, he wasn't about to settle for clinging to a geriatric horse that probably felt sorry for him. Whatever it took, he vowed, by the time he left this place, he would be a competent horseman.

"How are you doing?" Kira called over her shoulder.

"I think I'm getting the hang of it. But how do you steer this old boy?"

"Easy. You just move the reins in the direction you want him to go. That puts pressure on the bit, and he'll turn to get more comfortable. Just a touch is enough. You don't want to hurt his mouth."

"And if I want him to stop?"

"You pull on the reins and say 'whoa!' Just a gentle tug—there's no need to pull hard. Dynamite knows what to do."

Jake tried a couple of moves. The old horse responded to his touch. "Hey, it's kind of like driving a stick shift," he said, making a lame joke.

Kira's laugh was musical. "It's even easier than that," she said. "Come on, let's try the trail now. Just give him his head. He knows the way."

They passed under the ranch's high gate and headed down the trail, riding single file. The path wound among jutting clumps of rock, lacy mesquite and paloverde trees, and stands of blooming cactus, all silvered by the moonlight. The old horse's gait was sure and steady, the slight rocking motion strangely soothing. Jake found himself shifting his balance in time, matching the horse's rhythm.

They reached the flat rock where he and Kira had sat and talked on his first day here. The lights of Tucson glowed in the distance. He was expecting Kira to stop and turn back. Instead she swung her mare to the right and vanished downhill, into the shadows of the canyon.

The new trail was steep. Jake had to lean back to keep from sagging forward over the saddle horn, but he soon adjusted to the slanting posture. Surefooted as ever, Dynamite plodded along the switchbacks. The air felt cooler here. Leaves fluttered in the canyon breeze. From somewhere below came the splash of water and the trill of frog calls.

Farther down, where the trail leveled out, Kira signaled a halt. "We'll tie the horses and walk from here," she said. "It isn't very far."

Following her example, Jake swung out of the saddle, dropped to the ground and looped the reins around a sapling. His legs felt rubbery from straddling the horse. He was going to be sore in the morning.

"Where are we going?" he asked.

"It's a surprise. One of my favorite places. Come on."

He followed her along a path that was too rocky and narrow for the horses. The moonlight, shining through the trees, made lacy patterns on the ground. The splash and gurgle of water was close now, but still out of sight.

"We aren't going skinny-dipping, are we?" he teased, thinking to lighten the moment.

"You could try it," she said. "But the water's cold. You'd freeze."

"So what's so special about the place?"

"Nothing. It's just beautiful—and peaceful. So please don't spoil it by asking questions."

Jake followed her in silence. They emerged moments later through a thicket of willows into a clearing, where a trickling waterfall cascaded over the rocks into a shallow pool. The golden disk of the moon cast a shimmering reflection in the dark mirror of the water.

"See? Didn't I tell you?" Kira whispered.

"You were right," he said. "No more questions."

A cool night breeze blew down the canyon. Kira shivered in her light cotton shirt. Acting on impulse, Jake stepped behind her and wrapped his arms around her shoulders. "You're cold," he said.

"I'm fine," she responded, but she didn't pull away, even when his arms tightened around her.

"Thank you for sharing this place with me." Jake could feel her heart pounding against him. She smelled of the lavender soap stocked in the guest cabins. But on her skin, the aroma became sensual, even arousing.

"I like to come here when I'm feeling stressed," she said. "It reminds me that the world isn't such a fearful place after all. Sometimes I bring Paige along. She loves it, too."

He resisted the impulse to turn her in his arms and kiss her right then. Instead he asked, "What do you find so fearful about the world, Kira? What are you afraid of?"

She was silent, thinking. After a moment, she spoke. "Losing the people I love, or hurting them. Not being there to keep bad things from happening."

"You can't keep bad things from happening. Maybe some, but not all of them."

"I know. That's what scares me. It scares me all the time."

He did kiss her then, lifting her chin with his

thumb and pulling her gently around so he could find her lips. A brush, a nibble, he took his time, tasting her, slowly deepening the contact. A quiver passed through her body as he flicked the tip of his tongue into her mouth—pausing just there, knowing that to push too far, in this isolated place, could give her the wrong idea. Better to leave her curious, maybe even wanting more.

For the space of a breath, he held her, then freed her to back away. The kiss had been gentle, almost chaste, but they were both breathing hard.

"Don't say that didn't happen," he said. "Believe me, it did."

"I know." She faced him, with moonlight sculpting her features as she pulled herself together. "But that isn't why I brought you here."

"I had a feeling it wasn't," he said. "I'm listening."

"When Dusty brought you here, I was afraid you'd be nothing but trouble. But that's changed. Now I'm asking you to stay. Not for me, but for Paige."

"Kira—"

"No. Hear me out. I know you're planning to leave. But that little girl needs her father. If you don't care enough to be part of her life, she'll feel that loss forever. It will affect her self-esteem, her trust, her future relationships with men. . . ."

"Stop it, Kira. You know I can't stay, and you know why."

"I know you think you can't get well. But look around you—the beauty, the peace of places like this. Flying Cloud Ranch is your best chance to heal, maybe your only chance. You owe it to your daughter to try."

"And what if it doesn't work?" Jake thrust his hands into his pockets to keep them still. "You don't know how bad this thing can get. You've barely seen the tip of the iceberg. The foul words that come screaming out of my mouth, the things I throw and hit and break—I've punched my way through doors, through walls, even through people. That's how I landed in jail. Do you think I want Paige to see me like that?"

"Of course not. But if you're not ready to stay, maybe you could try the VA again. Spend some time. Let them work with you. Then you could come back here. You'd always be welcome."

Jake shook his head. "The VA was a dead end for me. Counseling was a waste of time, and medication only made me dopey. The best I can do on my own is try to keep the bad spells under control. Most of the time, I manage. But sometimes I can't help it. Something triggers me and all hell breaks loose. I've got an engineering degree, but I can't hold down any kind of decent job, let alone be a decent father."

When she didn't reply, he walked to the edge of the pool and stood for a moment, listening to the splash of the waterfall and the drone of frog calls. "You've worked with vets. You've heard about the hell over there and what it did to some of us. The real thing was a hundred times worse than what you read about or saw on TV. But I was able to handle it as long as I knew Wendy was waiting for me back home. Hearing her voice, seeing her face when we managed to Skype—she kept me grounded. If she'd been there through that last deployment, I think I might have been all right. But without her, there was nothing to keep the nightmares out."

"I'm sorry." Kira's whisper was laced with anguish.

"The accident wasn't your fault. But it happened, and I don't know if I'll ever be right again."

As soon as the words were out of his mouth, Jake knew he'd said the wrong thing. But the damage was done. A moment of tense silence passed before she spoke. "We should go. Dusty will be needing our help."

Jake followed her as she led the way back to the horses. Saying little, they mounted and rode single file up the trail.

Sensitivity had never been one of his strong points, but he'd just hit a new low. After enjoying that tender, passionate kiss, he had pretty much slapped her in the face.

Should he apologize, or would that only make things worse?

Never mind. He felt like a jerk, but what was done was done. He had just added one more item to his list of reasons to leave here.

As they rode under the ranch gate, Kira forced the past hour's happenings into one of her mental boxes and locked it tight. She'd battled tears most of the way up the trail. But it was time to forget how Jake's kiss had stirred her. Time to put aside what she'd felt when he'd told her how he'd de-

pended on Wendy's support to give him hope—
and how he'd fallen over the edge after he'd lost
her.

Jake was still in love with his beautiful wife. She
should have reminded herself of that when he
took her in his arms. Instead she'd responded to
him—and left herself open to humiliation. There
was more to Wendy than Jake knew. But she would
never tell him. Why cause more pain when he'd already suffered so much?

"You can go on up to the house," he said as they
neared the stable. "I'll put the horses away."

"Thanks." Kira dismounted, making an effort to
act as if nothing had changed between them. "I'm
sure Dusty could use a hand with the students.
We'll be doing more groundwork in the morning.
I'll see you then."

"One request," he said. "Your students have
picked their horses. Is it okay if I choose this old
boy for mine?" He patted Dynamite's shoulder.
"He's no Derby winner, but he's growing on me."

"I was hoping you'd say that," she said. "Dynamite's a great horse."

"And can I take him out for practice whenever I
get time?"

"Sure. He's yours for the duration—or even for
keeps if you change your mind about sticking
around."

"Let's table that," Jake said. "I've got a loan to
repay and a bike to fix. I won't be leaving anytime
soon."

"Fine. Turn off the light and bolt the stable door
when you're finished with the horses." Emotions

wearing thin, Kira strode off toward the house. Jake had put her through the wringer tonight. Maybe in the morning, she'd feel calm enough to deal with him. But tonight she couldn't get away fast enough.

As she neared the front porch, she saw Paige sitting on the top step with her arm around the dog. Concerned, she hurried toward the little girl.

"What are you doing out here alone, Paige? Is everything all right?"

"Everything's fine," Paige said, sounding very grown-up. "And I'm not alone. Tucker's here with me."

"Why aren't you watching the movie?"

"I've seen that old movie about a hundred times. Seabiscuit always wins." She scratched the dog behind the ears. "Where did you go with Mister Jake?"

"Just down the canyon. He's learning to ride a horse."

"Doesn't he already know how?"

"He wasn't around horses before he came here. That's why I let him ride Dynamite."

"I bet I could ride Dynamite, too, if I had longer legs."

"You can ride when you're older. I know you'll be good at it. You already know a lot about horses."

Paige twirled a lock of hair around her finger, suddenly pensive. "I thought Mister Jake was my friend. Why doesn't he like me anymore?"

Kira sighed. She should've known this conversation would come up. "How could anybody not like a nice girl like you? Mister Jake likes you fine."

"No, he doesn't. Today when I brought him a cookie and some root beer, he told me to go away. He said it wasn't good for me to be with a bum like him. I told him 'bum' was a bad word. Then Tucker ate the cookie, and Mister Jake made me go. It made me feel bad."

"Oh, honey." Kira slipped an arm around the small shoulders. Sometimes the only safe answer was the truth—or part of the truth, at least.

"There's something you need to understand about Mister Jake," she said. "He was in a war."

"Like my daddy." It wasn't a question.

Kira's breath caught. "Yes . . . like your daddy. And some really bad things happened to him over there—things that made him scared and angry and sad."

"What kind of things?"

"Things like bombs blowing up, seeing people die and having his friends get shot. Mister Jake remembers all those things. Sometimes he remembers too much. When that happens, he can get upset." Kira took a breath. Explaining post-traumatic stress disorder to an innocent child had to be one of the hardest things she'd ever done.

"Upset how?"

Kira sighed. "He can get really mad, or really unhappy, or he can even feel like he's still in the war and has to fight. That's why he doesn't want you with him. He's afraid he might scare you, or say bad words you shouldn't hear."

"But I wouldn't be scared. I would know it was because of the war."

"Maybe. But he's afraid to take that chance. So

you're to leave Mister Jake alone, because that's what he wants. Understand?"

Her small hand lay still on the dog's head. Tears glimmered in her eyes. Slowly she nodded. "But he still likes me, doesn't he?"

Kira gave her a squeeze. "He likes you very much. But promise me you won't bother him anymore. Okay?"

She hesitated. "Okay. But can I say a prayer for him? Maybe that will help him get better."

"That would be the very nicest thing you could do." Standing, Kira took the small hand in hers. "Let's go on inside. It's past your bedtime."

As she followed Jake's daughter into the house, Kira couldn't help wondering whether she'd said too much. Paige was a bright little girl who'd spent her life surrounded by adults. She was mature beyond her years. Still, understanding something as complex as Jake's condition was a lot to ask of a child.

Or maybe not. In her wise young way, Paige had taken what she'd been told and made her own truth of it.

The war had hurt Jake. She would say a prayer for him.

In the stable, Jake finished toweling Kira's mare, closed the gate and walked down the row of stalls to the gentle chestnut that had carried him down the canyon and back. He'd already removed the saddle and bridle and replaced them in the tack room, and the horses had been fed before dinner.

But he wanted to reward Dynamite with some extra attention.

He'd learned about grooming along with Kira's students. Now, with a currycomb, a brush and a towel, he stepped into Dynamite's stall and began.

None of the horses in the stable wanted for care. But because Dynamite was an extra, he hadn't received a daily grooming like the students' horses. A shudder of pleasure passed through the old gelding's body as Jake combed the loose hair from his coat. He snorted and shook his hide in clear enjoyment. As Jake followed with a soft brushing, he began to talk to the horse.

"So you like that, do you, old boy? Well, you've earned some special treatment. Any horse that'll let me on its back without a fuss is one classy animal. . . . Say, maybe we can get to be friends, if you don't mind a man who gets crazy sometimes. Could you handle that? I'll bet maybe you could. . . ."

Jake rambled on, letting the words flow as he brushed the horse. The stable was quiet, the air fragrant with hay and horses and fresh manure. The only sounds were peaceful sounds—horses moving in their stalls, breathing, munching. The stillness and the warm, earthy aroma gave him an unaccustomed sense of safety. As he worked, he found himself talking about things he'd kept to himself—not about the war, but about the loneliness and frustration of not being able to let go and just live life. Talking to a blasted horse that was listening like he could understand every word.

This was crazy, he thought. But somehow it felt all right.

Jake finished grooming the horse and walked outside, closing the stable behind him. The lights were on in the house. He knew he'd be welcome to join the students for post-movie donuts and Kira's briefing about the next day's activities. But right now, it felt good to be alone and enjoy a rare few moments of peace.

The full moon had crested the sky, flooding the hills with light. Jake found himself walking under the gate, back down the trail where he and Kira had ridden earlier. He stopped at the flat rock with a view of the valley and took a seat. The sky was clear, the breeze cool. Still wearing their crowns of white blossoms, the saguaros stood like silver sentinels in the moonlight. A gray fox paused in a pool of light, then vanished into shadow.

Why not stay here? an inner voice whispered. Where else would he have a better chance of healing his tormented soul? Where else could he be a father to the little girl who meant more to him than anything in the world?

He was needed and welcomed here. He had meaningful work, friends, a decent place to live. And there was Kira, whose brusque manner hid a woman's tender passions—passions barely glimpsed, barely tasted.

He could love her if he let it happen. Maybe, in a way, he already had.

His thoughts went back to the kiss they'd shared and then to how he'd spoiled the moment by talking about Wendy. Why couldn't he have left well enough alone?

As his thoughts changed, Jake could feel the darkness closing around him. Once more, he went over what Kira had told him about the events leading up to Wendy's accident—how Wendy had called her from the party across town because her friends were drinking and wanted to stay.

Strange, he thought, remembering. Kira had mentioned that Wendy was sober and wanted to go home. But the Wendy he remembered had loved a good party. More often than not, she would be among the last to leave. And she'd enjoyed drinking. Not that she was an alcoholic. He'd never seen her sloppy drunk. She'd always had her drinking under control. In fact, when she was pregnant with Paige, she'd stopped drinking altogether because it was bad for the baby.

Bad for the baby.

Something shifted in Jake's mind—like the drop of a coin or the click of a switch. He stared into the night, his hands clenching into fists as he grappled with the truth.

CHAPTER ELEVEN

"**L**et me see your arms, Lanie." Kira kept her tone friendly and informal, masking her concern. Nine days had passed since this group of students had arrived at the ranch. Lanie had been among the first to be interviewed. At the time, the razor slashes on her arms had been scabbed and raw. Now, as the petite, dark-eyed girl rolled up her sleeves, Kira saw that the cuts were mostly healed.

"Good for you. How about your legs? Sorry, you know the drill." Kira had cleared this inspection with the girl's parents.

Lanie stood and dropped her jeans below her knees. No new cuts on her thighs, either. "I'm not cutting myself here at the ranch," she said. "I only feel like doing it at home."

"Why's that, do you think?" Kira asked, although she knew at least part of the answer.

"My mom and dad aren't here." Lanie pulled up her jeans and fastened them. "When I'm home, they fight all the time. It makes me feel awful. That's why I cut myself."

"How does that make you feel, cutting yourself? Doesn't it hurt?"

Lanie twisted the hem of her shirt. "Well, sure. But it takes my mind off the fighting. And when they catch me at it, they, like, freak out, and I say, 'Well, if you wouldn't fight, I wouldn't cut.' "

"Does it help?"

The girl shrugged. "Maybe, for about ten minutes."

"So you can't really control your parents."

"I guess not. But I can make them feel bad."

"You can punish them by cutting yourself. Does that make you feel better?"

"I guess."

"You punish them by hurting yourself. How smart is that? Think about it."

Lanie sighed, nodded and changed the subject. "How soon do we get to ride our horses?"

"When everybody's acquired the skills they need. Maybe by the weekend, if all goes well. Meanwhile, all of you need more practice saddling and bridling. And there's no such thing as too much groundwork. Run along now. I'll meet you at the stable in forty-five minutes."

Kira accompanied the girl to the front porch and watched as she crossed the yard to her cabin. Lanie was gaining confidence here, working well with the horses, and getting along with the other students. The challenge would come when it was time for her to return home. Kira had recommended marriage counseling for the parents, to be followed by family sessions for the three of them. But there was no guarantee that her suggestions would be carried out. Lanie could return to a home environment as toxic as the one she'd left. Kira could only hope that the horse therapy would build the girl's self-reliance enough to deal with her parents and move forward on her own.

From the direction of the stable, the sound of hammer blows rang on the sunlit air. Jake had finished organizing the contents of the shed and started on the stable roof, replacing the worn and missing cedar shingles. That job, and the ongoing need for his help with the horses, had left him with little free time for the motorcycle. But he'd cleared out a sheltered area in the shed where he could work on the machine. Kira was also aware that he'd spent some late nights searching online for sales of vintage parts.

They'd had few private words in the two days since the night of their canyon ride. Even on the outing to Organ Pipe Cactus National Monument, he'd barely spoken to her. It was as if Jake had closed a door between them. He seemed more determined than ever to repay his debt to Dusty, get the bike operational and then leave. But there was more than that to his behavior. It didn't take a therapist to see that something was seriously wrong. Jake was sullen and withdrawn. He looked as if he'd barely slept. Kira recognized the warning signs of a meltdown.

Now, as he pounded the nails into the shingles, she could sense the pent-up anger in each blow, as if he were beating on some invisible enemy—most likely his own inner demons. She could imagine his pain. She could almost feel it.

In her practice, she'd learned to distance herself from her patients and their emotional issues. But Jake wasn't a patient. His trouble was personal—maybe too personal.

This man was the father of the little girl she loved like her own child—a man who'd held her in his arms and kissed her until she burned with womanly hungers. But he was also a broken man—a man still in love with the memory of his dazzling wife. She couldn't let any feelings for him cloud her judgment. She had to step back and look at him with her clinical eyes.

The reality was, Jake needed intervention before he spiraled out of control. He wouldn't welcome her meddling. But she had every reason to step in. There was the welfare of her students to consider. She was responsible for their well-being. That meant not only keeping them physically safe but also shielding them from upsetting situations. And Paige was the most vulnerable of all. Kira would do anything to protect her.

Even more urgent was the danger to Jake himself. Suicide was all too frequent among war vets. If he were pushed to the breaking point, anything could happen.

If she approached him, would he listen to her? Or would her concern only make him more defensive? She needed backup, Kira decided. That would mean involving the one person who had the best chance of reaching him.

The backyard patio, built on the site of the filled-in swimming pool, was a private family place, surrounded by a brick wall. Consuelo's cooking herbs grew here in pretty Mexican pots. There was a play area for Paige and a clothesline for drying linens in the sun. There was a doghouse with food and water bowls for Tucker, as well as a small picnic table and colorful outdoor chairs for sitting.

Kira found Dusty dozing in a lounge chair. His color was better than when he'd first come home, but he still seemed to need plenty of rest. She was about to turn and go, but then he opened his eyes.

"Sorry, I didn't mean to wake you," Kira said. "Go ahead and sleep. I can come back later."

"No, I'm fine." He levered the chair to an upright position, reached for the glass of iced sweet tea, which was on the side table, and took a sip. "Sit down. Tell me what's on your mind."

Where do I begin? Kira glanced in the direction of the stable, where the hammer blows were still ringing from the roof.

"Is it Jake?" Dusty asked, reading her body language.

Kira nodded. "He seemed fine until a couple of days ago. And he was so excited when he found that old motorcycle. But something's changed. I think he needs help."

"You're the expert," Dusty said.

"I'm supposed to be. But I'm finding it hard to be . . ." She groped for the right word. "Objective."

"So it's getting personal, is it?"

"It's always been personal. He's not a patient. He's Paige's father. He's more like family."

"Are you saying you've fallen for him?" Dusty's words rocked her, but the old cowboy had always spoken his mind.

"That would be crazy." Kira dropped her gaze to hide the rush of heat to her face. She couldn't deny the chemistry between them. But Jake wasn't a man any woman should "fall" for.

"Crazy happens to the best of us, girl," Dusty said.

"Well, that's not why I'm here," she said. "Jake needs to talk to somebody he trusts. And right now, that isn't me. Things are pretty . . . tense between us."

"So you want me to talk to him."

"Could you try?" Kira seized her grandfather's hand. "Jake respects you. He trusts you—at least as far as he trusts anybody. And I'm truly worried about him. Listen to those hammer blows. He sounds as if he's about to explode."

Dusty squeezed her hand. "All right. I can see how much this matters to you. Give me a pull up and I'll head out to the stable. Maybe Jake would go for a ride into town."

Jake shimmed a cedar shingle into the empty slot, positioned the nail and drove it down with a couple of solid hammer whacks. He'd had roofing jobs before, so he knew what to do. The work was hot and physically hard, but it didn't demand much thinking. Most of the time, that was all right. But today he would cheerfully beat his head with the hammer if it would blot out the question that played and replayed in his mind in a loop that wouldn't stop.

Had Wendy been pregnant when she died?

If the answer was yes, there was no way the baby could've been his. He'd been in Afghanistan for ten months when he was given leave to fly home for the funeral. The baby's father would have been some other man.

If there even *was* a baby.

What if he was tormenting himself for nothing? Maybe Wendy had given up drinking because she had a young child to care for. Or maybe she just hadn't felt like getting drunk with her friends that night. Either way, he had no proof. Since nothing could bring Wendy back, why not give her the benefit of the doubt and move on?

Jake had tried that line of thinking. But his gut instinct argued for guilt. A stunning, vivacious woman with a long-absent husband, lonely and craving some excitement—how could it *not* have happened? And how could he not have realized it would? What a clueless idiot he'd been.

The hammer crashed down, splitting the wood and barely missing his fingers. He tossed the splintered shingle aside and reached for another. He'd been pounding out his frustration on the roof all afternoon, but it hadn't helped. He could feel his anger simmering, heating to rage, building toward an explosion.

"Hey, Jake!" Dusty's voice, coming from below, was a welcome distraction. "I could use a trip to the hardware store and the bank in Tucson. Want to drive me? There's a double sirloin burger and a milk shake in it for you."

"Sure. I could use the break." Jake secured the bundled shingles and made his way along the sloping roof to the top of the ladder. Since Dusty wasn't supposed to drive until after his next checkup, it made sense that he'd ask for help. But knowing the old cowboy, Jake suspected he could easily have something more up his sleeve. Jake was prepared to be cautious. But at least the drive might take his mind off Wendy for a couple of hours.

In his cabin, he peeled off his shirt, splashed away the sweat on his face and upper body and pulled a clean black tee over his head. Dusty was waiting in the Jeep when he came outside.

"Thanks for chauffeuring me," he said as Jake climbed into the driver's seat. "I do have errands, but mostly I just need to get out. I'm sick of being cooped up like some damn fool ninety-year-old in a rest home."

"I get that," Jake said, starting up the vehicle. "I could use a getaway myself. Does Kira know we're going?"

"I mentioned it to her. She's fine with it." Something in his tone roused Jake's suspicion that Kira might have put her grandfather up to this trip. If that was the case, he could probably expect more lobbying for him to stay.

He would listen out of respect, Jake resolved, but it wouldn't make any difference. He had already made up his mind to leave—the sooner, the better. This place was a minefield of complications and entanglements, all threatening to catch him, hold him and tie him down. It was time he moved on.

They drove out the side gate and down the road through the foothills. The afternoon sun, coming from the west, was so bright that Jake had to lower the visor to shield his eyes. But the clouds rolling in above the distant city were dark. Rain, maybe, he thought.

They made small talk on the way to Tucson. In town, Jake picked up more roofing supplies at the Home Depot and piled them in the back of the Jeep while Dusty waited. The bank stop was a drive-through, where Dusty cashed a check.

"Is there anything else you need?" Jake asked the old man.

"I could use a good, rare steak, if you're up for it," Dusty said. "You treated me to dinner in Flagstaff. Today it's my turn."

"I bought you a burger," Jake said. "And that's what you promised me today."

"Well, I lied." Dusty's blue eyes twinkled. "Consuelo's a fine cook, but for her, the only way to serve meat is well-done. So I sneak into town when I get a craving for the good red stuff. I hope you won't deny me the pleasure of sharing."

"You're sure it's all right with your doctor?"

"He said I could eat anything that didn't eat me first."

Laughing, Jake gave in. He liked a good steak himself, and it had been a long time since he'd had one. "Show me the way," he said.

They drove to a rustic steak house on the way

out of town. Dusty said he'd tried it before and the food was excellent. Something told Jake he was being softened up for whatever the old cowboy had in mind, but he'd already agreed to this. Might as well enjoy it and deal with the consequences later.

The restaurant was quiet at this hour, and the hostess showed them to a booth. After asking Jake, Dusty ordered two rib eyes, his own rare and Jake's medium rare, with salads and loaded baked potatoes. They were buttering their hot sourdough rolls when Dusty cleared his throat.

"I've never been one to beat around the bush," he said. "Kira's been worried about you the past couple of days. She's got me a little worried, too. Is everything all right?"

"Everything's fine," Jake lied. He'd be damned if he was going to share his suspicions about Wendy with her grandfather.

"You're sure?" Dusty asked. "You were bangin' in those shingle nails mighty hard."

"She's worried because I was hammering too hard?" Jake muttered a curse. "Is that all?"

"Kira's a perceptive woman. She's worked with PTSD, and she knows what to look for. She's afraid you're headed for a crash."

"So why doesn't she come talk to me herself?" The server had just set a fresh mixed-green salad in front of him. But Jake's appetite was fading.

"She doesn't think you'll want to talk to her. According to her, things have been 'tense' between the two of you lately—her word, not mine."

"Tense"? He remembered Kira in his arms, her lovely body molding to his, her lips softening with

his kiss—and how he'd spoiled the mood afterward.

"Any idea why she'd say that?" Dusty asked. "Did you have an argument?"

Jake took a forkful of salad and forced himself to chew it before he answered. "She tried to talk me into staying for Paige," he said. "I told her it wasn't possible, and things went downhill from there. But it's not as if we had a fight. We've been working together fine."

They just hadn't been talking much. Or touching. Or even making eye contact. Was that her doing, or was it his?

"Are you sleeping all right?" Dusty asked.

"I'm sleeping fine." He wasn't, but that was nobody's damned business.

"How about Paige? Is she upsetting you? Do you think she suspects who you are?"

Jake shook his head. Whatever Kira had told his daughter, it must've sunk in. Paige hadn't been coming around to see him anymore.

"Take a day off, if you feel like it," Dusty said. "Take a hike, or take the Jeep to town if you want. Go to a movie. Hell, go to a strip club. I don't care. Whatever makes you feel better."

"Dusty, I'm fine." Jake reached across the table and put a hand on the old man's arm. "I don't know why Kira should be concerned about me."

"She's concerned because she cares about you."

"She cares about everybody."

"I know." Dusty took a sip of ice water. "Kira's the most caring person I've ever known. She gives so much of herself it hurts—to Paige and me, to the horses and to those poor mixed-up kids she tries to help. But with you, it's something more. If you want to know the truth, I think she's falling in love with you."

Jake gave the shock a moment to sink in. *Kira in love with him? The old man had to be imagining things.* "No way," he said. "Look at me. I'm a nervous wreck, with no money, no stability, nothing to offer a woman. And Kira's a smart lady. She's got a lot more sense than that."

"Take it from a man who's lived as long as I have," Dusty said. "When it comes to a woman's heart, sense has nothing to do with it."

Jake stared down at the edge of the table. "If what you say is true—and I can't believe it is—the best thing I can do is leave before I ruin her life."

"Leaving isn't the answer to everything. Maybe you've been running away for too long." Dusty stopped talking as the server set two platters on their table. The thick, juicy steaks, still sizzling from the grill and accompanied by baked potatoes topped with bacon, cheese, chives and sour cream, halted the conversation for now. Jake gave a silent sigh of relief as Dusty reached for his fork and steak knife. "Dig in," the old cowboy said.

Emotional turmoil had taken the edge off Jake's appetite, but the food was good and he was hungry enough to eat most of it. By the time they'd finished the meal, topped off with apple pie a la mode, he was feeling stuffed.

Dusty paid the check. Jake thanked him on the way outside. Roiling black clouds had moved in to fill the sky. Lightning flashed across the horizon, followed by the roll of thunder. Jake's reflexes jumped, but he held himself in check. There was no danger, he told himself. It was only a storm.

As they drove out of the parking lot, the clouds burst. Rain pelted the Jeep, streaming down in wet gray sheets. Jake turned on the windshield wipers. Water sprayed beneath the tires as he drove the water-slicked highway. Rain in the desert was rare, but when it came, it could pour like the biblical deluge, flowing along the streets, pooling in yards and sending flash floods roaring down the canyons. As he drove, he thought about Kira and Paige, the students and even the horses and the dog. He could only hope they were all in a safe place, out of the storm.

He cared, too, Jake realized. He cared about the ranch, which was already becoming like home to him—a place where he was accepted and valued. *Maybe even loved.*

The idea that Kira was in love with him was too far-fetched to be believed. The two kisses they'd shared had been delicious. But Kira was a smart woman, ruled by her head, not her heart. If she were to let herself fall in love, it would be with somebody who could offer her a future—say, a college professor, a scientist or maybe a doctor, like her father had been. She was way out of Jake's league.

Even if the sparks between them were to grow into something more, he'd be a fool to think it could last. Sooner or later, he was going to screw up—have one of his crazy episodes and scare somebody, maybe even hurt somebody. Get involved with

Kira, and she would only end up hurt. He had to get out of here before something bad happened.

Lightning sizzled across the sky, chased by a boom of thunder so loud it shook the Jeep. Jake clenched his teeth.

It's all right. It's only thunder. It won't hurt you.

"I guess I should've stayed and finished the roof," he said to Dusty. "I hope the stable isn't leaking."

There was no answer. When Jake glanced over at the old man, he saw that Dusty was fast asleep, a little snore escaping his lips as his chest rose and fell.

Jake returned his gaze to the road and the storm-swept mountains. How did a man live as long as Dusty and still keep his faith in people? Had the old cowboy just been lucky, or had he learned to forgive and move on?

Jake's thoughts returned to Wendy—the wife who'd been his rock while he was overseas. Her smile and her loving voice had given him a refuge from the horrors that he faced every time his unit went out on patrol. And seeing his baby daughter on Skype had been one more reminder of the happy life that waited for him at home.

Had it all been a lie?

How long had Wendy been cheating on him? he wondered. *Had she met someone toward the end of her life and fallen in love, or had she been playing around the whole time?*

Or was his wife as blameless as he'd long believed her to be?

Jake's hands tightened on the steering wheel,

gripping so hard that his knuckles ached. He'd tried to dismiss the question, telling himself it didn't matter anymore. But the truth was, it was driving him crazy. One way or another, he needed closure.

And his only chance of getting it lay with the person who'd known Wendy longest—Kira.

The storm had caught the students leading their horses down the easy trail that snaked along the hills above the ranch. Kira had turned them back at the first distant roll of thunder, but the fast-moving storm had reached them fifteen minutes short of shelter. By the time they'd crossed the graveled yard and reached the barn, they, along with the horses, were soaked and cold.

All to the good. It was time for an important lesson.

In the stable, she turned on the overhead lights and passed out thick, dry towels—two towels each—to the shivering boys and girls. "These aren't for you," she said. "They're for your horse. You take care of your horse before you take care of yourself. That's a rule you never break—otherwise, you could end up with a very sick horse. Now get those wet saddles and pads off them, and give them a good rubdown with the towels. Then make sure they've got food and water before you leave."

Teeth chattering, the students went to work. Nobody complained or argued. Kira was proud of them. They were learning about responsibility and about putting the welfare of others before their own.

Once the horses were dry and comfortable, she

excused the students to go and change out of their wet clothes. There would be hot chocolate and donuts waiting for them in the house, and free time to play video games, read or do schoolwork before dinner.

Consuelo had lit a fire in the fireplace. When Kira came inside, Paige was sitting on the hearth with the baby book, the dog stretched out at her feet. "You look like you got rained on, Aunt Kira," she said.

"We did." Kira stood next to the fire for a moment, soaking in the warmth. "We all got wet, but we made it back okay and put the horses away. What have you been up to?"

"Drawing pictures and helping Consuelo make enchiladas. But I got tired. Where are Grandpa and Mister Jake?"

"They went to town. They should be back soon, unless they waited for the rain to stop."

"Good. Grandpa promised he'd read me a story."

"Great." Kira knew the little girl was lonely. Next fall she'd be starting school. She was more than ready to be in a classroom, learning with children her own age. A bus would pick her up, down on the main road. She was already talking about it, asking every few days how much longer she had to wait.

Now she turned a page in the baby book. "Why aren't there any pictures of my daddy in here?" she asked.

"He was in the army when these pictures were taken," Kira said.

"Why didn't he come back?"

"He did, when your mother died. He came home for the funeral. Do you remember him?"

Paige shook her head. "No. Maybe—I don't know. I just remember somebody in a brown soldier suit, with a hat."

"You don't remember his face from the funeral?"

Paige shook her head again. "Why doesn't he come back now? He's been gone a long time."

Kira's throat tightened. "Maybe he can't. Maybe they need him. Or maybe he's sick."

Paige closed the baby book. "Or maybe he doesn't want to," she said.

CHAPTER TWELVE

It was still raining when Jake drove into the yard. After a stop at the front steps to let Dusty out, he pulled around to the vehicle shed and parked the Jeep next to Kira's Outback.

The yard was empty, the barn door closed. Kira and the others would most likely be in the house, keeping warm and dry while they waited for dinner.

With a mutter of impatience, he stepped out into the rain. The need to question Kira about Wendy was eating him alive. But he had little choice except to wait until he could catch her alone. For now, since he wasn't hungry and didn't feel like socializing, he would just go to his cabin. It would feel good to pull off his wet boots, stretch out on the bed and maybe watch something on the antiquated TV.

He splashed across the graveled yard. The rain was coming down so hard that by the time he reached the cabin door and unlocked it, he was wet to the skin.

Inside, the cabin was cold. There was an electric heater below the window, the kind Jake had seen in motel rooms. He switched it on and turned the heat dial up all the way. Shivering, he stripped off his clothes and hung them over the back of a chair, pulled on his sweats and propped himself on the bed pillows with a quilt over his legs.

As the room warmed, he could feel his tension easing some. But the questions about Wendy kept his thoughts roiling. Alone in the stillness, with the rain droning overhead, Jake could feel himself becoming more agitated—a danger signal. He needed a distraction. Anything.

He found the remote on the nightstand, clicked on the TV and scrolled through the channels. Not much available—infomercials, college basketball, which he didn't care about, and a kiddy channel showing *SpongeBob*. He finally settled on a local cooking show, which featured an annoying woman with poufy blond hair. Even that was better than the silence.

Closing his eyes, he let the gushy voice flow into his head, filling up the dark hollows like water until, finally, blessedly, he began to drift.

In the house, dinner was long over, but with the rain still misting outside, most of the students had chosen to stay by the cozy fireplace or to share video games on the big-screen TV in the den. Paige had fallen asleep and had been carried off to bed.

Dusty, who'd skipped dinner, had taken refuge in his corner armchair, with one of the large-print Western novels he enjoyed. That was where Kira found him.

He glanced up from his book as she stepped close. "How was Jake today?" she asked in a low, private tone.

"Fine. We ran some errands and had a good steak dinner. I think he enjoyed the break."

"Did anything seem to be bothering him?"

"I asked him. He said everything was fine—including his relationship with you."

"But he didn't come inside tonight."

"I told you, we had dinner. He was probably just tired."

Dusty's gaze dropped to his book again. Kira sighed. The old man might not be worried about Jake, but she still was.

"I'm going out and check on him," she said. "If I don't come right back, don't worry. Maybe he'll feel like talking."

"I wouldn't count on that." Dusty spoke without looking up. "Jake strikes me as a man who plays his cards pretty close to his vest."

"I'll keep that in mind." Kira grabbed a light rain jacket from the coatrack by the door and went outside. The rain had slowed to a light drizzle. Stars glimmered through the parting clouds.

The security light came on as she strode across the yard. She could see Jake's cabin, faint light flickering through the curtained front window. That would be from the TV. Everything else appeared dark.

She gave a light rap on the door. There was no

answer. Maybe he'd fallen asleep with the TV on. Or maybe he was in the bathroom. Cautiously she turned the latch. The door was unlocked. She opened it a few inches.

"Jake?" There was no answer, no sound except from the TV. The door creaked as she opened it a few more inches and stepped into the warm room. She could see Jake now, sprawled on the bed in ragged gray sweats, half-covered by the quilt. He appeared to be fast asleep.

For a moment, she stood gazing down at him. His hair clung to his forehead in damp curls. Rumpled and unshaven as always, he looked exhausted. *Was there a chance he'd taken some kind of medication?* Kira was weighing the wisdom of checking in the bathroom, when he opened his eyes.

He blinked drowsily, as if unsure of where he was. Then, suddenly, he jerked bolt upright, wild-eyed and wary.

"It's all right, Jake," Kira said in a calm voice. "It's me. It's Kira. You're fine."

The fight went out of him. He exhaled, sagging back against the pillows. "What are you doing here, Kira?" His voice was a muzzy growl.

"Sorry I woke you. I just came by to make sure you were all right. Now I'll leave." Kira turned toward the door.

"No—stay. Just give me a minute to get my bearings." The remote lay next to him on the bed. He picked it up and turned off the TV. In the dark room, Kira could see him silhouetted against the white pillows.

"I've been waiting for the chance to ask you something. It's about Wendy." He reached down to smooth the wrinkled quilt. "Sit down. I won't bite you."

Feeling uneasy, Kira pushed back her rain hood and sat on the edge of the bed. She hadn't expected this, and she had no idea what Jake meant to ask her. But she couldn't help feeling that something was about to change.

"I need the truth," he said. "Will you give it to me?"

"I will if I know the answer." She fell silent, waiting.

"When you told me about the accident, you mentioned that Wendy wasn't drinking."

"I told you she didn't seem drunk. I can't say for sure whether she'd had any alcohol."

"Then this is what I need to ask you. Did you have any reason to believe Wendy was pregnant?"

Kira took a moment to let the words sink in. She should have been prepared for Jake's question. But it had slammed into her, catching her off guard.

"Kira?"

"Yes," she said, knowing that nothing but the truth would satisfy him. "I knew Wendy was pregnant. She told me the week before the accident."

"And the father?" His voice was cold enough to be frightening.

"Nobody you'd know. She called him 'Drake.' I don't even know whether it was his first name or his last name. She was going to bring him around to meet me, but . . . the accident happened first."

"So this wasn't just a one-night stand. It was serious."

"Yes." Kira was grateful for the darkness that hid his face from her as she spoke. "Wendy had divorce papers drawn up and ready to file. She was going to give them to you when you came home."

Jake's silence was broken only by the patter of rain on the tile roof of the cabin. Kira kept still, waiting for him to speak again.

"Was he at the funeral—this man, Drake?"

"I wouldn't have known if he was," Kira said. "I'd never met him."

Silence again, and the whisper of rain before he spoke. "You can go, Kira. Don't worry about me. . . . I'll be fine."

"How can you be fine after what I just told you?"

"Why shouldn't I be?" he said. "Knowing what Wendy did won't make any difference. It won't bring her back."

She rose, put up her rain hood and moved to the door. "You're sure you're all right?"

He dismissed her with a mutter of impatience. "I'm not one of your students, Kira. Go back to the house and leave me alone. I'll see you tomorrow."

She left him then, closing the door behind her and splashing across the yard in her rain-soaked sneakers. Jake had insisted he'd be all right. But the kind of news she'd given him would devastate most men. He'd been calm and controlled, but she hadn't missed the undertone of wounded anger in his voice.

This wasn't a safe time for him to be alone. But as he'd angrily reminded her, he wasn't one of her students. She had no right to make choices for him.

That didn't mean she wasn't worried sick.

She returned to the house, leaving her dripping shoes on the front porch. Dusty and Consuelo had gone to bed. The students were still inside: Faith and Brandon were playing games on their phones; Calvin was on the couch reading a book; the others were watching a sitcom in the den. Kira roused them, saw them into their jackets and watched from the porch as they crossed the yard to their cabins. Once they were safely inside, she went back into the house and spent a few minutes putting the rooms back in order. That done, she checked on Paige and listened at Dusty's door for the sound of his snoring. She even checked the doghouse on the back patio, where she found Tucker curled in cozy sleep, his legs twitching as he dreamed.

Everything was peaceful, everyone safe.

Except Jake.

It's over. She's gone. It doesn't matter anymore. . . .

Lying on his back, staring up into the darkness, Jake let the words flow like water through his mind.

It doesn't matter . . . Maybe if he repeated the thought long enough, he'd begin to believe it. But it wasn't getting any easier. He kept remembering Wendy's lovely face on Skype, her lying lips telling him how much she loved and missed him, while she was thinking about her lover the whole time.

Drake.

Jake wanted to beat the man to death with his bare fists.

He imagined Drake and Wendy making love, her long, white legs clasping his hips as he pumped into her, her cries of pleasure as he brought her to a shattering climax.

The son of a bitch hadn't even cared enough to use protection.

It's over. . . . It doesn't matter . . .

Jake tried to concentrate on the words, repeating them like a mantra, but he could feel the rage building inside him. Wendy had betrayed him, betrayed her marriage vows and her family. But angry as he was, he couldn't blame her. Even with a baby to take care of, she would have been lonely, starved for attention and excitement. And during his last time home, he'd been withdrawn and unsympathetic to her needs, the man he'd once been already lost to the war.

He couldn't even blame the bastard who'd taken advantage of her. Who could resist a woman like Wendy? Whether she was married or not, what man could look at her without wanting her?

His real fury was focused inward, on himself.

A beautiful, passionate woman, left alone too long—how could he have missed what was happening? He'd taken Wendy for granted, drawing on her strength, her love, to give him courage—and he'd given her next to nothing in return. Everything had been about him, about the war, about the danger and his homesickness.

Stupid, stupid, stupid!

It was as if he'd killed her himself.

The darkness was closing. Desperate for distraction, Jake found the remote and switched on the TV again. By now, it was after midnight. Nothing was on the air but infomercials, a tacky jewelry sale and, on the last channel to come on, a wild-eyed evangelical doomsday rant that became part of his nightmare. Outside, more rain had moved in, hammering the roof and lashing the windows with a sound like AK-47 fire. Jake's head amplified the racket to a scream of sound.

Incoming!

He had to end it, had to make it stop. . . .

Lunging off the bed, he grabbed a wooden chair and smashed it with all his strength into the TV screen.

Kira had tried to sleep, but she'd been too concerned about Jake to relax. After what seemed like hours of restless tossing, she'd thrown her flannel robe over her pajamas and stepped out onto the front porch. From there she could see across the side yard, through the pelting rain, to Jake's cabin. The flicker of light through the curtain had been reassuring. Maybe he was just watching TV. Maybe he was all right.

Or maybe not.

The window curtains were closed, but the light that filtered through told her the TV was still on. Suddenly, outlined against the curtains, a silhouette rose and swung something hard. Almost in the same instant, the window went black.

She'd left her wet sneakers on the porch. Pulse slamming, she jammed her feet into them and plunged down the steps. As she raced out into the rain, the security light came on, its gleam reflecting in the rain-specked puddles.

She was halfway across the yard when Jake's door opened. Barefoot and still wearing his sweats, he walked out into the storm and stood under the gutter spout that drained the water off the roof, letting the water stream over his head and down his body.

Was he trying to calm himself? Maybe wash away some awful memory? Did he even know what he was doing?

She hesitated. Jake didn't appear to be injured, thank heaven. But if he was having a severe episode, he could be like a wounded animal—a danger to himself or even to her. In a treatment center, like the one where she'd trained, she'd have called for someone to back her up before approaching him. But he could be in pain and needing her help— and this was Jake, a man she'd come to care deeply for, maybe even to love, if such a thing was possible.

Speaking his name, she walked straight toward him. Rain streamed down his face as he watched her come. His dark eyes were lost in pits of shadow. Kira's own eyes felt the sting of tears, blending with the rain. This good man had wanted nothing more than to serve his country and return home safe to the family he loved. Through no fault of his own, he had lost everything.

He stood rigid, not responding as she opened her

arms, pulled him close and drew him away from the pouring water. She could feel him quivering against her, feel his heartbeat galloping hard, driven by the adrenaline pumping through his body.

"You're cold, Jake," she said gently. "Let's go inside and get you warm."

He mouthed a string of profanities, but he didn't fight her as she turned him toward the open doorway of the cabin. Still swearing, he allowed her to guide him onto the stoop and over the threshold until she was able to let go and close the door behind them. The security light shone through the loose weave of the curtain, illuminating the upended chair and the broken TV, with a gaping, glass-edged hole where the screen had been.

Glass shards were scattered on the floor. Jake wasn't wearing shoes. He could have glass embedded in his feet and not even be aware of it. She would have to check, but first she needed to get him calm and comfortable.

She thought about flipping on the overhead light switch next to the door, but decided to wait. The sudden brightness might startle Jake.

He was shivering in his rain-soaked sweats. Kira noticed a basket of clean, folded laundry on the luggage rack next to the bathroom door. After rummaging for a towel, a cotton tee and a pair of boxer shorts, she hurried back to him. "We've got to get you out of those wet clothes. I'm going to need your help. All right?"

When he didn't answer, she grabbed the hem of his dripping sweatshirt and pulled it partway up. His skin was icy. At the touch of her fingers on his bare ribs, he shuddered as if coming to life. With a rough exhalation, he took over the job, pulling the sopping garment over his head, then tossing it on the tile floor.

The soaked sweatpants would have to come off next. Kira tugged at the knotted cord that held the waistband, preparing to avert her eyes when the pants dropped. He pushed her hand away. His chilled fingers fumbled with the tight, wet knot until, with a muttered curse, he yanked the frayed string with his fist and broke it.

The uneasy moment was saved when the timer turned off the security light outside, plunging the room into darkness. Stepping back, Kira heard the sound of fumbling, heard something wet dropping to the floor. Moments later the three-way lamp on the nightstand came on low, throwing a soft light into the room. Jake had turned it on. He was sitting on the edge of the bed, wearing the shirt and shorts and toweling his wet hair. His eyes were bloodshot, his expression unspeakably weary. The worst of the episode appeared to be over, but the haunted look was still there.

"I can handle this." His voice was a rasp. "Go back in the house."

"Not yet." Kira stood her ground. "I'm not leaving until I know you're all right."

"I'll be fine. And I don't need a damned audience. I like to keep my craziness private."

"I've seen far worse," she said. "Right now, I need to look at your feet. You could've stepped on glass from the TV."

"I'll look." Still sitting, he inspected one foot, then the other. "No glass. And I'll pay for the TV."

"Don't worry about it. That old set was junk before you broke it."

"I'm not your charity case. I'll buy you a new one."

Kira hung the wet clothes over a rod in the shower, then found a broom and dustpan in the back of the closet and swept up the broken glass. She was wet, too. The rain had soaked her bathrobe and dampened the pajamas she wore underneath. Even in the warm room, she was beginning to shiver.

"You need to get some sleep, Jake." She replaced the broom in the closet.

"I can handle this like I always do. So leave me the hell alone." He was a wounded animal, still defiant.

"I'll leave when you're calm and resting—really resting."

"I'm not your patient—or your problem!" he snapped. "Why can't you just mind your own damned business?"

"Because I care. I care about you. And I want you safe."

Had she pushed him too far?

His expression darkened as he rose and moved toward her. Kira resisted the impulse to back away. She couldn't let herself believe that Jake might hurt her.

Facing her, he caged her jaw between his hands. His eyes burned into hers. "Sweet Kira." The words held an edge. "Taking care of everything and everybody. Tell me something. Who takes care of you?"

Her heart seemed to stop as his lips closed on hers in a deep, rough, searching kiss. This was a mistake, the voice of caution shrilled. The man had no real feelings for her. He'd learned that his wife had been unfaithful, and he was reacting to the pain, that was all. He wasn't in his right mind.

But the hunger that rose in her body was too powerful to be denied. The need surged and burned as she stretched onto her toes to deepen the kiss. His hands released her face as his arms slid around her, molding her body to his. He was big and hard-muscled, his skin cool and firm, his body smelling of clean rain. Heaven help her, she wanted him. All of him.

The voice was still shouting in her head. *Don't be a fool! He's ill! You can't let this happen!*

Kira forced herself to listen this time. She steeled her resolve to pull away, but before she could move, he released her and stepped back. They faced each other in the soft glow of lamplight, both of them quivering.

"I should go," she said, turning toward the door.

"Yes, maybe you should." His voice was flat. He made no move to stop her. "Go on. I'll be fine."

She paused and looked back, one hand resting on the doorknob. He stood where she'd left him, his expression unreadable. Without another word, Kira stepped outside and closed the door behind her.

The rain had slowed to a drizzle. Holding up

the hem of her robe, she started for the house. She'd gone only a half-dozen steps when the security light came on. If anybody had been looking outside at this hour, they'd have seen her leaving Jake's cabin in her nightclothes. Never mind. She'd done nothing to be ashamed of. But she was still worried about Jake.

Had that shattering kiss been his way of getting her to leave? But why else would he kiss her? Jake knew her all too well. Threats wouldn't budge her, but one kiss from a half-undressed man in his bedroom would send her fleeing into the storm like the devil was chasing her.

A clever plan. But that didn't mean the episode was over. He could still be in danger.

She paused in the glare of the security light, rain streaming off her hair and down her face. If anything were to happen because she'd left him alone too soon, she would never forgive herself.

Squaring her shoulders, she turned, walked back to the cabin and opened the door without knocking.

The lamp had been turned off, but with the security light shining through the drapes, Kira could see into the room. Jake was huddled on the edge of the bed, his head clenched in his hands, his body quivering.

She closed the door quietly and moved to his side. If he'd seen or heard her, he gave no sign of it. But when she laid her hands on his shoulders, she felt a shudder pass through him.

"Jake, I'm here," she said.

He twisted his shoulders, shaking off her touch. "I can deal with this. Just leave me alone till it's over."

"No." She reached behind him and turned down the bed. "Lie down and stretch out. You'll feel better." She pushed him sideways, toward the pillows. He was far stronger than she was, but he showed little will to resist as she laid him on his side and covered him with the sheet and the blankets. He straightened with a long sigh.

"Kira . . . ," he said. "I'm sorry for this mess. Hearing about Wendy—I was primed. I thought I could take it, but everything went a little crazy."

"Do you want to talk?" she asked.

"No."

"Can I get you some water, maybe a Coke?" There was a mini fridge stocked with sodas under the TV stand.

"No." He was still shaking beneath the covers.

In her rain-soaked robe, Kira was so cold, her teeth were chattering. She took a moment to peel the soggy garment off and drape it over a chair near the heater; then she blotted her wet hair with Jake's discarded towel. Her cotton pajamas were slightly damp, but not too wet to wear. Not having anything else, she decided to keep them on.

What she decided to do next would take courage. But Jake needed it. Maybe she did, too.

Jake's eyes were closed, but it was too soon for him to be asleep. After leaving her wet sneakers by the door, she walked around the double bed to the far side. She took a breath to gather her resolve.

Then, lifting the blankets but leaving the top sheet over Jake, she slipped into bed beside him.

"Kira?" His voice was a mumble.

"I'm cold," she said, and spooned against his back.

He flinched at the first contact through the sheet. "Lord almighty, you *are* cold."

"I'll be warm soon." She snuggled closer. "Is this all right?"

"It's . . . fine. It's nice."

With a little murmur, she laid an arm over him and nestled closer. He tensed like a wary animal being stroked for the first time. Then, little by little, his taut muscles relaxed. His breathing became deep and regular, and she knew he was sinking into sleep.

Kira cradled him against her through the sheet, feeling warm and surprisingly safe. This wasn't about sex. They were both too raw, too vulnerable for that. This was about something deeper—something that might not even have a name.

Comfort, perhaps. But no, it was more than comfort.

Drifting, she closed her eyes.

CHAPTER THIRTEEN

Jake stirred and opened his eyes. The room was still dark, but Kira was already gone. He rolled onto his back and lay still, remembering her warmth and the sound of her breathing, like a silken whisper in his ear.

Maybe he'd only imagined her sweet body spooned against his back, her arm cradling him as he eased into sleep. But no, he could feel the slight dampness her hair had left on the spare pillow. His angel had been real.

And he'd needed her. Lord, how he'd needed her—for reasons that had little to do with sex. Not that he would've complained if it had happened. But forget that—the chaste bedsheet between them had made her intent clear.

Lifting his head, he checked the luminous clock on the nightstand: 4:33. Not quite dawn. But he'd had a decent sleep and, except for a slight headache and the vague emptiness that tended to follow a bad spell, he felt calm and alert.

Last night he'd dreamed about Wendy—a murky sort of dream in which he'd seen her from a distance, walking away from him. He'd called to her, but she hadn't even looked back. He'd been trying to run after her when he'd awakened to a dark room, with Kira spooned against his back. Still foggy, he'd nestled against her warmth and gone back to sleep.

No doubt Wendy would haunt his dreams for a long time to come. In a way, he would always love her, just as he would always mourn her. But the truth was finally sinking in. He had lost her long before the accident that took her life.

Raking a hand through his tangled hair, he sat up and swung his feet to the floor. Last night had changed some things—maybe a lot of things. He needed time to himself, to get his head on straight before he faced Kira again. For that, he'd need to get away to someplace peaceful, where he could be alone.

A glance through the window told him the rain had stopped. Hurrying now, he dressed in riding clothes and pulled on his socks and boots. Framed by jagged, broken glass, the empty hole that had been the TV screen was a mocking reminder of last night's meltdown. Later today he would haul the set outside and pile it with the last of the junk from the shed, to be hauled to the landfill. He would do fine without TV until he could afford to buy a replacement.

Stars were fading above the mountains as he crossed the yard to the stable and unlocked the door. With the sky already dawning and his eyes accustomed to the darkness, Jake didn't bother to turn on the light. He didn't want to startle the horses or alert Kira that somebody was in the stable.

The place was fragrant with hay and the odor of fresh manure. Horses dozed or munched, a few of them raising their heads as he passed on his way to the stall at the farthest end.

Dynamite pricked his ears and nickered at Jake's approach, as if the two of them were already friends.

"Good morning, old boy." Jake reached over the stall gate and stroked the satiny neck. "How about you and me going for a ride this morning?"

He retrieved the saddle, pad and bridle from the tack room. Getting the gear on the horse was still awkward for him, but Dynamite was patient. The old horse stood quietly, giving Jake time to check the cinch and the leathers before easing into the saddle.

Jake had ridden once with Kira, but this was his first time alone. For the first few minutes, sitting on the tall, swaying animal made him nervous. But the feeling didn't last. By the time they passed under the ranch gate, he was getting used to the easy motion.

"Just keep moving, boy." Somehow it felt natural, talking to a horse. "You're the teacher here, and I'm the classroom dunce. I've got a lot to learn, so thanks for putting up with me."

Jake gave Dynamite his head, letting the horse pick his way along the familiar trail. The ground was wet, the air cool and fresh with last night's rain. Above the mountains, the sky was brightening from deep onyx to mother-of-pearl. Soon sunrise would streak the clouds with the brief glory of rose, gold and amber, and the day would begin.

Overnight the rain had brought the desert to bursting life. The land was fresh, green and blooming. Saguaros and chollas glistened with diamond drops of moisture. Lupines, budding yesterday, were opening into bloom. Birds swooped low to drink from rain pools that would shrink and vanish with the heat of the sun.

Jake had not known peace since the war. What were his chances of finding it here, in this starkly beautiful place? He pondered the question as Dynamite took the right-hand trail, down the canyon.

As the trail wound downward, he could hear the waterfall—not the gentle, flowing sound he remembered from the other night with Kira, but a powerful hiss, as the runoff from the storm funneled down the canyon. Curious, he tethered the horse in the willows, as he'd done before, and made his way up the rocky trail and over the top.

The clearing—magical when he'd seen it by moonlight—was a different place this morning. The rushing water had scoured the canyon bottom, stripping away plants and silt. A gnarled, dead mesquite, roots and all, had been washed over the falls. Now it lay in the pond, its bare branches sticking above the brown water like groping fingers.

Jake stood at the edge of the flooded pond. Water roared over the rim of the falls in a muddy torrent that hid the rocks beneath. From the look of the canyon, there'd been even more water at the height of the storm, enough to do some heavy damage.

"It's amazing how a place can change overnight, isn't it?" Kira's voice startled him. He hadn't heard her come over the trail to stand beside him. Aside from some weariness about her eyes, she looked fresh and ready for the day. Jake struggled against the memory of her tender warmth in his bed. This would be the daytime Kira, he reminded himself. The driven, micromanaging woman who challenged him at every turn.

"You followed me?" Charm had never been his strong point.

"Guilty as charged. I saw you leave and wanted to make sure you were all right."

"I'm fine. You don't need to mother me, Kira."

"Is that what you think I'm doing?"

He stayed silent for a long moment, watching the chocolate-brown water pour over the falls. "Thanks for last night," he said. "You didn't have to stay. I'd have been fine."

"Maybe." She watched a wren light on a branch of the drowned mesquite and flutter away. "What now?"

Was she asking about their relationship or his future at the ranch? Jake decided to address the safer, second choice.

"I'm feeling pretty good this morning—even thinking I might like to stay for a while—maybe work with the horses and see if I can lick this thing. If it doesn't take, I can always change my mind."

"That's great news," she said. "But don't expect the moon. For most PTSD cases, there's no guaranteed cure. There are techniques to help you manage it. But in the end, you make it through one day at a time—and if you slide back, you just pick yourself up and move forward again. You'll need to accept that, maybe for the rest of your life."

She gave him that measuring look, her eyes silvery in the dawn light. The old Kira was back, taking charge as usual. But that didn't mean he'd forgotten how she'd felt next to him in bed. He was still battling the urge to seize her in his arms and kiss her until that warm, sexy Kira he remembered surfaced and came back to him.

"What do you really want, Jake?" she asked.

Thinking, Jake poked at an exposed root with the toe of his boot. "Just normal things," he said. "Holding down a decent job, having the means to take care of other people, instead of being taken care of. Most of all, I guess, I'd like to have a relationship with my daughter—one where I don't have to worry about losing control and scaring her, or even hurting her."

And a relationship with a woman crazy enough to put up with me.

Leaving that thought unspoken, Jake picked up a rock and skipped it across the swollen pond. "What the hell, I know better. Maybe the best I can hope for is to be free, with nobody to care, nobody to hurt, nobody to cry over me when I'm gone."

She laid a hand on his arm, her touch butterfly

light through the fabric of his sleeve. "Look around you, Jake. You saw this spot before the flood came down the canyon. Now look at it."

Jake's gaze took in the brown water, noticing the places where the creek's high bank had washed away, exposing the tangled roots of trees and the layer of silty mud, which coated everything, leaving no trace of green. The place would make a good setting for a zombie film, he thought.

"What happens to all the floodwater?" he asked, pretending not to notice her lingering touch on his arm.

"It flows down the canyon into a wash. From there it runs through a culvert under the road and spreads out onto the plain. You can see the silt fan from that flat rock on the upper trail."

Her fingers tightened on his arm, the contact triggering a warm tingle. Jake resisted the urge to turn and brush back the tendril of light brown hair that had stolen across her cheek. Leave it be, he thought. It softened her finely drawn profile and made a pretty contrast with her rose petal skin.

Looking at her now, he wondered how he could have seen her as plain for so long. Standing in the pale dawn light, her face bare of makeup, her cheeks flushed from the cool morning air, she was enchanting.

"Would you believe this canyon gets flooded almost every year?" she said. "Right now, it looks ruined. But ride down here in a few weeks, and you'll see clear water, grass growing, flowers blooming. . . . It never comes back quite the same as it was. Some things are lost. Other things are new. But the canyon always comes back."

It didn't take a genius to figure out what she was trying to tell him, Jake thought. If the canyon could come back and thrive after a disaster, so could he.

She made it sound so simple. But Jake felt as if she were talking to him the way she might talk to one of her students. As a therapist, she should know that his PTSD had been etched into his brain with needles of pain, guilt and shock. It had become part of him—who he was and would be for as long as he lived.

He could call her on it. But that would only stir up tension between them. And right now, he didn't want to talk about his PTSD. He was here with this compassionate, spirited, maddeningly beautiful woman. All he really wanted was for her to stop lecturing and let him hold her, maybe even taste those warm, ripe lips again.

But he was fantasizing now. And Kira had already released his arm and stepped out of reach.

"I have to go," she said. "My students will be waking up soon. You can take your time getting back. We won't need you until after they've had breakfast and the stable's cleaned out."

"Go ahead. I won't be long." He watched her as she disappeared up the narrow pathway. Moments later, Jake heard the sounds of her mare going back up the trail toward the ranch.

He gave her time to get a head start before he returned to Dynamite and mounted. He wouldn't be going back to the ranch just yet. He had too much thinking to do. For that, he needed time and solitude—and the company of a wise old horse.

At the top of the canyon trail, he took the left-hand fork that wound along the foothills and down to the flat below, where glistening saguaros stood like a vast army of giants. In the east, the sunrise streaked glory across the sky. Losing himself in the majesty of the morning, Jake rode on.

Kira rode in under the ranch gate, dismounted and, after a quick rubdown, loosed her mare into the paddock. She'd thought about Jake all the way up the trail, remembering how her desire had surged as he kissed her and how she'd held him through the night, feeling his chest rise and fall with the sound of his breathing. She'd felt so warm and safe, that it had been all she could do to ease herself away from him and go before dawn.

Was she falling in love with the troubled soldier—or was she drawn to him simply because he needed her?

Jake was a proud man—especially now, when pride was all he had. He would never settle for a relationship in which he was the needy one. Maybe that was why, in the long run, nothing between the two of them could possibly last.

When it came to boyfriends, Kira had lost out to too many clingy, dependent girls not to know that her strength drove most men away. Maybe that was why she'd never had much of a social life, let alone anything close to marriage. But she was who she was. When something needed doing, or when somebody needed help, she took charge.

A domineering woman and a proud, dysfunctional man—it was a recipe for disaster. The worst of it was, as she confessed to herself, she'd never wanted any man the way she wanted Jake.

As she walked toward the house, she could see her students gathering for breakfast. Forcing herself to close the mental box that held thoughts of Jake, she refocused on her job—helping these young people find the peace and self-confidence they needed to live productive lives.

Paige was waiting on the front porch with the dog. She was dressed in a mismatched shirt and Jeggings, her fiery curls scrunched up in a lopsided ponytail. Her shoelaces trailed behind her sneakers as she walked.

Kira sighed. She needed to spend more time with this much-loved little girl. Consuelo kept an eye on her while Kira was working, but she was too busy with kitchen and housekeeping duties to do much more than make sure Paige was safe. Dusty adored his small great-granddaughter, but he couldn't be expected to dress and feed her, or take her where she wanted to go. And Kira had a strict rule against letting her students babysit. It wasn't the best use of their time, and, more important, given their issues, it might not be safe for Paige.

"Where have you been, Aunt Kira?" Paige held still so Kira could tie her sneakers.

"Just out for a morning ride. I needed some quiet time."

"Maybe you could take me with you next time. I could sit on the horse with you and hold on tight. If you wanted quiet, I wouldn't make a sound."

"Oh, honey . . ." Kira finger-combed Paige's hair and fixed the ponytail. The flowered top and striped Jeggings would have to do for the day. At least they were clean. "I'll take you riding one of these days, maybe after the students go. But hey, tomorrow we'll be going into town for the day, to see the fiesta and the old mission and have tacos for lunch. You get to come along."

Her small face lit. "Is Mister Jake coming with us?"

"Not this time." Kira had sensed that the question would come up. By now, Dusty was well enough to make the trip as long as Kira drove the vehicle. The old man had been eager to go, which meant that Jake could be left behind—less awkward for him, for her and for Paige.

"But I want Mister Jake to come. I won't bother him, I promise."

"Somebody has to stay here and take care of the ranch. Besides, your grandpa will be going. You can hang out with him. Okay?"

Paige sighed, looking down at her feet. "Okay."

"Fine." Kira took her hand. "Let's go wash up and get some breakfast."

"Aunt Kira?" Paige paused at the door. "Why doesn't Mister Jake ever shave? I think he'd look nice without a beard."

Kira's pulse stumbled. Did Jake's daughter suspect the truth? "Maybe Mister Jake likes the beard," she said. "Besides, those short, scruffy beards are in style these days. A lot of movie stars have them."

"Do you think he'd shave it off if I asked him to?" Paige persisted.

"I don't know. But you're not going to ask him because you promised not to bother him."

"Are you mad at me, Aunt Kira? You sound like it." Paige's dark eyes were as innocent as a puppy's.

Kira bent and hugged her. "I could never be mad at you. But you must promise that you won't bother Mister Jake about his beard."

"All right, I won't bother him. But I still think he'd look nicer if he shaved." She sighed as Kira ushered her into the house.

Paige was an intuitive child. Raised among adults, she was more aware of things going on around her than most people realized. How much longer, Kira wondered, could she be protected from the truth about Jake? Was her question about his beard a sign that she was already watching him, wondering whether he was hiding something?

Maybe it would be wise to tell her the truth before she guessed it on her own. But that decision wasn't Kira's to make. It was Jake's, and she knew he wasn't ready.

She owed it to Jake to warn him that his daughter might be getting suspicious. What happened next would be up to him. She hoped he wouldn't just shoulder his pack and leave. But Kira was learning that Jake was his own man; there were many things she couldn't control.

After the emotional start to Kira's day, the rest of the morning had its own ups and downs. From the beginning, Kira had told her students that they would move ahead together or not at all. Today, as they practiced saddling and bridling their horses in the paddock, she noticed them assisting each other—Calvin helping Faith untangle her bridle, Brandon helping Lanie lift the heavy saddle onto her horse, Heather checking Patrick's cinch. This was an important part of the program, working together for the good of the group. It pleased her to see how well the youngsters were learning their lessons.

Only Mack still seemed to be having problems. The husky fifteen-year-old, who'd come here with anger issues, had chosen a docile paint gelding named Patches. A few days ago, when Patches had misunderstood a command, Mack had yanked hard at the lead rope and yelled curses at the horse. Unaccustomed to such behavior, Patches had become wary of the boy.

Today, as Mack tried to get the bit into the horse's mouth, Patches was having none of it. The brown-and-white gelding was snorting and jerking away, and Mack was becoming more and more frustrated. To make matters worse, none of the other students had offered to help. Mack was the person nobody wanted to work with.

Kira could sense the boy's anger building. Much more of this, and he was liable to punch the horse or pick a fight with one of the other students—either of which could get him sent home.

She was about to intervene and suggest a break, but Jake, who was there to help supervise, stepped between the boy and the horse.

"Whoa, there," he said. "Look, Mack, this horse is scared of you. Back off for a minute or two. Give yourself and Patches some breathing space. Then try to show him that you're his friend."

Mack backed away a few steps, but his face was flushed, his breathing agitated. "That horse hates me," he said. "I want a different one."

"Horses don't hate," Jake said. "And you stay with the horse you chose, that's the rule."

"It's a dumb-ass rule," Mack said.

"You might think so," Jake said. "But if you give up on this horse now, he's won. You need to show him that the two of you can still be partners. Don't worry about the bridle for now. Just put it aside. Pet him and talk to him until he calms down. Then try the bridle again."

Kira watched Jake talk the boy through the process of calming the horse and putting on the bridle. Jake had learned a lot about horses from listening to Dusty, and he was a natural with the students. If she could talk him into staying, he could prove to be a real asset to the therapy program.

But getting Jake to stay would involve a lot more than just giving him a job. It would mean giving him a home and a family—and getting him to accept those things.

With time and patience, Mack was finally successful. Kira praised her students. She had them remove and stow the tack, then dismissed them for lunch. They were getting impatient to ride. But, as she reminded them, only after every one of them could saddle and bridle a horse without supervision would they be ready to mount up and take their first trail ride.

As the students scattered to get ready for lunch, Kira caught up with Jake outside the paddock fence. "You were terrific with Mack," she said. "I was getting worried about him."

"The kid just needed to back off and cool down," Jake said. "I hope he learned a thing or two."

Side by side, they started toward the house, walking slow enough to talk.

"You could stay and do this—manage the students and help them with the horses," she said. "You're good at it, Jake."

"I thought I was just filling in for Dusty."

"Dusty can still teach. But I don't know when, if ever, he'll be strong enough to take over the active work. If there's nobody else to help, he'll try. But he's an old man. I don't want him to push himself into another heart attack."

"Are you offering me a job, Kira?" His dark eyes seemed to mock her.

"If you want it. We can negotiate your pay. You're too valuable to be just a handyman."

"Whoa!" He stopped her. "I never said yes. Besides, do you really want a part-time maniac working with your students? What happens if something gets to me and I take a dive off the deep end?"

She scuffed at the gravel with her boot. "I was hoping that your being here with Paige and working with the horses would help keep you calm."

"It might. But what you saw last night was just the tip of the iceberg. When my nerves start misfiring, things can get ugly. I could tell you stories. . . ." His voice trailed off. He began to walk again. "I get the impression that your liability insurance is already high. What would happen if your insurer found out you'd hired a man who smashes chairs into TV screens?"

She sighed, keeping pace with him. "Will you at least give it some thought? You'll be here awhile yet. We can see how it goes. Meanwhile, know that the offer still stands."

"I'll keep it in mind. But no promises." He turned away and walked off toward his cabin. Torn, Kira watched him go. Jake was a good man in so many ways. But he was right about his condition. He knew what he was capable of, and he knew the risks even better than she did.

She recalled his first morning here, when the sound of dynamite blasting had triggered a reaction. He had flung himself on top of her, protecting her with his life from what he perceived as a deadly danger.

How could she not trust him?

But how could she trust the safety of her students, her practice and the child she loved to a broken man—a man who fought a never-ending battle with the demons in his head?

And how could she trust the safety of her own heart?

CHAPTER FOURTEEN

On that afternoon, Kira's scheduled interview was with Mack. Good timing, she reflected as she waited in her office. After his morning frustration, they'd have a few things to talk about.

He walked in a few minutes later, a stocky blond boy with a round face and blue eyes that never quite made contact. Kira had met his parents. The father, who owned a Cadillac dealership in Scottsdale, was a pushy glad-handing man, a former football star at Arizona State. The mother was a petite woman with rigidly coiffed blond hair, designer clothes and redneck grammar. Kira made it a rule not to judge people, but after meeting them, she sympathized with their son.

"Sit down, Mack." She opened a chilled Dr Pepper, which she knew he liked, and gave it to him. "I was proud of you this morning, the way you stuck with bridling Patches and didn't give up until you got it done."

"I wanted to quit," he said. "But Jake wouldn't let me. Besides, I knew the other kids would be mad if I didn't finish. That's a dumb-ass rule, that we can't ride till everybody can saddle and bridle a horse. They all hate me because I'm slowing them down."

"Nobody hates you, Mack."

"Yes, they do. They all hate me. Even that stupid horse."

"What about your roommate? How are you getting along with Brandon?"

Mack chugalugged his soda. "Okay, I guess. But he keeps to himself. We don't have much to talk about. Why can't I trade? I'd rather be with Patrick."

Mack and Patrick, two troublemakers in the same cabin. Not likely, Kira thought.

"So Brandon doesn't seem to hate you, and Patrick doesn't hate you. And I don't think Calvin hates anybody."

"No, but those snooty girls hate me. At first, I thought Lanie was kind of cute. But she won't even look at me."

Kira suppressed a sigh. "What's really on your mind, Mack? If you could tell me one thing, what would it be?"

He gazed down at the empty soda can, crushing it between his hands. "I guess I just don't like horses much," he said. "My mom and dad made me come here. They said it would help me get along better—you know, with other people. But it isn't working."

"I'm sorry to hear that," Kira said, meaning it.

"But thank you for being honest with me. Are you saying you want to go home?"

He shook his head, looking miserable. "Home isn't much fun. Dad's always after me—to make something of myself, he says. And my mom's always at the spa or out with her friends. I'd rather stay here. But can't I do something else, like maybe help with the work? I feel stupid when my horse won't mind. And then I get mad."

Kira could understand the boy's loneliness and frustration. Her natural impulse would have been to give him a hug, but that was another rule she couldn't afford to break. And Mack's parents had paid to have him work with the horses. She could hardly turn him into a helper, even if that was what he wanted.

"Tell you what," she said. "I know you had a tough morning. If you're not feeling up to it, I'll give you and Patches a break for the rest of the afternoon. Tomorrow we'll be going into town to visit some historic spots and watch a fiesta celebration. That'll be a nice change for you. After that, if you want, we can talk about ways to help you enjoy your horse."

She walked him to the porch, Mack scuffing his feet. The boy needed a way to feel good about himself. How could she give him that?

After he'd gone, she went back inside. She'd promised to read Paige more of *Charlotte's Web,* a book the little girl loved. At two p.m., the students, with Dusty helping supervise, would be doing more groundwork with their horses. Then, with

Kira in charge, they'd walk them along the easy mountain trail above the ranch.

Consuelo had already gone home for a break. Dinner tonight would be another cookout, and Kira would fix a light breakfast tomorrow morning. With the group spending much of the day in town, Consuelo wouldn't be needed until they returned at dinnertime.

All through lunch, Kira had listened to the sound of hammering on the stable roof. She knew Jake had wanted to finish the repairs so he could spend time on the motorcycle. So far, he'd been too busy to pin down the engine problem. Once he found it, he could take the next step, finding and ordering the parts he needed online.

Now the sound of hammering had stopped. A glance through the window confirmed that the ladder was gone from outside the stable. Jake probably hadn't taken the time to eat. She could bring him a sandwich—but no, she'd promised Paige she'd read to her. Jake could get his own sandwich if he was hungry. She had to stop micromanaging the man. It would only annoy him.

"Aunt Kira!" Paige came bounding down the hall, waving the well-worn book. "You promised!"

"So I did." Kira accepted the small hand and allowed herself to be led to the sofa.

Jake was checking the starter on the bike when he realized someone was watching him. He glanced up to see Mack standing just outside the open shed. "Hey, Mack," he said.

"Hey." Mack watched in silence for a few moments. "That's a cool bike. What're you doing with it?"

"Trying to figure out why it won't run." Jake reached for a screwdriver.

"Can I come in and watch?"

"Aren't you supposed to be working with your horse?"

"Kira said I could take a break this afternoon. So can I watch you? I won't get in the way."

"All right, but stay out of my light and keep still."

Mack walked into the shed and leaned over Jake's shoulder, his shadow falling across Jake's hands. "Not so close," Jake said, reminding himself that the boy wasn't one of his army recruits.

"Maybe it has a dead battery," Mack said, backing up a couple of steps. "Or maybe it just needs new spark plugs."

"Maybe so," Jake said. "It sounds like you know a little bit about motorcycles."

Mack grinned. "My mom's brother has an old Harley. He lets me help him work on it when I'm at his place. He's even let me drive it a few times when there weren't any cops around. I want to get my own bike as soon as I'm old enough."

"Well, don't rush it," Jake said. "They can be pretty dangerous to ride. I know some messed-up guys who got that way crashing their bikes."

Mack was silent, but only for a moment. "Maybe it's just out of gas," he said.

"Maybe." But Jake doubted it. McQueen wouldn't have left the bike here if it had just needed gas. But he'd bet money the tank had never been drained. It was likely to have some residue inside that would need cleaning out before the tank could be refilled. The fuel line was probably clogged, too. If he'd had any notion the old Indian would need only a simple fix, that notion was fading fast. This job could take weeks of part-time work.

"What can I do to help?" Mack asked.

"I'll let you know." Jake sighed. He understood that the kid needed validation. But he'd hoped for some time to himself to tinker with the bike and to try to figure out the problem.

He needed to figure out something else as well. He and Kira had been playing games long enough. Their damn-fool kiss, run and act-like-nothing-happened routine was getting old. This morning he had watched her, studying her lovely, serious face when she focused on her students, the warmth in her dove-gray eyes, and the way her smile deepened a dimple in her cheek. He'd found himself admiring the way her jeans fit her willowy body, and remembering the feel of that body in his arms. And he'd found himself wanting her, so much it hurt.

Kira had asked him to stay—to help with the program, to be here for his daughter and to work on controlling his PTSD.

He'd told her he would think about it. But what he hadn't told her—because he'd just begun to realize it himself—was that his answer depended on *her.*

Since the war, he'd settled for fleeting encounters with women he would never see again. Being with Kira made him yearn for something more. Not marriage—that would be asking too much. But something deeper and more lasting than empty nights in strange beds. Maybe even love.

Kira, his daughter and a peaceful place where he could be of value. Was it an illusion, like so many other things in his life—even, as it had turned out, his marriage?

Or was everything he needed just waiting for him, if only he could summon the courage to reach for it?

By the time Kira's students had finished the trail walk, rubbed down their horses and put them away with hay and water, the youngsters were tired and hungry. Kira was grateful to see that in their absence Jake had laid the fire, set up everything for the cookout and brought out a comfortable chair for Dusty. Mack appeared to be helping. She'd had second thoughts about giving him the afternoon off, but it must have been a good idea. This evening he was all smiles.

The students were still washing up when Dusty came outside with Paige and the dog. Dusty had brought his guitar, a surprise treat. Not only did he play well, but he had a great repertoire of old-time cowboy songs, which he sang in a gravelly baritone that added to the fun of listening. Kira had avoided asking her grandfather to entertain tonight, fearing it might be too taxing for him. But she was delighted that he felt up to it.

With the sun going down and the fire blazing in the pit, the students roasted their hot dogs and garnished them with mustard, cheese and chili. Then they wolfed them down with chips and potato salad.

Kira found a place next to Paige and helped the little girl cook and prepare her hot dog. Glancing up, she caught Jake watching them from the far side of the fire pit. He lifted an eyebrow and gave her a twitch of a smile. Was he smiling at her, she wondered, or at his daughter? Maybe at both of them.

With the fire burned down to coals and the students feasting on s'mores, Dusty picked up his guitar and strummed the opening chords of "I'm Ridin' Old Paint." By the time he began to sing, the low buzz of conversation and laughter had faded. The students probably had very different tastes in music, Kira reflected. But their respect for the old cowboy was such that they kept quiet and listened. Soon their faces began to smile, their bodies to sway a little with the music. It was as if the twilight air, the emerging stars, the glowing fire and the Western ballads had woven a spell over them.

Dusty sang "Strawberry Roan" and "Cool Water," followed by a funny song about a cowboy who couldn't get off his horse because some blankety-blank had put glue on the saddle. As his audience applauded, he put up his hand for silence.

"Now we've got a special treat for you," he said. "This talented young lady will be performing for the very first time. In a few years, when she's become a big star, you can all say you heard her here tonight. Let's give her a hand."

As Jake and the students clapped, Paige walked forward to stand next to her great-grandfather. Kira swallowed her surprise. She'd never heard Paige sing. But something told her the little girl had had some coaching.

Playing softly, so as not to drown out her voice, Dusty strummed the intro to "You Are My Sunshine." Right on cue, Paige began to sing. Her childish voice was sweet and true, her confidence total as she nailed not only the first verse but also the second and the chorus. Kira's eyes met Jake's across the circle of glowing coals. She saw pride there—pride verging on tears.

Perhaps that was the moment when she knew she loved him.

After the entertainment, Kira excused herself to get Paige ready for bed and tuck her in. "I was so proud of you tonight," she whispered as she pulled up the quilt and kissed the little girl's cheek. "You were amazing. I didn't know you could sing."

"Grandpa helped me." Paige turned her face toward the photo on the nightstand. "Aunt Kira, do you think my mom could hear me from up in heaven?"

Kira blinked back a tear. "I'm sure she could, honey. And I can just imagine how proud she must've been."

"Maybe someday my dad will get to hear me sing, too."

Kira looked away to hide a rush of emotion. When she turned back toward the bed, Paige had rolled onto her side and closed her eyes.

In the house, she turned off the security light. She would turn it on again before she went to bed. But the night was clear and peaceful. The glare would only spoil it.

By the time she came back outside, the cookout had been cleared away and the table folded. The leftover food, condiments and utensils had been boxed and carried into the house. The students had retired to their cabins. Dusty, too, had taken his guitar and probably gone off to bed. Only Jake remained. He was standing by the fire pit, gazing down at the glowing coals. At Kira's approach, he looked up.

"Thanks for cleaning up the mess," she said. "It's nice to come outside and find it done."

"The kids did most of the work. It didn't take long. Sit down and relax." He indicated a spot near the fire pit. "You look like you could use a rest. I could make you another s'more, if you want one."

Kira gave him a smile. The man could be endearing when he chose to be. "I've had enough to eat, thanks. Besides, everything's put away."

He sat beside her on the bench at a comfortable distance. His manner made her wonder if he had something serious on his mind. But if he did, he didn't seem to be in a hurry.

"Did you learn anything new about the motorcycle?" she asked, making conversation.

"Only that sitting in the shed all those years didn't do it any good. Dirty gas tank, dead battery and spark plugs, clogged fuel line, probably bad fuel pump, too—all things that'll have to be fixed before I can figure out what caused it to break down in the first place."

"I understand you had a helper." Dusty had mentioned seeing Mack out by the shed.

Jake chuckled. "I can't say he was much help. But the kid's really into motorcycles. Talked my ear off. I didn't have the heart to send him away."

"Mack looked happier tonight than I'd ever seen him. He has to keep working with the horses, but what he really needs is a way to feel good about himself. I hope you won't mind letting him help you sometimes."

"I had a feeling you were going to say that. Sure. He can hang around when he's not with the group. I'll even see that he gets extra practice with the saddle and bridle, so he can keep up."

"Thank you." She reached out impulsively and laid a hand on his arm. His skin was warm to the touch, the muscles firm and taut beneath. His breath caught slightly, but he didn't speak. In the silence, Kira could hear the chirr of crickets, the crackle and hiss of the dying fire. She liked touching him, liked the subtle electric current that seemed to flow from his skin to hers.

At last, he shifted on the bench and cleared his throat. "Our little girl did us proud tonight, didn't she?"

"Our *little girl*." *It sounded strange, but not really wrong.*

"I had no idea she could perform like that," Kira said. "Dusty must have spent some time with her."

"Whatever it took, she blew me away," Jake said. "It was all I could do to keep from hugging her and telling her how proud of my daughter I was."

"About that . . ." Kira let go of his arm and turned to face him on the bench. She'd been unsure of how to warn him about what might be Paige's growing suspicions, but he'd just given her an opening.

"Paige asked me why you don't shave your beard," she said. "She's a smart little girl. I don't know how much longer you can keep her from guessing the truth."

"That doesn't surprise me." He gazed into the dying fire.

"Kira, what would you think if I decided to stay—or to give it a try at least?"

Her pulse skipped. "I've already asked you to stay. You know it's what I want. It's what Dusty wants, too."

"You know the risks. What if I can't control this monster inside me?"

"Then we'll deal with it. But that doesn't mean you shouldn't stay. I can't help thinking that your best chance of getting better is right here."

"But what about Paige? It would kill me to leave her, but I can't stand the thought of her seeing me at my worst."

"I've already talked with her about your PTSD.

If you told her what to expect if you have an episode, I think she'd understand."

"Maybe. Still, it's damned scary."

"I know. When would you plan to tell her you're her father?"

"Not right away. Not until I can feel confident about staying. If this didn't work out, and I ended up leaving . . ."

Still gazing into the coals, he let the words trail off. Kira understood. To leave Paige as a stranger passing through would be one thing. To leave as her father could scar the rest of her life.

After a pause, he turned back to face her. "There's one more thing, Kira. I want an honest answer."

Kira waited in the silence. Whatever Jake was about to say, she sensed, it was weighing heavily on him.

"You and me," he said. "We've been playing these chicken games long enough. I need to know whether there's anything more—anything that would give me a reason to stay."

Kira's pulse stuttered. She fumbled for words—but words wouldn't be enough. Jake needed more.

Looking into his shadowed eyes, she cupped his cheek with her hand, leaned forward and pressed her lips to his.

She felt his breath catch. Then his arms went around her, crushing her close. The kiss warmed and deepened, drawing her into him. She ached with yearning, wanting the dark room, the soft bed and Jake loving her.

His fingers fumbled with the buttons of her

shirt. She reached up to help him, wanting his intimate touch, his hands, his mouth. . . .

"Something tells me we're in the wrong place," she murmured against his ear.

With a raw laugh, he caught her waist and swept her across the yard to his dark cabin.

Inside, with the door securely locked, they took up where they'd left off, their kisses hot and hungry, their hands seeking sweet, forbidden places. Kira's blouse slipped to the floor, followed by her bra. The touch of his callused hands on her bare skin brought tears to her eyes. She moaned, arching against him, feeling his hard need against her hips. All she could think of was wanting more—wanting all of this strong, wounded man and what he could give her.

Her eager fingers tugged at his belt. With a mutter, he unhooked the buckle, unsnapped his jeans and let them drop to the floor, kicking off his boots as he stepped out of them.

Breathless in their haste, they left a trail of clothes across the tiled floor before they fell into bed, wrapped in each other's arms.

His skin was cool, his flesh pitted with the scars of war—each one a memory of pain. Kira brushed them with tender fingertips. If only she could love that pain away, she thought. And then, as her body welcomed him home, her thoughts were lost in a burst of wonder. This was Jake—her antagonist, her friend, her soul mate. He was making love to her, healing her in the deepest way—perhaps healing himself as well. She gave in to the shimmering sensations, rode the swell to a soaring peak. She cried out, then drifted slowly back to earth.

Spent, they lay side by side. Kira nestled against him, listening as his breathing deepened and he fell asleep. Then, knowing she must, she eased away from him, pulled on her clothes and prepared to leave. For a moment, she stood looking down at him. She loved this man, loved what he'd given her. At this moment, she couldn't have been happier. But for Kira, happiness held its own terrors.

The future loomed dark with uncertainty. Jake's struggle to control his PTSD would likely last the rest of his life. But at least he had a chance—*they* had a chance, she reminded herself. For now, that would have to be enough.

The next morning, Jake was up with the students to make sure the stable was clean and the horses cared for before the trip to town. He could have easily done the job himself, but the youngsters had to learn that, even on a holiday, they couldn't neglect their animals.

"Why can't I stay here with you?" Mack cornered Jake outside his horse's stall. "I'd rather help you work on the bike than go to a stupid old fiesta."

"I have other jobs to do first," Jake told him. "And anyway, you're not here to work on motorcycles. You're here to work with your horse and do things with your group. That's what your parents paid for. So go and have fun."

"That's not fair!" Mack kicked at the side of the stall. "I never get to do what I want to!"

"You can help later, but only if you stop complaining. The world doesn't revolve around what you want. The sooner you get used to that, the happier you'll be."

Jake shook his head as Mack stomped off to get his shovel. Had he boosted the boy's self-esteem by letting him help with the motorcycle? Or had he just created one more demand? But that question was Kira's department. She was the therapist, not him. Thank heaven.

He gave himself a moment to remember last night and the way he'd felt making love to her. Lord, how he wanted to keep that feeling! To be here, with his little girl and a woman to love, would be his idea of heaven. But could he make that heaven last? Could he find the strength to control the horrors in his head—the nightmares, the rages and the awful black bouts of depression?

With everything he'd ever wanted on the line, he had to try.

This morning he joined Dusty, Paige and the students for breakfast. Kira had laid out a cold buffet of cereal, rolls, fruit, cheese, juice and milk. Her gaze met his, briefly, across the dining room. They didn't speak, but her warm look said it all. Nothing had changed since last night.

The new challenge would be finding time alone with her.

After breakfast and a quick bathroom break, everyone piled into the big Jeep—Kira driving, Dusty in the passenger seat, Paige behind them belted in her booster seat, and the students filling the remaining spaces on the three bench seats. Jake, with the dog standing at his side, watched them drive out the side gate and down the road. He felt strangely lonesome, being the only person here. But he had plenty to keep him busy. Much of the day would be spent brushing a coat of protective oil on the newly repaired stable roof. After that, if the job didn't take too long, he might have time to spend on the motorcycle.

But first he owed himself some needed peace and pleasure.

In the stable, he took a saddle, a pad and a bridle from the tack room, then walked down the row of stalls to the very last one. Dynamite nickered at his approach.

"Hello, old boy," Jake said, opening the gate of the stall. "How would you like to take me for a nice morning ride?"

By the end of the outing, Dusty and Paige were tired, and even the students were winding down. But Kira was satisfied that the break from routine had been worth the time. They'd strolled through the historic section of town, touring the San Xavier Mission, visiting a craft market and enjoying a fiesta staged by a church group, featuring traditional food, music and dancing.

While Dusty rested on a bench in the plaza,

she'd also given her students time to explore the shops, gardens and galleries.

As on their earlier trip to the Arizona-Sonora Desert Museum, she made it a practice to watch how her students were interacting socially. There'd been some interesting changes. Most surprising was the friendship between Brandon and Heather. The two of them—opposites in many ways, but each an outsider—were walking apart from the group, talking earnestly. Had Brandon come out to the brash, attention-starved girl? That could be a good thing. Both of them needed support, and they appeared to be getting it from each other.

Faith and Lanie were hanging together, sporting identical French braids—also a good sign. Both girls needed friendship. Patrick and Calvin, who seemed to be getting along, were trailed by an unhappy-looking Mack. Of all her students, Mack worried Kira the most. Last night, after spending the afternoon with Jake, he'd appeared happier than she'd ever seen him. Today he looked as if he wanted to punch somebody.

Most of Kira's students finished the horse therapy program with renewed self-esteem, empathy for others, and a heightened sense of responsibility. Nearly two weeks into the course, she could see that happening with most of these young people. But not everyone succeeded. Some went home for rule breaking. A few, with serious issues, needed more help than she could give them. Still others simply refused to cooperate. She was far from ready to chalk up Mack as one of her failures, but she needed a better way to reach the boy.

She was loading everyone into the Jeep when her cell phone rang. The caller was Consuelo.

"I wanted to let you know I was back," she said. "I'll have dinner ready by the time you get here."

"Have you seen Jake?"

"He's out in the shed, working on that bike. Do you want me to call him?"

"No, that's fine. We're just getting ready to leave, so we'll be home soon."

"Oh, one more thing," Consuelo said. "I picked up the mail from the box on my way in. Mostly just bills and things. But there's a letter addressed to Dusty. It looks like it's from somewhere in Africa."

At the mention of *"Africa,"* a knot formed in the pit of Kira's stomach. Her aunt Barbara—Dusty's daughter and Wendy's mother—was in Africa with her minister husband. There'd been little contact with them over the years, so why a letter now? What if it was bad news?

Maybe she should open the letter before giving it to Dusty, so she could prepare him for whatever it held. She'd never approved of opening other people's mail, but the old man was fragile. An emotional shock could be dangerous to his health.

Thanking Consuelo, she ended the call. Dusty had settled in the passenger seat. He looked worn-out. He'd probably overdone it today. She would give him the letter after dinner, when he'd had a chance to rest.

After buckling Paige into her booster seat and making sure her students were safely belted in, Kira started for home. Everyone was tired. By the time they passed the outskirts of Tucson, Dusty had fallen into a doze, his silvery head drooping forward over his chest.

By the time they reached the ranch, it was getting dark. Kira pulled into the yard and let her students out of the Jeep, so they could wash up in their cabins and come back to the house for dinner. Dusty had awakened. He yawned, climbed stiffly to the ground and headed for the front porch.

Paige, still in her booster seat, was fast asleep. Kira had climbed out, opened the side door and was unbuckling the straps when she felt someone behind her.

"Let me carry her inside for you," Jake said, close to her ear.

She stepped aside to let him scoop Paige out of the seat and lift her in his arms. Roused by the motion, Paige opened her eyes, looked up at Jake with a sleepy smile and drifted off again.

Kira saw his jaw tighten, saw his throat move as if gulping back emotion. She moved with him into the house, holding the door so he could pass through with his precious bundle

In Paige's room, Kira turned down the bed and pulled off Paige's sneakers. For now, the soft leggings and tee she wore would do for her to sleep in. Jake eased her onto the bed. As he slipped his hands away, Kira pulled up the covers and tucked them around her.

They stood for a moment, looking down at the child they both loved. Jake's arm stole around Kira's waist and pulled her close to him. How would it feel, she wondered, to be a real family, sharing moments like this every night?

The mood was shattered by the sound of Dusty's raised voice from the living room. "Where did this letter come from, Consuelo? How long has it been here?"

With a moan of dismay, Kira tore herself away from Jake and rushed back down the hall.

CHAPTER FIFTEEN

Kira had planned to wait for the right time before giving the letter to her grandfather. Now it was too late. By the time she reached the living room, Dusty had torn open the exotically stamped envelope and unfolded the single handwritten page.

As he read the letter, the old man went pale. Crumpling the thin paper in his fist, he collapsed onto the sofa.

"What is it?" Kira flew across the room to his side.

He stared into the empty cavern of the fireplace, as if seeing some presence there. "Barbara's gone," he said. "The letter's from her husband. She died of a fever three weeks ago. All this time—you'd think that, as a father, I'd have some kind of sense that it had happened. But no, I've felt . . . nothing."

Wordless, Kira sank down beside him and wrapped

him in her arms. She'd expected something like this when she'd heard about the letter. But that didn't lessen the shock, especially for Dusty, who'd now lost his wife, his two daughters and a beloved granddaughter, all before their time.

Kira hadn't seen Wendy's mother in years. The woman she remembered as a pretty, talkative blonde had changed after marrying a stern preacher. She'd disowned Wendy for getting pregnant, and hadn't even come home from Africa to attend her daughter's funeral. Paige would never know the grandmother she'd just lost.

But Kira's grief was mostly for her grandfather, who felt so frail as she held him. His aging frame shook with the strain of holding back tears.

"Will her body be coming home?" Kira asked, thinking that a funeral service might at least bring some closure.

He shook his head. "They buried her in a little plot behind the mission. She'll never be coming home again. I'll never even get to visit her grave."

Kira's arms tightened around him. Glancing up, she saw Jake standing in the entrance to the dining room. He would have heard enough to know what had happened. "The students will be coming to eat," he said. "I'll bring them in through the kitchen and keep them quiet."

"Thanks." Kira's lips moved, barely voicing the word.

"And tell Dusty how sorry I am. If there's anything I can do—"

"You're already doing it." She met his gaze and saw the warmth and sympathy there. Then he disappeared in the direction of the kitchen, probably to tell Consuelo what had happened and to intercept the students before they could burst into the house, laughing and talking.

She stayed with Dusty for a while, letting him reminisce about Barbara and her growing-up years. When the old man was talked out, she steered him gently off to bed and waited outside his room until she knew he was settled for sleep. Then she checked on Paige and wandered back through the living room. Opening the front door to step out onto the porch, she nearly bumped into Jake, who was standing on the threshold.

"Whoa there!" He steadied her with his hands on her shoulders. "I was just about to knock." He stepped inside, closed the door behind him and gathered her close. Kira nestled against his chest, taking comfort in his solid strength.

"I'm sorry," he whispered against her hair.

"I'm sorry, too, even though she wasn't my favorite person," Kira said. "Especially after the way she treated Wendy. It's Dusty I'm grieving for. He's lost his whole family now."

"He's got you and Paige."

"But that's not the same. Barbara was his daughter. He'd always hoped to see her again when she came home. But now, as he said, he can't even visit her grave."

He eased her away, far enough for her to see his face. "That's part of why I'm here," he said. "Your students want to do something for him tomorrow morning. A surprise."

"'A surprise'?"

"It was Calvin who came up with the idea. It might be a little over-the-top, but their hearts are in the right place. I'm all for letting them do it."

"You're asking my permission? Without telling me what it is?"

He nodded, still holding her. "They'll need an hour or so after the horses are taken care of. I'll have my eyes on them the whole time. It won't be dangerous, and it won't hurt anything. Trust me, this could be good for them, and I hope for Dusty. He can even come out and watch if he's feeling up to it."

Kira looked up into his earnest eyes. *"Trust me,"* he'd said. How long had it been since she'd felt free to trust—to let go and let someone else take control, however briefly? Could she do it now? What if something were to go wrong?

"Trust me."

Her trust, Kira realized, was what this broken man needed most. It was the one vital, healing gift she could give him. Starting now.

"You're sure they'll be all right?" she asked.

"They'll be fine, Kira."

"Go ahead, then. Just be careful."

He opened the front door, gave her a lingering kiss and vanished into the darkness.

The next morning, after a sleepless night, Kira rolled out of bed at her usual five thirty a.m. By six, she'd showered, dressed, pulled her hair back, applied sunscreen and lip balm, strapped on her wristwatch, made her bed and left her room, ready for the day.

Ordinarily, she would have gone outside to make sure her students were up. But this was no ordinary day. With the tragic news from Africa still fresh, she would need to be here for Dusty and Paige.

After nearly two weeks in the program, the students would know the routine, and Jake would be there to keep them in line. This morning her own small family had to come first.

Peeking into Paige's room, Kira saw that the little girl was still curled in sleep. Dusty's room was empty, his bed made, his flannel robe hung neatly on its customary hook behind the door.

The dining-room table was set for breakfast. No one had come in yet, but she could hear Consuelo stirring in the kitchen and smell the aromas of bacon and coffee.

She found Dusty sitting at the kitchen table, sipping his coffee. He looked haggard, his eyes bloodshot. But he was shaved, combed and neatly dressed in a fresh shirt and jeans.

Stepping behind him, she bent and pressed her cheek against his. Consuelo, scrambling eggs at the stove, gave her a quiet smile. Kira walked to the counter, poured coffee into a mug, added some milk and took a seat across the table from her grandfather. "How are you this morning?" she asked. "Is there anything I can do for you?"

He shook his head. "Not much to be done. Only thing that's changed is what we know. So I reckon we'll just go on with the day as usual."

Kira sipped her hot, bitter coffee. "The students wanted to do something special for you. Jake said it was to be a surprise, but since I don't know what it is, I thought I'd better prepare you."

"That's nice of them. I'll at least pretend to be pleased." He spoke as if every word were an effort. "You and Paige are my only heirs now. This ranch will be all yours when I pass on."

"I hadn't even thought about that," Kira said, which was true.

"I'd wondered how to handle it if Barbara came back and wanted her share, most likely in cash. Guess I won't have to wonder anymore." His voice cracked slightly.

"We don't have to talk about this now." Kira reached across the table and covered his hand with hers.

"I don't even have a picture of her that isn't ten or fifteen years old," he said. "She's just . . . gone."

At that moment, Paige wandered into the kitchen. Still dressed in yesterday's shirt and leggings, she yawned and rubbed her eyes. Her gaze fixed on Dusty. "Why do you look sad, Grandpa?" she asked.

He gave her a melancholy smile. "Just some sad news, honey," he said. "Your aunt Kira can tell you about it."

Taking her cue, Kira rose. "Come on, Paige, let's get you bathed and ready for the day," she said, leading the little girl back to the bedroom. While Paige splashed in the tub, Kira did her best to explain the passing of the grandmother she'd never met.

"So my grandma is up in heaven with my mom now," Paige said. "I bet they were really happy to see each other."

"Let's hope so." Kira helped Paige out of the tub and wrapped her in a towel. "Now let's go and get you dressed."

By the time Kira returned to the kitchen with Paige, Dusty had gone to sit on the porch with the dog. The students had finished eating and were busy with morning chores. If the planned surprise was going to happen, it would have to be soon. She had her own full agenda for the day.

When Paige had finished breakfast, Kira took her outside. The students had finished with the stable and turned the horses loose in the paddock. Now, wearing work gloves and carrying shovels, hoes and rakes, they headed toward the hills that rose behind the ranch yard.

The nearest hill was a small one, low with an easy slope, and slightly rounded top. The trail, where Kira's students had led their horses on past outings, wound around its base. That hill was where the young people were headed now.

"What the devil's going on?" Dusty had risen and walked to the porch rail, where he could see what was happening.

"It's a surprise." Kira picked up an empty chair from the porch and carried it to a shady spot at the side of the house with a view of the hill. "Come on down here, where you can watch them."

Dusty came down off the porch and took his seat. Tucker followed him, resettling himself at the old man's feet. The dog seemed to sense his distress. He had stayed close to his master all morning.

Paige climbed onto his lap to watch as the students began clearing an area, about six feet across, at the top of the hill, smoothing the earth and edging it with a circle of stones. With that done, they began searching the slope, bringing back rocks to pile at the center of the circle in a narrow pyramid shape.

"What the blazes are those kids doing?" Dusty muttered.

"Calvin calls it a memory cairn." Jake had come from around the house to stand behind them. "They're building it to honor your daughter, Dusty. When you look up there and see it, you'll remember her. And after it's done, every person who goes up the hill to visit it can bring a rock and add it to the cairn, so it will grow over time."

Dusty blinked away the first tear Kira had seen him shed. "I'll be damned," he said. "That's right nice."

"I want to help!" Paige scrambled off Dusty's lap and raced across the yard toward the hill. Kira was about to call out and stop her, when Jake touched her arm, his message silent but sure.

He was right. Paige was fine, and she wanted to be part of this. *Let her go.*

Still, she kept her eyes on the small figure as Paige stopped to pick up a pebble, then dashed up the hill to place it on the cairn. Now the students were giving her high fives. Kira couldn't have been more proud of them, working together to do something unselfish for a grieving old man.

They had learned one of the most important lessons her course had been designed to teach them—and they had earned an early reward. This afternoon she had a surprise in store for them. They would finally get to ride their horses.

Six days had passed since the building of the cairn. From under the overhang of the shed, where he was replacing the fuel pump on the motorcycle, Jake watched Paige and Kira walk up the hill. Each of them carried a small rock. Paige had insisted on climbing up to the cairn every day, sometimes more than once. Usually, Kira went with her, but Dusty had made the pilgrimage a few times as well. The old cowboy was getting stronger now, insisting that it was time to stop treating him like an invalid.

Dusty's recovery had given Jake more time to work on the bike. He'd long since given up the idea that a single replacement part would get the old Indian running again. After more than thirty years in the shed, none of the mechanical or electrical parts could be counted on to work. Jake had had little choice except to replace almost everything except the engine, which might still need a rebuild. He'd found the parts online, paid for them with his debit card and had them shipped express to the ranch. The purchase had wiped out his last benefit check, but getting the vintage machine operational would be worth every cent.

"Got it working yet?" Mack's question cut into his thoughts.

"Nope." Jake tightened a small bolt, grateful that the ranch had most of the tools he'd needed, rusty but still serviceable.

"How much longer do you think it'll take?" Mack asked.

"Don't know. A couple of days, at least. And then I might have to take it somewhere and test it. I promised Dusty I wouldn't rev it up around the horses."

"I could go with you," Mack said. "To test it, I mean."

"Don't count on it. You've got plenty of other stuff to keep you busy." Jake had tried to be patient with the boy and to let him help a little. But the kid never seemed to stop talking, especially when Jake was trying to think things out. Mack was becoming a nuisance.

"Will you give me a ride on it when it's ready?"

"Nope. That's against the rules. Do you know what liability is?"

"Yeah. It's like my folks could sue you if I get hurt."

"That's right. And that's why I can't let you on this bike." Jake glanced toward the stable, where the students were gathering, waiting for Kira. "Looks like it's time for your afternoon trail ride," he said.

"Can't I stay here and help you?"

"Maybe later. Right now, that's not what you're here for."

Muttering and dragging his feet, Mack headed for the stable. Kira had dropped Paige off at the house and was hurrying to meet her students. She flashed Jake a secret smile as she passed the shed. Things had been good between them since that night after last week's cookout—so good that he'd dared to wonder if there was a real chance for things to work out here. Watching the easy flow of her jeans-clad hips from the back, he remembered holding her in his arms last night, every curve and hollow of her sweet woman's body molding to his in the darkness. It had been heaven—or damn close to it.

But was all this too good to last?

He was still riding Dynamite almost every morning and doing his best to stay calm. He'd even tried meditating—a practice he'd learned in the VA hospital. So far, it seemed to be helping. But it was too soon to know for sure. Only time would tell whether he was making real progress.

If he could keep himself under control, he might be lucky enough to find a life here with Kira and Paige. If not, he told himself, it would be time to face the truth: the people he loved so much would be better off without him.

With just a few days left in the course, time was moving fast. Now that the students were comfortable in the saddle, they were on the trail every day, their outings getting progressively longer. Kira took pride in seeing their confidence. They'd learned new skills, formed new habits and made new friends.

Kira had made it clear that there would be no running or jumping the aging trail horses. Not only was it dangerous for both the horses and their young riders, but it was contrary to the peaceful goal of the course. Most of the students accepted that rule. Only Mack had argued. "What's the fun of riding a stupid horse if you can't race it?"

"Sorry, Mack," Kira had replied. "If you want to race a horse, sign up for riding lessons when you get home and learn to do it safely."

Mack had made progress here, but his stubborn temperament remained an issue. Kira had long ago learned that there were some problems not even the horses could remedy.

Today their outing would be the longest so far. They'd be riding up to a beautiful alpine meadow for a lunchtime picnic and getting back in time for dinner. Jake would be coming along to bring up the rear and lend an extra hand.

He joined the group at breakfast, looking fresh and well-rested. Kira knew he'd taken Dynamite out for an early-morning ride. As he took his seat, their eyes met across the table. They'd had precious little time together in the past few days, but his warm look told her nothing had changed between them.

"How's the motorcycle coming along?" she asked.

He grinned. "Would you believe I finally got it running? Yesterday while the horses were out on the trail, I started it up and took it for a slow drive around the yard. It still needs fine-tuning and a lot more work, as well as new tires and new brakes. But those things will have to wait until I can afford them."

"Wow, you finally did it!" Mack reached for the last strip of bacon.

"With a little help from you," Jake said. "Too bad you won't be here when it's licensed and ready for the road."

Paige, who'd been eating breakfast in the kitchen, wandered in to stand beside Kira. "Aunt Kira, can you walk up to the cairn with me now?"

Kira sighed. "Sorry, honey, I need to help get the horses ready for the trail ride. We can go tonight, when I get back."

"But I want to go this morning." Paige's lower lip jutted. She turned toward Jake. "Can you go with me, Mister Jake? I'm not supposed to go by myself."

Jake shot Kira a questioning look. Early on, they'd agreed that he shouldn't spend time alone with his daughter, but a lot of things had changed since then.

"It's all right—that is, if you don't mind taking her," Kira told him. "Since your horse is already saddled, you can join us when you're done."

Jake finished his coffee and half a piece of toast. "All right, Miss Paige, you're in charge," he said, pulling back his chair. "Lead the way."

Jake followed the small figure across the yard to the foot of the hill. "We'll need rocks," she said, looking around. "Here's a good one for me." She picked up a flat, rust-colored chunk the size of her hand. "And there's one for you." She pointed to a larger stone. "It's too heavy for me, but you can carry it fine."

Jake picked up the stone, touched by his daughter's amazing sense of purpose. This task had become all-important to her; and right now, nothing mattered more to him than the chance to share it. "Is this all we need?" he asked her.

"We'll need more. But we can find them on the way." Clutching her rock, she darted up the faint trail that had been worn among clumps of brittlebush, owl's clover and Mexican poppy. Jake followed close behind, picking up extra stones as she pointed them out. This would be his first visit to the memory cairn. He'd made excuses, telling himself he was too busy to go. But the truth was, his few memories of his late mother-in-law were bitter. The woman had cursed him for getting her daughter pregnant and broken Wendy's heart when she refused to attend the wedding or even acknowledge Paige's birth.

But Paige didn't need to know that. She was a happy little girl honoring her grandmother.

He reached the cleared circle a few steps behind her. The cairn the students had started was growing with the pebbles and small rocks that had been added every day. Following Paige's example, Jake added one of the stones he'd brought, choosing a place where it would balance. That done, he was about to turn back, but caught sight of something else.

A few steps away from the cairn, but still inside

the circle, was a miniature pile of stones—colored pebbles carefully stacked. "What's this, Paige?" he asked her.

"This is a cairn I'm making for my mom." Paige added two small rocks to the pile. "Do you want to help me, Mister Jake?"

Jake's throat tightened. This was the last thing he'd expected, but he could hardly say no. As he took the rocks they'd gathered and helped Paige arrange the pile into a pyramid shape, he remembered Wendy—her flaming beauty, her laughter, her reckless passion. Wendy, who had given him this wonderful child. Wendy, who had lied, cheated and betrayed him in the cruelest way.

She was who she was, and nothing could change that, Jake reminded himself. It would be his choice to hate her for the rest of his life or to forgive her and move on.

His choice.

As he took each stone from Paige's hand and placed it on the new cairn, he felt forgiveness, and healing, begin.

The narrow trail wound upward through the foothills above the ranch and into the heart of the Santa Catalina Mountains. Changing with the altitude, desert scrub gave way to mesquite groves, then to oak, juniper, cottonwood and Arizona sycamore. The morning was bright, the crystalline air musical with birdcalls.

With Kira leading on Sadie, the students rode

single file. Their horses knew the trail and needed little guiding. The young riders were free to look around, enjoy the fresh air and spectacular scenery. Today they had made their own lunches, filled their canteens and packed their saddlebags with things a rider would need. If things went well today, the final event at the week's end would be an overnight trip and a campout with their horses.

As they approached a bend in the trail, Kira glanced back along the queue of riders. Jake, who was bringing up the rear, gave her a hand sign. All okay back there—for now, at least.

They'd both been concerned about Mack, who seemed to be having one of his bad days. Back in the stable, while they were saddling up, Patrick had taken Mack's usual bridle by mistake. Mack had yelled at the other boy. Kira had stepped between them just in time to avoid a nasty fight.

As a precaution, when she'd lined up the riders for the trail, she'd placed Patrick at the front, right behind her. She'd put Mack at the end, just ahead of Jake. Mack had grumbled about eating dust and riding through poop, but Kira had chosen to ignore his complaints.

With the sun at the peak of the sky, they reached the grassy meadow where they planned to rest and have lunch before starting back. It was a beautiful spot, rich with long grass and dotted with red and purple lupines. By now, the students had been in the saddle for almost four hours. They were sore and tired. Some of them groaned good-naturedly as they dismounted and slipped to the ground.

Patrick was about to climb off his horse, when

Mack broke out of the line and rode up next to him. "Race you to that big stump," Mack said, pointing to a dead tree on the far side of the meadow. "Loser's a stinkin' coward!"

With that, he kicked Patches hard in the flanks. The startled horse whinnied, reared and was off like a shot.

Kira had already dismounted. *"Stop!"* she shouted.

Patrick, still recovering from his surprise, heard her and reined to a halt. But Mack, clinging onto Patches, was out of control. There was no way he could stop his panicked horse.

Jake, still mounted at the rear of the line, could do little except watch in horror. The ground in the meadow would be like a sponge, pitted with holes and burrows, where a horse could easily catch a leg and go down. Patches was too fast, and too far ahead, for Dynamite to catch up with him; and even if Kira were to leap into the saddle and give chase, she'd be too late to stop the runaway, especially given the risk to her mare.

Telling the students to stay put, she took off on foot, racing through the grass. Leaving his horse, Jake charged after her.

Two-thirds of the way across the meadow, Patches stumbled and pitched forward onto his knees. Mack flew out of the saddle, went over the horse's shoulder and landed in the grass.

Adrenaline surged through Jake's body as he ran. Mack was wearing his helmet, but that wouldn't save the fool boy from a broken neck or even worse. Kira, he knew, would be frantic.

Patches lurched to his feet, shook himself and wandered off to graze. Jake could make out a streak of red across one knee. At least the horse didn't appear to be badly hurt. But what about Mack?

Kira had nearly reached the boy as he sat up. Cursing with relief, Jake sprinted toward them and caught up. Mack was stunned, but moving his arms and legs. Jake extended a hand and pulled the boy to his feet. He was pale and shaken, but nothing appeared to be broken.

Kira was white with fury. Jake had never seen her so angry.

"You were lucky!" she snapped. "You could have killed yourself and that poor horse, or put yourself in a wheelchair for the rest of your life!" She turned to Jake. "Take him back to the others and keep him there. I need to get Patches and look at his leg."

With Mack beside him, Jake started back across the meadow, to where the other students waited. "What the devil were you thinking?" he demanded. "You should've known better than to race off like that."

"I was just bored," Mack said. "All we have around here is rules, rules, rules. Aren't rules meant to be broken sometimes?" He gave Jake a smile, hoping for approval. Jake didn't smile back. It was all he could do to keep from grabbing the young fool by the shoulders and shaking some sense into him.

The other students stood silent, most of them watching Kira lead Patches back across the meadow. Only Patrick stepped forward as Mack reached the group. He was grinning. "Boy, you really screwed up this time. I'll bet you're gonna get sent home for this."

"Then I don't have a friggin' thing to lose, do I?" Mack took a step, swung and crunched his fist into Patrick's eye.

CHAPTER SIXTEEN

Still dressed in her dusty riding clothes, Kira faced Mack across her desk. "You know the rules, Mack. Any student who hurts an animal or another student has to leave the ranch. Today you did both. I'm about to phone your parents. Do you want to tell them what happened, or would you rather I do it?"

Mack had been slumped in the straight-backed chair, eyes sullen, lower lip thrust outward. Now tears welled in his eyes. "Please don't call them!" he begged. "My dad will kill me! Please—he'll lock me in my room and take my phone away for a month! He won't even let me watch TV or go to the gym. And he'll yell at me—you've never heard anybody yell like he does!"

Kira hated the process of sending a student home, but she'd done it enough times to know what to expect. "You should have thought of that before you broke the rules," she said.

"Please give me another chance!" He was gripping the edge of the desk, almost on his knees. "I'll be good, I promise!"

"Tell that to Patrick. Jake had to take him to the doctor in town to get his eye checked. You'd better hope the damage doesn't turn out to be serious."

"It was Patrick's fault, too. If he hadn't made me mad, I wouldn't have hit him."

"Patches cut his knee when he stumbled. He could've broken his leg. What if we'd had to call the vet and have Patches put down? Would that have been his fault, too?"

Mack stared at the floor, saying nothing.

Jake had left the meadow early, riding double with Patrick on Dynamite and leading Patches, who was still too skittish to be ridden. The other students had eaten their lunches, then headed back down the trail with Mack riding Patrick's horse. The outing should have been fun for the students. But by the time they got back to the ranch, nobody was in a good mood. They'd put away their horses, eaten dinner and gone to their cabins—except for Mack, who had to face the consequences of what he'd done.

Kira picked up the phone. "Last chance. Do you want to make the call?"

Mack shook his head.

"Fine. You stay right here until I excuse you." Kira dialed the Phoenix phone number on Mack's program application. It was his mother who answered. She seemed more annoyed by the inconvenience of having to pick him up than by her son's misbehavior. "I've got a salon appointment tomorrow morning," she said. "Maybe his daddy can come get him. Hold on."

The exchange of voices was loud enough for Mack to hear. He shrank in his chair, as if trying to hide. A moment later, his mother was back on the phone. "He says he'll be there by eight thirty. Tell Mack he'd better be ready on time."

Kira ended the call and escorted Mack to the cabin he shared with Brandon to pack and get some sleep. He was under strict orders to stay put until morning. She felt sorry for the boy, but rules were rules. Mack had earned his dismissal from the program.

On her way back to the house, she glanced at her watch. It was after nine. Hours had passed since Jake had ridden down the trail with Patrick. Dusty, who'd put Patches and Dynamite away and dressed the shallow cut on Patches' knee, had confirmed that Jake had taken her Outback to drive the boy to the ER. Patrick's eye injury hadn't looked that serious, but it needed to be checked by a doctor.

Waiting in the ER could take a long time, Kira knew. But it was getting late, and she was becoming worried. What if something had happened on the road—or what if Jake had suffered an episode? He didn't carry a cell phone, and, since students' phones weren't allowed on the rides, Patrick's phone had been left in his cabin. She had no way to call either of them.

She'd reached the porch, and was about to go look in on Paige, when she caught sight of headlights rounding the last bend in the road. A moment later, her wagon drove through the side gate and pulled around the house. Jake and Patrick climbed out, both looking weary.

"The eye is okay," Jake said before Kira could ask. "But he's got one heck of a shiner."

Patrick turned to face her, grinning. The bruise around his eye had morphed into an ugly ring of blues and purples. He was showing it off like a trophy.

"You're sure you're all right, Patrick?" Kira asked.

"I'll live. Can't wait to get my phone and send out some selfies."

"We stopped for shakes and burgers on the way back, so we won't need to eat," Jake said. "How's Patches?"

"Not too bad. But he'll be out of action until his leg heals. Patrick, you look like you could use a shower and a good night's sleep. We'll take it easy tomorrow."

"What's happening with Mack?" Patrick asked. "He's not a bad kid, you know. He was just having a crappy day. Is he going home?"

"I'm afraid so, but we won't talk about that now," Kira said. "Run along. Get some rest."

By the time Jake had parked the vehicle in the shed and returned to the porch, Kira was alone. He mounted the steps two at a time and gathered her into his arms. She softened against him, feeling warm and protected. "Sorry," he murmured, his lips brushing her forehead. "I know you've had a hell of a day."

"It could've been worse," she said. "At least Mack didn't break his neck. And Patrick and the horse will be okay. But I hate having to send a student home, especially after he seemed to be making such good progress."

"Like Patrick said, he was just having a crappy day. Believe me, I know how that feels."

"Speaking of that, how have you been?" She looked up at him, raising a hand to cup his cheek. His beard was rough against her palm. She loved the feel of it.

"So far, so good," he said. "Having a steady girl-friend seems to be helping—and Dynamite de-serves some credit, too."

Kira closed her eyes, inhaling the manly smell that had seeped into his shirt. At times like this, with Jake's arms around her, it was hard to imag-ine that anything could go wrong.

"I was about to check on Paige," she said. "Want to come with me?"

"Sure." He followed her inside and down the hall, where they peeked into her room. Paige was sleeping like an angel. Not wanting to wake her, they moved quietly back to the living room.

"I can't get enough of looking at her," Jake said. "She blew me away this morning going up that hill. She was amazing."

"You've got to tell her who you are, Jake," Kira said. "Paige is a sharp little girl. She's going to guess the truth, if she hasn't already. And then she'll wonder why you kept it from her."

"I plan to," Jake said. "I want her to know."

"So when are you going to tell her?" Kira had turned to face him.

"Tomorrow," he said. "I'll tell her tomorrow—when I shave off my beard."

She walked out onto the porch with him, to say good night. The sky was clear, the stars hung like jewels on black velvet, but the night breeze carried the fresh smell of rain.

Once more, he gathered her in his arms. His kiss was filled with promise. "I love you, Kira," he whispered.

Her arms tightened around his neck. "I love you, too. And whatever happens, we'll work it out."

Her gaze followed him as he walked away and crossed the yard to his cabin. *Jake loved her*—it was like a dream come true. But how could she dare feel this way, when so many things in her past had come to a bad end? Right now, she was as happy as she'd ever been in her life. But at the same time, she was terrified.

With so much good in her life, how could something not go wrong?

By the time she'd checked her e-mail and set up tomorrow's agenda, with contingency plans for rain, Kira was so exhausted that she could barely stay awake in the shower. After toweling herself dry, she pulled on clean pajamas and crawled into bed. Her head had barely settled on the pillow before she sank into dreams—strange, jumbled dreams filled with ringing phones, crashing cars and sirens screaming through the night.

A rap on her bedroom door jerked her out of sleep. At first, she thought she'd imagined it. But no, there was the rap again. Her heart lurched. Was somebody in trouble? Paige? Dusty? One of the students?

Sitting up, she glanced at the bedside clock: 3:15. "Who's there?" She sprang out of bed and rushed to open the door.

"It's me, Brandon." The slim, dark boy stood in the hallway, faintly silhouetted by the security light that fell through the living-room window. "Mack is gone. He's nowhere in the cabin, and his backpack is missing."

"You didn't hear him leave?"

"I was asleep," Brandon said. "A couple minutes ago, I got up to use the bathroom. That's when I noticed he wasn't in his bed. He'd lumped the pillows to make it look like he was there, but I could tell it wasn't him."

"Go get Jake! Hurry! I'll be right out." As Brandon raced off, Kira scrambled into her clothes. Why hadn't she guessed that Mack would run away rather than face his father? Until he was picked up, the boy was her responsibility. Anything that happened to him would be her fault.

Still zipping her jeans, she rushed out of the bedroom—to face a small figure clad in pink pajamas.

"What's the matter, Aunt Kira?" Paige asked. "Is somebody sick?"

"One of the students ran away." Kira knew better than to lie. "I have to help find him. Go on back to bed. Grandpa and Consuelo will be here. You'll be fine."

Paige didn't go, but Kira had no time to argue. Leaving the little girl in the hall, she dashed outside. Jake, in sweats and sneakers, stood with Brandon in the glare of the security light. "Any sign of him?" she asked.

"Not yet," Jake said. "Maybe he's just hiding on the property. Brandon, you stay and keep your eyes open. If anybody else wakes up, keep them here. I'll check the sheds and vehicles. Kira, can you look in the stable?"

Kira was off before he finished speaking. Mack could be hiding in a stall or in the tack room. But what if he'd taken one of the horses? He could ride up one of the mountain trails; or worse, he could ride the horse down to the highway, abandon the poor animal and hitch a ride into Tucson. She didn't even want to think about what could happen to him as a runaway boy on the streets. If he wasn't found soon, she would have to notify the police—but now she was getting ahead of herself.

The stable door was closed, nothing disturbed in the tack room. The horses were safe in their stalls, with no sign of Mack anywhere. Kira had gone back outside and was closing the door; then she heard a shout from Jake. She ran back, meeting him in the yard.

"The motorcycle's gone." He was out of breath. "That crazy kid's taken it."

"Wouldn't we have heard it start?" Kira asked.

"He wouldn't have started it here. Too loud. My guess is, he would've wheeled it out of the gate and partway down the road, then started it there. Come on." He grabbed Kira's arm, pulling her toward the vehicle shed where he'd parked her wagon, leaving the key under the floor mat. "The engine's still tricky. With any luck, he won't be able to start it."

"What if he can get it started? Does he know how to ride a motorcycle?" Kira asked.

"He thinks he does. But that's not the problem. The damned bike doesn't have any brakes. There's no way he can ride it down that road without crashing."

"Dear God . . . ," Kira breathed a prayer.

They'd almost reached the shed when a sound—distant but unmistakable—froze them in their tracks.

It was the sudden cough and bellow of a big motorcycle engine.

"You drive, I'll watch." Jake sprang into the passenger side of Kira's wagon, reached for the keys under the floor mat and thrust them into the ignition for her. The vehicle shot backward out of the shed, spitting gravel as Kira swung around and headed for the gate.

"Can you hear anything?" she asked.

Jake rolled down the window. From somewhere below, he could still hear the sputtering roar of the old engine being revved. He could only hope it would lose power and quit before the kid had a chance to put it in gear. He'd inspected the brakes just yesterday. The decades-old brake pads had disintegrated over time. Planning to order new ones, he'd removed them and thrown them in the trash. The motorcycle Mack had stolen had no brake function at all.

The road from the ranch to the highway below was a series of hairpin curves with steep-sloping drop-offs below—no problem for a careful driver going at a safe speed. But for a crazy kid in the dark, who had no idea of the danger . . .

Jake tried to blot the images from his mind—the mangled bodies of young men under his command, broken and bleeding, the desert dust settling over them. He could feel the adrenaline rising, shooting electric currents through his body. Muscles tensed, nerves pulsed.

Kira was driving as fast as safely possible, headlights on high beam. From below, Jake could still hear the roar of the engine. But now, the pitch had changed. The bike wasn't just revving. *Oh, Lord, it was moving.*

He could tell Kira to drive even faster, or honk the horn. But the approaching vehicle might cause the boy to speed up. Panic surged through Jake's body. Barring some miracle, when Mack came to a curve, unable to stop or slow down, he'd go flying off the road in a crash that nobody could survive.

Jake listened as the bike gained distance. Then, suddenly, he realized he could no longer hear it. Kira glanced at him, her face pale and questioning. He shook his head. All they could do was keep going.

As they came around the next bend, the headlights outlined a stocky figure standing next to the road. It was Mack.

Kira pulled off the road, jumped out of the vehicle and ran to him. Fighting to control his emotions, Jake followed more slowly. Mack was bruised and scraped, his hands bloodied, his jeans and jacket ripped. His backpack hung from one shoulder. There was no sign of the motorcycle.

"What happened?" Kira asked in a shaky voice.

"I . . . fell off the bike," he said. "Scraped myself pretty bad on the road."

"Where's the bike now?" Jake demanded, reeling as waves of relief and anger washed over him.

"Down . . . there." Mack pointed to a nearby spot where the shoulder of the road dropped off a good seventy feet into a dry wash. There was a flashlight in Kira's wagon. Jake found it, brought it back and directed the beam down off the roadside. Steve McQueen's priceless vintage Indian motorcycle lay scattered on the rocks below, broken into so many pieces that it wouldn't even be worth climbing down to pick them up.

Jake strode back to the Outback and opened the back door. "Get in," he ordered Mack. "Don't you say another word."

Kira found a place to turn around, and they drove back up the road to the ranch. Jake was seething, his temper threatening to explode. Losing the bike was bad enough. But this fool boy, with no regard for safety, honesty or common sense, could have died tonight. He'd missed death by a stroke of fate—

and he was probably too clueless to even realize how close he'd come.

Jake remembered his third deployment and the nineteen-year-old corporal who'd snuck outside the wire one night to see a girl. Jake's patrol had found his body the next morning, hacked to pieces in the most obscene way imaginable. It appeared that the young man had been alive through much of it. Such a hellish, senseless, stupid way to die—and for nothing.

That image boiled to the surface, flooding Jake's senses with bloodred heat as the wagon pulled into the yard and stopped short of the house. Clinging to his last thread of self-control, he opened the back door for Mack. The boy looked up at him and grinned.

Something snapped. Jake was suddenly back in the combat zone, and he was screaming—screaming obscenities at the young corporal who'd died and at all the others who'd died on his watch—the brave ones, the stupid ones, he was seeing them all, the blood, the shattered bodies and missing limbs of the ones who would never be whole again. He cursed heaven. He cursed the foolish boy who'd almost died tonight—and would have died for nothing. *Nothing*.

Now, at last, he could feel himself winding down, getting tired. He became aware of Kira, holding him from behind, wrapping him in her arms, and a white-faced Mack, cowering in terror against the side of the vehicle.

Then, as he turned, he became aware of something else—a small figure in pink pajamas, standing speechless on the porch.

Holding him, Kira felt him break. He groaned, his body crumpling against her, and she knew it was because he'd seen Paige.

"Get me out of here," he muttered, his voice hoarse from screaming. With her arms still around him, she walked him to his cabin. By the time they reached the door, she could tell from his breathing that the worst of the episode had passed.

"Don't turn on the light," he said. "Just go. I'll be all right."

"You're sure?" Her arms released him as he sank onto the edge of the bed.

"You're needed out there," he said. "Don't worry, I'm just going to lie down."

"I'll be back." She moved to the door, half-afraid to leave him. But he was right. Paige was out there, as well as Mack, Brandon and any other students who might have awakened. She could only hope that Dusty and Consuelo, whose rooms were on the far side of the house, had slept through the racket.

"Kira." She heard his voice behind her and turned.

"I'm sorry," he said. "God, I'm sorry."

"It wasn't your fault. Rest, now."

She closed the door and hurried outside. Mack was still standing by the vehicle. The students, roused by the noise, were standing outside their doors as if uncertain what to do next.

She took charge. "You, Mack, go in the house and wait. The rest of you, back to bed. Everything's under control. We'll talk about this in the morning."

Kira gave the students a moment to disperse. Then she hurried onto the porch, lifted Paige in her arms and sat down with her in a chair. The little girl was calm, but her cheeks were wet with tears. Kira held her close, rocking her gently. "I'm sorry you had to see that, sweetheart. Remember what we talked about, how Mister Jake might get upset and imagine he was back in the war? That's what happened to him tonight."

"I know," Paige said. "Poor Mister Jake. He must have been so scared."

"Scared": Kira had never thought of Jake's affliction that way, but his daughter was right. At some level, he must have been terrified.

"Will he be all right?" Paige asked.

"I think so. But it could happen again."

"Can we help him?"

Kira thought of Jake's plan to tell Paige the truth tomorrow. Now that wasn't likely to happen. "We can try to help him. But mostly he'll have to help himself." She stood, lowering Paige's feet to the porch. "Come on. Let's tuck you back in bed."

Mack was waiting in the darkened living room, slumped in a chair. Kira put Paige to bed, then returned to him. Jake's wild tirade had taken all the fight out of the boy. He submitted meekly when Kira washed his skinned hands and applied antibiotic ointment to the abrasions. "Mack, I'm too tired and too angry to lecture you," she said. "Since I can't lock you up like a prisoner, I'm taking you back to your cabin to get some sleep. Leave again, and I'll call the police and press charges for stealing the bike. Understand?"

He nodded. Kira escorted him back across the yard to the cabin and saw him safely inside. She'd left the Outback parked, with the keys in the ignition. Now she took a few moments to put the vehicle in the shed and lock it. Then she went to check on Jake.

When she opened the door, the room was quiet. Jake lay on the bed, sprawled in exhausted sleep. Kira covered him with a spare blanket, bent close and brushed a kiss on his forehead. Tomorrow, when he was rested, they would deal with what had happened and try to move on.

She stepped outside again, closing the door behind her. In the sky, dark clouds hid the stars. Far to the west, sheet lightning flickered across the horizon.

Inhaling the cool, fresh air, Kira walked back to the house. She was bone weary and emotionally drained. But with dawn so near, sleep would only make her groggy when she was facing what was sure to be a difficult day. She would make some coffee, maybe catch up on reading the professional journals she subscribed to or update the files on her computer. The quiet time would be welcome while it lasted. Morning would be here soon enough.

* * *

By seven that morning, the rain was pouring down in a steady drizzle. The soot-black clouds and rumbling thunder in the west gave warning that the weather would only get worse. Kira woke her students for chores and breakfast, then gave them free time to sleep, do schoolwork, read or play video games in the den.

At seven forty-five, Paige wandered into Kira's office, her shirt buttoned crooked and her shoelaces dragging. A chocolate milk mustache on her upper lip confirmed that she'd had her breakfast.

"Where's Mister Jake?" she asked. "Is he okay?"

"He was tired last night. I didn't want to wake him this morning. He's probably still asleep." But it wouldn't hurt to go and look in on him, Kira thought. She needed to make sure he was all right.

She rebuttoned Paige's shirt and tied her shoes, then took her into the bathroom to wash her face and run a brush through her curls. She was about to go and check on Jake, when she heard the loud honking of a horn as a big red Cadillac pulled up to the porch. Mack's father had arrived early to pick up his son.

Heedless of the rain, Kira rushed outside. The beefy man at the wheel was in no mood for pleasantries. "Get my boy!" he growled through the open window. "You were supposed to fix the kid! Damned waste of time and money!"

Mack was nowhere in sight. Kira found him playing games in the den. He had his rain jacket, but his pack was still in the cabin. "Go get it— hurry," Kira ordered him. "Your father's waiting."

Mack went to the cabin, but didn't hurry. He returned, dragging his feet through the rain puddles and carrying his pack as if it weighed a hundred pounds. Kira had hoped for a final interview, to make sure the father understood why his son was being dismissed and how the boy might be helped. But given the man's impatience, that wasn't going to happen.

Kira watched the Cadillac pull away through the rain with Mack inside. Fighting tears, she remembered each day of his time here, the struggles, the accomplishments, the rare moments of sweetness. He wasn't a bad boy, just desperately unhappy; and in the end, she had failed to give him what he needed. She could only hope Mack would find the hidden spark inside him—that given time, he would outgrow his roots and become the man he was meant to be. But that was out of her hands now. She had done what she could for him, and it hadn't been enough.

By now, it was after eight—time she checked on Jake.

Already wet, she sprinted across the yard to his cabin. The door was unlocked, as she'd left it. As she stepped inside, her heart dropped. The bed was neatly made, Jake's pack and clothes missing from the room.

Jake was gone.

A folded sheet of guest stationery was tucked between the pillows. Her legs failing her, Kira sank onto the edge of the bed. Her hands shook as she unfolded the paper and began to read.

Kira,

I'm sorry, but after a long night of thinking, I know this is for the best. I will always love you and Paige. But it wouldn't be fair to inflict my illness on people I care so deeply about. For your sake and mine, I'm moving on. Please tell Dusty that I haven't forgotten what I owe him. As soon as I find a job somewhere, I'll send monthly checks until he's paid off.

Thank you for making me part of your lives these past weeks. I will never forget you.

Jake

CHAPTER SEVENTEEN

The rain was a steady downpour, but Jake was used to bad weather. Water sheeted off his hooded poncho as he trudged down the winding, graveled road toward the highway. Just ahead was the spot where the motorcycle had gone off the road. He passed it without looking down. It didn't matter anymore. Whatever had happened last night was behind him. He'd learned not to look back.

The red Cadillac had swerved around him, going downhill a few minutes ago, splashing him with muddy water as one wheel swished through a puddle. He'd recognized Mack in the passenger seat. At least the fool kid was alive. But Jake had known better than to try and thumb a ride. He'd be better off in the rain.

He thought about Kira. By now, she would have discovered he was gone. He could almost picture her beautiful face as she read the letter he'd written.

He forced back a rush of emotion. Leaving Kira and Paige had been like cutting off his arm. But it had to be for the best. Now that they'd seen the monster lurking inside him and heard the obscenities that poured out of his mouth, they wouldn't want him on the ranch.

Kira wouldn't come after him, he knew. She had her pride, and she was smart enough to know that he mustn't stay. Being around him wouldn't be good for Paige. And what would happen to Kira's practice if word got out that she had a crazed army vet working with her students?

Lightning flashed across the sky. An earsplitting boom triggered more rain, pelting hard enough to sting. Jake had planned to walk down the three-mile road to the construction site and maybe get a ride into town with one of the workers when they finished their shift. But they wouldn't be working in this weather. He'd have to hitchhike, or shelter in one of the open equipment sheds until the storm passed—nothing he hadn't done before.

Pausing, he turned and gazed uphill toward the ranch, now veiled by a gray curtain of rain. He was moving on, as he always did. But this time would be different. He would be leaving his heart behind.

Kira was soaked by the time she reached the front porch. The dog got up and greeted her, wagging his shaggy tail. She gave him a pat and hurried inside. Ignoring the students lounging by the fire in the living room, she rushed down the hall. Coming out of the dining room, Dusty gave her a startled look as she passed him.

In her room, she toweled her hair, stripped off her wet cotton shirt and replaced it with a warm sweatshirt. Her damp jeans, she decided, would have to do for now. She would change them later.

Jake's letter was folded inside one hip pocket. She had taken it out, unfolded it and flattened it on the bed to dry. She soon heard a light tap on the door, followed by her grandfather's voice. "Kira, are you all right?"

She sighed. Sooner or later, Dusty would need to know everything. "Not really," she said. "Come in and I'll tell you about it."

Dusty walked in and closed the door behind him, leaving it ajar. "What's the matter?" he asked, seeing her stricken face.

"Jake's left." Kira forced herself to speak calmly.

"On foot? In this rain?"

"You know that wouldn't stop him."

The old man sank down on the foot of the bed. "I was afraid something like that might happen," he said.

"Did you know he had an episode in the night?"

"I heard it, all the commotion. I stayed in bed because I figured he didn't need me for an audience. But it sounded pretty bad."

"It was. When he didn't show up this morning, I went to check on him. His things were gone, and I found this on his bed."

She handed Dusty the letter. He read it, sadness creeping over his features. "Does Paige know yet?"

"I haven't told her. But she was there when he lost control. She saw and heard everything. I think that's what really got to Jake. And I think that's the reason he left."

"She still doesn't know he's her father?"

"He was going to tell her today. Before all this happened, he'd told me he was planning to stay."

Dusty glanced at the letter again, then laid it on the bed. "Are you in love with him?"

The question almost shattered her. She glanced away to hide a rush of painful emotion. "It doesn't make any difference now, does it?"

"It could still make a difference. Go after him. Bring him back so we can talk some sense into the man. He couldn't have gotten far in this storm."

Could her grandfather be right? For an instant, hope flickered. But no, she knew better. Kira shook her head.

"Jake's a proud man. After what happened last night, he won't come back. He wouldn't—not even if I asked him to. Not even if I begged him. He's gone—and all I can do is respect his decision."

She stood, fighting tears. "It's time I checked on my students. And I'll need to tell Paige that Jake's gone. She's bound to be upset."

She walked back to the living room. Calvin was reading a book. Brandon was teaching Heather how to play chess. Faith, Lanie and Patrick were playing a video game in the den. Nothing had changed—except that part of her world had just crumbled away like a stream bank in a flood.

Desperate for distraction, Kira wandered into her office, switched on her computer and spent a few minutes scrolling through a meaningless list of e-mails. Unable to focus, she ended up staring out the rain-spattered window.

Why hadn't Jake trusted her to be there for him, no matter what? Why hadn't he realized that she would understand, and that Paige, in her childish wisdom, would understand, too?

She loved him unconditionally. Why hadn't that been enough to keep him here?

Did the answer to that question lie with Jake, or with something in herself?

She remembered his protectiveness, his drive to prove himself, his annoyance when she fussed over him. To Jake, pride was all. Maybe what he craved was not so much to be loved as to be *needed*.

When was the last time she'd allowed herself to need anyone—to let go of her fears and trust someone else to be there for her?

Only now that he was gone did she realize how much she needed Jake in her life—and how much she needed to let him know it. She had to take a chance. She had to go after him.

But first she had to find Paige and tell her what had happened.

In the kitchen, Consuelo was making Rice Krispies Treats for the students. Paige was nowhere in sight.

"I haven't seen her since breakfast," Consuelo said in response to Kira's question. "I thought she must be with Dusty."

Worry gnawed at Kira as she checked the bathroom and Dusty's room. Dusty was alone there, watching his TV from his rocking chair. Kira decided not to worry him. Surely, Paige would be somewhere in the house. She wouldn't go out in this weather.

Suddenly Kira remembered the conversation with Dusty in her bedroom. Had he closed the door all the way when he'd come in? Was there any chance that Paige could have been in the hallway, listening to what was said?

Or could she have gone looking for Jake herself and found his cabin empty?

Frantic now, she hurried into Paige's room. The bed was unmade, as Paige often left it. The closet door was open, her child-sized yellow rain slicker missing from its hanger.

Kira was about to rush out of the room again, but then she noticed something else.

A felt-tipped marker from her office lay on Paige's nightstand next to the wedding photo of her parents. But something was different. Kira's breath stopped as she realized what it was.

Paige had taken the marker to the framed glass, carefully inking a short beard and longer hair onto the image of her father.

The young soldier in the picture had become the man she'd known as Mister Jake.

It was still raining when Jake rounded the last bend in the gravel road. A hundred yards ahead, next to the highway, he could see the construction site, the huge machines idle, like yellow dinosaurs drowsing in lakes of mud. He saw no cars or pick-ups. No one moving. But at least he should be able to find a place out of the rain until the storm passed.

He paused, listening. From somewhere behind and above him, a big vehicle was coming down the road, fast enough to spit gravel on the curves. Since there was nothing above here but the ranch, the driver had to be coming from there.

And unless Dusty was driving the Jeep against doctor's orders, it had to be Kira.

Jake willed himself to ignore his quickening pulse. He'd hoped to get away clean. That, evidently, wasn't to be. But if the driver was Kira, he was surprised that she'd come after him. His letter had made it clear that their relationship was over. And much as he might want her to, she wasn't the kind of woman to chase him down and beg him to change his mind.

Anxious, he stepped out of the road and waited. Now he could see Dusty's big Jeep swinging around the last bend, Kira at the wheel. She pulled up with a squeal of brakes and rolled down the window.

"Get in," she said. "Paige is missing. We think she went looking for you. We need you to help find her."

His gut clenched as two words registered: *"Paige. Missing."*

Without a beat of hesitation, Jake strode around to the passenger side, tossed his pack into the backseat, sprang in beside her and slammed the door. He could find out what had happened on the way back to the ranch. "Go," he said.

She turned the Jeep around and roared back up the road.

"How long's she been gone?" He fired the question at her.

"We just missed her a few minutes ago, but the last time I saw her was after breakfast. Dusty has the students searching around the ranch. But we need you." She paused. "Jake, she knows you're her father."

"You told her?"

"I didn't have to. She figured it out."

Jake stared through the windshield wipers at the road. He'd assumed he could just walk away from here, like he always had. How wrong he'd been.

"Any idea where she might go?" he asked.

"If she'd gone by way of the road, I'd have seen her on my way down here. She may have taken one of the trails below the gate. But she doesn't know her way out of the canyon. We've never let her go down there alone."

Jake pictured his little girl wandering through the rain, lost and scared, looking for her father—for *him*.

"Could the dog track her?" he asked, grasping at any faint hope.

"Tucker's missing, too. We think he must've followed her." She glanced at him as the Jeep pulled through the side gate of the ranch. "Here's what I'm thinking. You and I can follow the trail down to where it forks, then take separate directions. If that's where she's gone, it's our best chance of finding her."

"Makes sense." Jake thought about taking horses, but swiftly realized that saddling them would take time, and horses could spook or slip in the storm. He and Kira would be better off on foot.

They pulled up to the house and climbed out of the Jeep. Dusty was waiting for them on the porch. He shook his head. No sign of Paige.

"Let's go," Kira said. Leaving his pack in the vehicle, Jake followed her toward the high gate at the top of the trail. Dressed in sneakers and a light nylon jacket, she'd be soaked within minutes. Pulling off his waterproof poncho, Jake stopped her and slipped it over her head. She started to protest, but he touched a finger to her lips.

"Just go," he said.

With Kira leading, they passed under the ranch gate and took the winding trail down the canyon. Thunder cracked overhead. Rain drummed around them, turning the trail dust to slippery mud. With every step, Jake thought about his little girl, out here somewhere in the storm, cold and frightened, maybe even in danger. He'd never been much of a praying man, but he prayed silently that Paige would be safe and that they would soon find her.

Minutes later they reached the lookout rock where the trail forked—one branch winding along the foothills, the other going down toward the small side canyon with the waterfall. They paused, as if both of them had suddenly realized that once they separated, they'd have no way to communicate. No phone, no gun or flare to shoot. Kira glanced at her wristwatch. "Forty minutes and we meet back here," she said. "If one of us doesn't make it, the other one goes for help. All right?"

"Fine." Jake checked his own watch, then moved toward the steeper, more dangerous trail leading downhill to the waterfall.

At the sound of his name, he looked back. She was watching him, fear and love mingled in her gaze. "Be careful," she said.

"You too." He started down the trail. At the first bend, he paused and glanced back. *I love you,* he wanted to say. *We'll find her and everything will be all right.* But it was too late for that. Kira had already gone.

Heedless of the pelting rain and the slippery trail, Jake lengthened his stride. He remembered that little canyon all too well—first its beauty, then the total devastation after the last rainstorm, when the runoff from the mountains had scoured it bare and left everything coated with mud. Anyone in the path of that flash flood would have died. Now it could easily be happening again. If Paige had gone this way, she could be in terrible danger.

Flash floods tended to happen later in a storm, after the mountain runoff had found a path and built up enough current to race downhill with devastating force. Could he reach the waterfall before the flood came surging over the top of it with the momentum of a freight train, sweeping up rocks, trees and everything in its path?

Driven by fear, Jake began to run, leaping roots and boulders, skidding through mud. Once, he fell, tumbling down the brushy slope. Scraped and bruised, he scrambled back to the trail and plunged on.

He was getting closer, when he heard a sound that sickened him with dread—the hiss and roar of water rushing down the canyon bottom. The flood had beaten him in his desperate race. But he couldn't stop. If Paige was down there, he had to find her.

Sides throbbing with effort, he ran on. Suddenly he heard another sound. He paused, breath rasping, ears straining. Had he imagined it? No, there it was again, faint but distinct. It was the bark of a dog.

Paige was down there. She had to be.

He reached the place where he and Kira had left the horses and climbed up the rocky path. After he reached the top, the first thing he saw was Tucker, wet and muddy, barking frantically on the bank of the creek. Silt-laden water poured over the falls to churn and swirl in the overflowing pond before roaring on down the canyon.

Jake moved closer, heart pounding, eyes searching. It took him barely seconds to spot Paige.

Somehow she'd made it to the top of a high boulder in midstream. She was clinging to the top, her clothes wet, her brown eyes huge and frightened. She must have climbed the big rock when the flood started rising. Now she was stranded, her childish strength barely enough to keep her from tumbling into the water.

She saw him. Her chilled lips moved. "Daddy, I'm scared," she said.

Jake felt his heart shatter. "Hang on," he said, making a quick survey of the situation. "I'm going to wade out to you. But I might not be able to reach all the way up to where you are. You'll have to let go and jump down to me. Can you do that?"

"I . . . think so." Her small voice shook. She would have to trust him—trust the father who'd been lying to her for weeks.

With no time to lose, Jake waded into the roiling flood. The water was deeper than he'd expected, the current powerful. He fought to stay upright on the treacherous bottom. If he lost his balance and went under, both he and Paige would die.

The boulder where Paige clung was out of the main current, but the eddying water was deep. By the time he reached the base of the steep rock, it was halfway up his chest. It was cold, too. So cold he could barely feel his legs now, which made balancing even more difficult.

Bracing as best he could, he held up his arms. Paige would have to jump out and down to reach him.

"Ready?" he asked her.

"I'm scared." She clung to the rock.

"Don't worry, I'm here, sweetheart. I'm going to count to three. On three you let go and jump. Trust me, I'll catch you."

Inwardly he made a promise. *If he could save this precious little girl, he would be her father forever—the best father he knew how to be. This was his chance, his only chance.*

"One . . . ," he counted. "Two . . . *three!*"

Paige let go of the rock, pushing away with her feet. For a breathless instant, she seemed to hang in space. Then Jake's hands touched her, seized her and pulled her into his arms. She clung to him, crying softly.

Getting out of the water was another struggle. When Jake was close enough, he hefted Paige onto the bank and used his arms to pull himself the rest of the way. For a moment, he lay on the muddy grass, gasping and exhausted. Then he forced himself to stand and lifted Paige in his arms. She was shivering and, wet as he was, he had nothing to warm her with. He held her against him as they started up the trail, with the dog tagging behind.

As they climbed, she recovered enough to talk. "Daddy, why didn't you tell me who you were?" she asked him, tears in her voice.

Jake weighed her question, knowing his answer would mean the world to her and that it would have to be honest. "I was scared," he said. "I was scared that I couldn't be a good father, and that I'd have to leave and hurt you. I almost did leave. But I'm back now, and I'm yours for keeps."

She shifted against him, turning her face upward. "Look, Daddy, the rain's stopped. The sun's coming out."

"So it is." Jake felt the warmth on his face.

Just then, the dog, with an excited bark, raced past them and bounded up the trail to greet Kira, who was hurrying around the bend toward them. At the sight of Jake and Paige, she broke into a headlong run, stumbling and sliding down the muddy trail. Reaching them, she flung her arms around them both, kissing them, shedding happy tears.

"Something told me I should turn around and come this way," she said. "I almost didn't listen. But I knew better."

She took off Jake's poncho and her jacket and wrapped Paige in them to keep her warm. Then, together they climbed the trail to the Flying Cloud Ranch—the place that, for Jake, had finally become home.

EPILOGUE

Six weeks later

By early June, the desert days were ripening into summer. The rains were gone, leaving the searing sun to hang like a jewel in the vast turquoise sky. The landscape glimmered gold in the afternoon heat, saguaros casting long shadows over the burnished earth. The spring blossoms had ripened into fruits and seeds that fed foraging birds and bats, rodents, ringtails and roving bands of javelina.

It was a quiet time at the Flying Cloud Ranch, but all that would change next week when a new group of students would be starting the summer session. Before they arrived, Kira wanted to make the most of her time with Jake and Paige.

This afternoon they were riding down the canyon to the waterfall for a picnic lunch. Jake rode in front on Dynamite, with Paige on the saddle in front of him. Kira brought up the rear on Sadie, with the picnic things in panniers. Tucker trotted alongside.

Jake and his daughter were chatting, with Paige teaching him the names of plants and birds she'd learned from Dusty. The old man would have been invited along, but he'd pretty much given up riding, because it bothered his arthritic hips. They had left him on the porch, sharing sweet tea with Consuelo's mother, Pilar, a handsome widow who'd moved in with her daughter and enjoyed visiting. Was a romance budding between the two seniors? Kira wasn't sure, and Dusty wasn't talking. But she'd noticed a new twinkle in his eye.

This afternoon, with Jake in charge, Kira let her mind wander. Although she'd needed this month-long break from work, she couldn't help missing the last group of students who'd been through so much with her. She'd heard from some of them. Calvin had transferred to a school for gifted youngsters, where he was fitting in well. Lanie and her parents were in counseling. Brandon had found a gay friend, and Heather had a date for spring prom. From Faith, Patrick and Mack, she'd heard nothing.

"I hear the waterfall!" Paige shouted. "We're almost there!"

A smile teased Kira's lips as she pulled her thoughts back to the present. She and Jake had brought Paige on this picnic, in what was still her favorite place, for a reason. They had some special news to give her.

They tied the horses in the willows and spread a blanket next to the pond. As always, the little side canyon had recovered from the spring floods. The waterfall was little more than a trickle now, but the water was clear, the pond a mirror that reflected the sky and the overhanging willows. Grass had sprouted along the bank. Moss and wild violets ringed the water.

They spread their picnic on the blanket and sat down to eat. Jake's eyes met Kira's. His mouth formed a silent question: *Now?*

Kira gave him a smile and a nod. "Paige," she said, "Jake and I have something to tell you. We've decided to get married."

"Yay!" Paige jumped up, spilling her can of root beer as she hugged them both. "When?"

"We were thinking later this summer," Jake said, "after the students are gone. Is that all right with you?"

"All right!" She clapped her hands, bouncing up and down. "I'll have a real mom and dad, just like other kids. I wish you could just get married tomorrow."

"So do I," Kira said. "But we need time to plan some things. Now sit down and have a sandwich."

Her eyes met Jake's through a ray of sunlight. Leaning close, she brushed his lips with hers in a tender, lingering kiss. She loved him so much. Some people might tell her this was a mistake, that Jake would always have issues with PTSD. But he would be there for her and for Paige when they needed him. And when bad memories stirred the demons in his head, she would be there for him, to hold him and understand.

Their marriage wouldn't be perfect, Kira knew. But she would settle for wonderful.

**Read on for an excerpt from Janet Dailey's
delightful holiday romance,
JUST A LITTLE CHRISTMAS!**

Believe in second chances this Christmas . . .

Ellie Marsden couldn't wait to shake the dust of
Branding Iron, Texas, off her heels and chase after
bright lights, big city, and a wealthy husband. Now
she's come home, divorced, a little disillusioned,
and a whole lot pregnant. Leave it to her one-time
high school sweetheart, cattle rancher Jubal
McFarland, to point out that citified Ellie is as out
of place in small town Texas as her teacup poodle.
So why is there something about being back—and
being with Jubal—that feels surprisingly right?

Jubal's seven-year-old daughter, Gracie, needs a
mother, but he hasn't found the perfect woman.
Or maybe the problem is that he *did* find her, and
had his heart broken when she left town. Gracie's
already falling hard for Ellie and that ball of fluff
she calls a dog. And no matter how hard the rugged
cowboy tries to resist, there's no denying the appeal
of first love and sweet new beginnings—especially
when there's a little Christmas magic in the air . . .

Late on a chilly November day, Ellie Marsden Thomas came home to Branding Iron, Texas.

Driving her BMW sedan along the two-lane road, she gazed across stubbled fields, dotted here and there with grazing cattle. Under a soot-gray sky, scattered houses, barns and silos rose out of a landscape that matched Ellie's bleak mood.

San Francisco was behind her, most likely for good. For the foreseeable future, she was right back where she'd started—smack dab in the middle of Nowhere, U.S.A.

When she'd left Branding Iron after high school, she'd vowed never to return except for brief visits to her mother. But now, ten years later, the small town had become her refuge. She had no place else to go.

A stray snowflake spattered the window as she neared the city limits sign. Just ahead, a worn dirt lane cut away from the asphalt. Ellie's memory traced its path through fields and stands of cottonwood, to the swimming hole where, one moonlit summer night, she'd almost surrendered her virginity to Jubal McFarland.

They'd been crazy about each other back then. But when he'd asked her to marry him, she found she didn't love Jubal wholeheartedly enough to spend the rest of her life herding cows on his family ranch. She'd turned him down and never looked back.

The last she'd heard of Jubal, he'd wed another local girl. By now he'd probably sired a brood of little blue-eyed McFarlands as handsome as he was.

And Ellie had gone off to law school and married cheating, lying Brent. End of story.

A plaintive *yip* broke into her musings. Harnessed into his booster-basket, Beau, her white teacup poodle, was due for a potty stop. Ellie blew him an air kiss. "Hang on, boy," she said. "We'll be there in a few minutes. Then you can do your business on my mother's nice, clean lawn."

Beau yipped again, dancing in place as if to let her know he was getting anxious. Ellie pressed the gas pedal, pushing the speed limit. Beau was well trained, but his tiny bladder could only hold out for so long.

Lately, it seemed, she'd been experiencing a similar problem herself.

Feeling a solid thump she glanced down at the rounded belly that barely cleared the steering wheel. Her unborn daughter was kicking up a storm. It wouldn't have surprised Ellie to learn that she was carrying a future Olympic soccer star—as if anything could surprise her after discovering that she was not only divorced but pregnant.

Brent had never been keen on having children. He'd always used protection. But during their disastrous trial reconciliation last spring, the unimaginable had happened. Now Brent was married to one of his wealthy law clients, and blissfully unaware that he was about to become a father.

Forcing the memory aside, Ellie drove down Main Street, where the traditional Christmas lights were already strung between the lampposts. Christmas in Branding Iron would be a far cry from the holidays in San Francisco—the glittering shops, the glamorous gowns, the cocktail parties and charity galas, which Ellie had always enjoyed. But that life was behind her now. The sooner she adjusted to her new reality, the better.

For better or for worse, the prodigal daughter was home.

Connect with U(s)

Visit us online at
KensingtonBooks.com
to read more from your favorite authors, see books
by series, view reading group guides, and more.

Join us on social media

for sneak peeks, chances to win books and prize packs,
and to share your thoughts with other readers.

facebook.com/kensingtonpublishing
twitter.com/kensingtonbooks

Tell us what you think!

To share your thoughts, submit a review,
or sign up for our eNewsletters, please visit:
KensingtonBooks.com/TellUs.

More from Bestselling Author
JANET DAILEY

More by Bestselling Author
Hannah Howell

__Highland Angel	978-1-4201-0864-4	$6.99US/$8.99CAN
__If He's Sinful	978-1-4201-0461-5	$6.99US/$8.99CAN
__Wild Conquest	978-1-4201-0464-6	$6.99US/$8.99CAN
__If He's Wicked	978-1-4201-0460-8	$6.99US/$8.49CAN
__My Lady Captor	978-0-8217-7430-4	$6.99US/$8.49CAN
__Highland Sinner	978-0-8217-8001-5	$6.99US/$8.49CAN
__Highland Captive	978-0-8217-8003-9	$6.99US/$8.49CAN
__Nature of the Beast	978-1-4201-0435-6	$6.99US/$8.49CAN
__Highland Fire	978-0-8217-7429-8	$6.99US/$8.49CAN
__Silver Flame	978-1-4201-0107-2	$6.99US/$8.49CAN
__Highland Wolf	978-0-8217-8000-8	$6.99US/$9.99CAN
__Highland Wedding	978-0-8217-8002-2	$4.99US/$6.99CAN
__Highland Destiny	978-1-4201-0259-8	$4.99US/$6.99CAN
__Only for You	978-0-8217-8151-7	$6.99US/$8.99CAN
__Highland Promise	978-1-4201-0261-1	$4.99US/$6.99CAN
__Highland Vow	978-1-4201-0260-4	$4.99US/$6.99CAN
__Highland Savage	978-0-8217-7999-6	$6.99US/$9.99CAN
__Beauty and the Beast	978-0-8217-8004-6	$4.99US/$6.99CAN
__Unconquered	978-0-8217-8088-6	$4.99US/$6.99CAN
__Highland Barbarian	978-0-8217-7998-9	$6.99US/$9.99CAN
__Highland Conqueror	978-0-8217-8148-7	$6.99US/$9.99CAN
__Conqueror's Kiss	978-0-8217-8005-3	$4.99US/$6.99CAN
__A Stockingful of Joy	978-1-4201-0018-1	$4.99US/$6.99CAN
__Highland Bride	978-0-8217-7995-8	$4.99US/$6.99CAN
__Highland Lover	978-0-8217-7759-6	$6.99US/$9.99CAN

Available Wherever Books Are Sold!

Check out our website at
http://www.kensingtonbooks.com